He bent down and kissed her lips.

She tasted of grapes and innocence, though he believed she was a sorceress in truth. Her body had grown stiff with the surprise of his touch, but quickly relaxed beneath it. Still, her movements were tentative and unschooled. She did not know how to tilt her head, or where to put her hands, or even when to breathe, and it quickly became clear that he was the first man to ever taste her lips.

And oh, by Jupiter, they were sweet.

Steady, he told himself. *Slow*. And yet they had no time at all. The others would be waiting. Soon one would come to see what was delaying them.

He pressed his lips harder against hers and as he kissed them, it was as if the burdens of his very life began to lift. All the things he needed to remember, all the things he was obliged to do, all of his secrets and all of his lies simply floated out the deckhouse doorway toward the stars.

He wrenched himself away and staggered backward. She had dealt him a blow in the dark. It was as if the pillow were a shield, and her lips two deadly swords. She had slain him, and he feared he would never be the same.

He pushed the knife h̶ ̶ ̶ ̶ ̶ ̶her palm. "Please, take it," he whispered you no harm."

Author Note

I admit it: I am one of the legions of people obsessed with Cleopatra. The last ruler of ancient Egypt features prominently on my bookshelves and among the false names I give when ordering fancy coffee drinks. I have never owned a female pet, but...you get the picture.

If you have cracked this book, perhaps you are also fascinated with Cleopatra. Or perhaps you are just Cleopatra-curious. Full disclosure: the heroine of this story is not Cleopatra, but an imagined character named Wen. Wen becomes Cleopatra's servant and adviser, while Cleopatra becomes her matchmaker, nudging Wen toward a certain Roman commander with brooding dark eyes.

I wanted to explore Wen's experience of love because the real Cleopatra may have never experienced it herself. There is no proof that Cleopatra loved either of her two famous Roman partners, though she had every reason to pretend she did. In this version of the history, Cleopatra gets to experience through Wen something she may have never had in real life.

And Wen gets to have something that even the richest, most powerful woman in the world would have envied—true, uncompromising, steamy-hot love.

I hope you enjoy the story!

GRETA GILBERT

—

In Thrall to the Enemy Commander

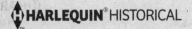

HARLEQUIN® HISTORICAL

Recycling programs
for this product may
not exist in your area.

ISBN-13: 978-1-335-52268-9

In Thrall to the Enemy Commander

Copyright © 2018 by Greta Gilbert

Printed in U.S.A.

Greta Gilbert's passion for ancient history began with a teenage crush on Indiana Jones. As an adult, she landed a dream job at National Geographic Learning, where her colleagues—former archaeologists—helped her learn to keep her facts straight. Now she lives in south Baja, Mexico, where she continues to study the ancients. She is especially intrigued by ancient mysteries and always keeps a little Indiana Jones inside her heart.

Books by Greta Gilbert

Harlequin Historical

Enslaved by the Desert Trader
The Spaniard's Innocent Maiden
In Thrall to the Enemy Commander

Harlequin Historical *Undone!* ebook

Mastered by Her Slave

Visit the Author Profile page at Harlequin.com.

For my dad: friend, mentor, sparring partner,
fearless leader, fellow dreamer, guiding genius,
benefactor, my superhero

Chapter One

Alexandria, Egypt—48 bce

She should have known better than to trust a Roman. She should have never listened to his honeyed speech, or considered his strange ideas, or dared to search his onyx eyes. Seth's teeth—she was a fool. *'Beware the heirs of Romulus and Remus,'* the High Priestess had always cautioned her, but the words had been but a riddle in her young ears. By the time she finally understood their meaning, it was too late. She was already in love and doomed to die.

She remembered the day she started down that terrible path. She was working at her master's brew house in Alexandria, Egypt's capital city. She had lived through one and twenty inundations by then and had been bound in slavery since the age of twelve. She had never tasted meat, or seen her face in a mirror, or touched the waters of the Big Green Sea, though the harbour was only streets away.

What she had done was toil. She awoke each day at dawn and worked without rest—stirring mash, cleaning pots, pouring beer—until the last of the brew house's clients stumbled out on to the moon-drenched streets. Then she would curl up on a floor mat outside the door of her master's quarters and welcome the oblivion of sleep.

That was Wen's life—day after day, month after month, from *akhet* to *peret* to *shemu*. It was a small, thankless existence, redeemed only by a secret.

The secret was this: she knew Latin. She knew other things, too, but Latin was all that mattered. Few people in Alexandria spoke Latin. The official language of Alexandria was Greek, the language of Egypt's Greek Pharaohs, though Egyptian and Hebrew were also widely spoken. But even Queen Cleopatra herself had sworn never to learn Latin, for it was the language of Rome—Egypt's enemy. The tongue of thieves, she had famously called it.

As it happened, the brew house in which Wen laboured was frequented by Roman soldiers who spoke only Latin. They were known as the Gabiniani—tolerated in Alexandria because they had once helped restore the late Pharaoh to his throne.

But the Gabiniani were villains—rough, odious men who belched loudly, drank thirstily and sought their advantage in all things.

She knew their depravity intimately, though she tried not to think of it. It was enough to admit that they were loathsome men and she was happy to keep her watchful eye upon them.

Thus she earned her bread as a kind of spy—an Egyptian slave serving Roman soldiers in the language of Plato. She pretended not to understand their Latin chatter and placidly filled their cups. But whenever one bragged about thieving beer or passing a false *drachma* for a real one, she would happily inform her master.

She had saved her master thousands of *drachmae* over the years in this manner and he was able to provide his family with a good life. It was for this reason, she believed, that he never used her body for pleasure, and always gave her milk with her grain. It was also why she knew he would never set her free. She began to see her life as a river, flowing slowly and inevitably towards the sea.

But the goddess who weaves the threads of fate had a different plan for Wen. One morning, a man entered the brew house wearing an unusual grin. He was as dark as a silty floodplain and handsome in an ageless way, as if he had been alive for a thousand years. She believed him to be Nubian, though his head was shaved like an Egyptian's and he wore a long Greek chiton that whispered across the tiles as he walked. A bracelet of thick gold encircled his arm and a heavy coin purse hung from his waist belt.

A tax collector, she thought. She was certain the man had come to collect taxes on behalf of the young Pharaoh Ptolemy, who was seeking funds for his war against his sister-wife, Queen Cleopatra.

'Please, sit,' she invited the man. 'Goblet or cup?'

He did not answer, but regarded her closely, first in the eyes, then quickly down the length of her body, lingering for a time on the scar that peeked out from beneath her tunic.

'How long have you been enslaved?' he asked.

'Nine inundations, Master. Since the age of twelve.'

'Then you are the same age as the exiled Queen.' Wen glanced nervously around the empty brew house.

It was dangerous to speak of Queen Cleopatra in Alexandria. Her husband-brother Ptolemy was currently preparing to attack her somewhere in the desert. 'You have a regal air about you,' the man continued jestingly. 'Are you sure you are not a queen yourself?'

'I am as far from a queen as a woman can get, Master.'

'That is not true. The roles and riches of this life are but—oh, how does that old saying go?'

'The roles and riches of this life are but illusions,' Wen said. 'They matter not.' It was a saying the High Priestess of Hathor had often repeated to her, though Wen had not heard it since she was a child.

The man's face split with a grin. 'Will you take me to your master?'

'My master is away,' Wen lied, as he had instructed her to do on such occasions. He despised tax collectors and would surely beat Wen if she let this man through to him.

But in that instant, her master emerged from his quarters and heralded the stranger, and soon the two men had disappeared into his office. When they reemerged, she noticed that the coin purse no longer dangled at the man's waist.

'Serve this honourable traveller what he requests,' her master told her, a rare smile beguiling his face, 'and do whatever he asks. He has paid in full.'

Do whatever he asks? She felt her *ka*—her sacred soul—begin to wither. Her master was not a kind man, but she had always believed him to be decent. It appeared that decency had been only in her mind, for he had apparently sold Wen's body for his own profit.

I could just run, she thought. *I could dash out the doorway and on to the streets.*

But the streets were more dangerous than ever. A Roman general had lately landed in Alexandria—a man they called Caesar—and was conducting diplomatic meetings with Pharaoh Ptolemy in the Royal Quarter. The General travelled with a legion of soldiers fresh from battle. They wandered Alexandria's streets in search of diversions. If Wen were not captured by slave catchers, then surely she would be captured by one of Caesar's soldiers seeking female company.

'What do you ask of me, then?' Wen whispered, speaking her words to the floor. She studied its cracked tiles, as if she might somehow mend the rifts in them.

But the man said nothing, nor did he attempt to lead her away. Instead, his stretched out his arms and held his hands open. 'You need not fear me,' he said in Egyptian, her native tongue. 'I am not here to take, but to give.'

Then, as if by magic, a large coin appeared between his fingers. He toyed with it for several moments, then tossed it in her direction. Her heart beat with excitement when she perceived its formidable weight. But when she squinted to determine its worth, she saw that it was stamped with an image of the exiled Queen.

'I am afraid that I cannot accept this generous gift,' she said carefully in Greek. 'Coins like this one have been forbidden by Pharaoh Ptolemy since Queen Cleopatra was exiled.'

'Then you view Cleopatra as the rightful ruler of Egypt?'

Wen felt her jaw tense. It was a question too dangerous to answer. Cleopatra had been the first in her family of Greek Pharaohs to ever learn the Egyptian language and the first of her line to have worshipped the sacred bulls. When the River had failed to rise, Cleopatra had devalued the currency to purchase grain for the starving peasants and had saved thousands of lives. In only two years since she had assumed the throne, the young Queen had shown a reverence and love for Egypt unheard of in her line of Pharaohs.

Of course Wen viewed Cleopatra as the rightful ruler of Egypt. But she would certainly never admit it to a stranger, especially in the heart of pro-Ptolemy Alexandria. 'No, ah, not at all,' she continued in Greek.

'You are a terrible liar, my dear,' the man said in Egyptian, 'though I sense much boldness in you.' He flashed another toothy grin. 'A cat with the heart of a lioness.'

'What?'

'I am Sol,' he said, sketching a bow.

'I am—'

'Wen-Nefer,' he interrupted. 'I already know your name, Mistress Wen, and much else about you, though I admit that you are more beautiful than I had anticipated.'

Wen-Nefer. That *was* her name, though her master never used it. Nor did the clients of the brew house. They preferred *you there*, or *girl*. It had been so long since she had heard her own name aloud that she had nearly forgotten it.

'I suppose you cannot read,' said Sol, producing a scroll from beneath his belt, 'so I will tell you that this scroll attests to your conscription by Cleopatra Thea Philopator the Seventh, Lady of the Two Lands, Rightful Queen of Egypt.'

His words became muffled—replaced by the loud beat of her heart inside her ears. He traced his finger down rows of angular Greek script and pointed to a waxen stamp. It depicted the same queenly cartouche that Wen had observed on the coin.

'Your master has been paid,' Sol continued, 'and has released you to me. I have been instructed to escort you directly to Queen Cleopatra's camp near Pelousion. Our driver awaits us outside.'

He was halfway through the open doorway when he turned to regard her motionless figure. 'I see,' he said with a sigh. 'I must have been mistaken about you. It appears that you support Ptolemy's claim to the Horus Throne.'

'What? No!'

'Then why do you not follow me?'

'I…' She paused. Her thoughts would not arrange themselves. How could she trust this strange man when his errand stretched the bounds of reason? 'Forgive me, but I must know, why would the Queen want…me?'

'It is my understanding that you have a special skill.'

Skill? She searched her mind. Beyond pouring beers and mixing brews, she had only one skill. 'Do you refer to my ability to speak Latin?'

'It must be that,' said Sol, 'though the Queen did mention something about your holy birth. Does that mean anything to you?'

'I am a child of the Temple of Hathor.'

'Ah! A child of the gods—it is no wonder the Queen summons you.'

Wen stood in confounded silence. Up until that moment, she had perceived herself unfortunate in her birth.

'I assure you that I mean you no harm,' said Sol. 'But neither do I have time to waste. You may come with me now or remain here for the rest of your days. It is your choice. Only choose.'

Wen turned the coin over in her hands. She studied the profile that had been etched into its golden metal. It was a woman's profile to be sure—a woman who, until only a year before, had ably ruled the oldest, most powerful kingdom in the world. She was a woman who had never known her own mother, had been neglected by her father and was hated by her husband-brother, who had lately put a price on her head.

If Sol was telling the truth, he would be leading Wen into mortal danger. Cleopatra was a woman surrounded by dangerous men, fighting to survive and likely to perish.

'Well?' asked Sol. 'Are you coming or not?'

The carriage was of modest size, but to Wen it seemed a great chariot. They raced past the grand colonnades of Canopus Street with such speed that the pedestrians paused to observe them, staring out from beneath the green shade cloths.

Wen's heart hummed. How bold she felt sitting on the bench with Sol—how wholly unlike herself. She undid her braid and let her hair fly behind her like a tattered flag.

Soon they had boarded a barge and were sailing upriver with the wind at their backs. Wen gazed out at the verdant marshlands as long-forgotten memories flooded in.

As a child, Wen had often travelled the River as part of the holy entourage of the High Priestess of Hathor.

It had been a great honor to travel with the High Priestess. As the goddess Hathor's representative on earth, the Priestess was required to attend ceremonies from Alexandria to Thebes. She would always select from among the children of the temple to journey with her, for she loved them as her own.

There were dozens of children to choose from and more every year. They were conceived during the Festival of Drunkenness, when high-born men were allowed to couple with the priestesses of Hathor and experience the divine. Any children that resulted from their holy act belonged to the temple, their paternity unknown, their maternity unimportant.

For each of her journeys, the High Priestess chose a different set of temple children to accompany her, but she never failed to include Wen. While they sailed, she would invite Wen beneath her gauze-covered canopy and instruct her in the invisible arts.

She called the lessons 'reading lessons', though they had nothing to do with texts. They were lessons on how to read people—how to look into a man's eyes and discover his thoughts.

She taught Wen how to spot flattery, how to uncover a lie and how to use the art of rhetoric to pull the truth from a man's heart. She told Wen wondrous tales—the *Pieces of Osiris*, she called them, for they were words gathered together to teach Wen lessons.

'You have the gift,' the High Priestess told Wen one day as they floated towards Memphis. She stared into the eyes of her golden-cobra bracelet as if consulting it, then gave a solemn nod. 'When you are ready, I will take you to meet the Pharaohs and we will find a place for you at the Alexandrian court. You will become a royal advisor, just as I have been.'

But that day never came.

Wen gazed at the silken water. So much had changed since then, though the River itself seemed unaltered. They skirted around shadowy marshes thick with lotus blooms, and floated past big-shouldered farmers who laboured in the deepening dusk.

Sol studied Wen with amusement as she gaped at the sights. 'You watch with the eyes of a child,' he mused, 'though a child you are not.' He glanced at her scar, which she had allowed to become exposed.

'It is a battle scar,' she offered, quickly pulling her leg beneath her skirt.

'And did you win the battle?'

'I am here, am I not?'

They travelled relentlessly into the night, moving from the gentle current of the river to the jarring bumps of unseen roads. Wen willed herself awake, fearful she might close her eyes and discover that the journey had been nothing but a dream.

She must have finally slept, however, for by the time she opened her eyes it was evening again and the souls of dead Pharaohs had already begun to salt the sky. Wen sat up and smelled the air. It was thick and briny, and she knew the sea was near.

They descended into a wide, flat plain where thousands of men loitered amidst a collection of tents. Sol explained that the men were soldiers—Syrian, Nabataean and Egyptian mercenaries who had been hired by Queen Cleopatra with what remained of her wealth. They were her only chance against her husband-brother's much larger army, which was stationed in the nearby town of Pelousion, preparing to strike.

They came to a halt beside a large cowhide tent, and Sol leaped to the ground. 'We have arrived. This is where we must part.'

'Arrived where?' asked Wen, taking his hand and jumping down beside him.

He flashed her an enigmatic grin, then motioned to the tent. 'Go inside and wait. The Queen's attendants will find you when her council concludes. No matter what happens, you must never address the Queen directly. You must wait until she speaks to you. Now go.'

'You are not going to accompany me?'

He laughed. 'The fate of Egypt will be decided in that tent.'

'Do you not wish to learn it?'

'The less I know, the better.'

'I do not understand.'

He shook his head. 'I think you do understand. You only pretend not to.'

He does not wish to be implicated in what is being decided, Wen thought. 'Sol is not your real name, is it?' she asked.

'No, it is not,' he said, smiling like a jackal. 'Good for you.' He bent and kissed her hand. 'It has been an honour, Wen-Nefer. Perhaps we shall meet again some day.' He gave a deep bow, then jumped back into the carriage.

'Wait! You cannot just leave me here!' she yelled, but he was already rolling away.

Chapter Two

He might not have seen her at all: the colour of her shabby tunic matched the colour of the sand and her hair was so tangled and dusty it resembled a tumbleweed. But the group of guards escorting him to the Queen's tent had grown larger as they passed through the camp, cramping his stride, and slowly he'd made his way to the edge of the entourage. As he passed by her, his thigh brushed her hand.

A shiver rippled across his skin. He wondered when he had last felt the touch of a woman. In Gaul, perhaps. Troupes of harlots always followed Caesar's legions and, as commander of Caesar's Sixth, Titus was allowed his choice from among them.

Not that he was particular. Women were mostly alike, he had found. Their minds were usually empty, but their bodies were soft and yielding, and they could provide a special kind of comfort after a day of taking lives.

Or at least—they had once provided him with such comfort. Now, after so many years of leading men to their deaths, even a woman's soft touch had ceased to console him.

The woman drew her hand away, keeping her gaze upon the ground. She was obviously a slave, but she was also quite obviously a woman—a woman living in a desert military camp where women were as rare as trees. He wondered which commander she would be keeping warm tonight.

He had a sudden desire that it might be him.

There was no chance of that, however. As Caesar's messengers, Titus and his young guard, Clodius, were under orders to deliver Caesar's message to Queen Cleopatra, then return to Alexandria immediately. It was dangerous for Romans in Egypt, especially Roman soldiers. They were viewed as conquerors and pillagers, and were unwelcome in military camps such as these, along with most everywhere else.

As if to underscore that point, the guard nearest Titus scowled, then nudged Titus back towards the middle of the escort. There, Titus's own guard, Clodius, marched obediently, his nerves as apparent as the sweat stains on his toga.

As was custom for sensitive missions such as these, Titus and Clodius had switched places. Clodius was playing the role of Titus the commander and Titus the role of Clodius, his faithful guard. This way, if Cleopatra chose to keep one of them for ransom, she would keep Clodius, whom she would erroneously believe to be the higher-ranking man, leaving Titus to return to Caesar.

'Hello, there, my little honey cake,' said a guard somewhere behind him. Something in Titus tensed and he turned to see one of the guards standing before the woman, pushing the hair out of her eyes.

She was not moving—she hardly even looked to be

breathing—and was studying the ground with an intensity that belied her fear. Clearly she was not offering her services to the man, or any other. Titus almost lunged towards the man, but he was suddenly ushered into the tent and directed to a place at its perimeter. The offending guard entered soon after him and Titus breathed a sigh of relief, though he puzzled over the reason for it.

He tried to put the woman out of his mind as his eyes adjusted to the low light. In addition to the guards, there were several robed advisors spread about the small space, along with a dozen military commanders and men of rank. They stood around a large wooden throne where a pretty young woman sat with her hands in her lap.

Queen Cleopatra, he thought. Titus watched as Clodius dropped to his knees before the exiled Pharaoh in the customary obeisance. 'Pharaoh Cleopatra Philopator the Seventh, Rightful Queen of Egypt,' announced one of the guards.

To Titus's mind, there was nothing Egyptian about her. She wore her hair in a Macedonian-style bun and donned a traditional Greek chiton with little to distinguish it from any other. She was surprisingly spare in her adornments and quite small of stature, especially compared to the large cedar throne in which she sat.

Still, she held her head high and appeared fiercely composed. It was an admirable quality, given that she was a woman. In Cleopatra's case, it was particularly admirable, for her husband-brother Ptolemy had made no secret of his determination to cut off her head.

'Whom do you bring me, Guard Captain?' asked the Queen. 'Why do you interrupt my war council?'

'Two messengers, my Queen,' said the head guard. 'They come from Alexandria. They bring an urgent message to you from General Julius Caesar.'

The Queen exchanged glances with two women standing on one side of her throne. The taller of the two bent and whispered something into Cleopatra's ear. The Queen nodded gravely.

Cleopatra was known as a goodly queen—one of those rare monarchs who actually cared about the people she ruled. Before her exile, it was said that she had done more than any of her predecessors to ease the lives of the peasants and to honour their ancient traditions.

Now that Titus finally beheld her, he believed that that her goodness was real. Her face exuded kindness, but also an intelligence that seemed unusual for one of her sex. She smiled placidly, but her eyes danced about the tent, never resting.

Still, Titus was careful not to venerate her. She was a woman, after all, and naturally inferior to the men who surrounded her. But even if she were a man, he would not make the mistake of supporting her rule. He knew the dangers of monarchs. One would spread peace and justice, then the next would spread war and misery. Kings and queens—or pharaohs, as they called themselves here in Egypt—were as fickle as their blessed gods and they could never be trusted.

There was a better way, or so Titus believed. It was a vast, complex blanket, woven by all citizens, that protected from the caprices of kings. They had been practising it in Rome for almost five hundred years and Titus understood it well, for his own ancestors had helped weave its threads.

Res publica.

Though now that glorious blanket was in danger of
unravelling. When Caesar had crossed the Rubicon
with his Thirteenth Legion, he had led the Republic
down a dangerous path. Generals were not allowed to
bring their armies into Rome. Nor were they allowed
to become dictators for life, yet that was exactly what
the Roman Senate was contemplating, for Caesar had
bribed most of its members. There were only a few
good men left in the government of Rome who remembered the dangers of monarchs.

Titus was one of them. He was one of the *Boni*—the
Good Men—and also their most powerful spy. His job
was to watch Caesar closely and, if necessary, to prevent the great General from making himself into a king.

And now that Caesar had defeated his rival Pompey,
there were no more armies standing in his way. What
better way to begin his rule than by occupying Egypt,
the richest kingdom in the world, and turn its warring
monarchs into tributary clients?

Or perhaps just murder them instead.

Titus could not guess General Caesar's intentions,
but he feared for the young Queen sitting before him
now. Much like the woman he had seen outside the tent,
she appeared to have no idea of the danger she was in,
or how very helpless she was.

It was growing darker outside the tent. Wen had
been ordered to wait inside, but could not gather the
courage to enter. She placed her ear between the folds
of the tent and listened.

'Caesar means to conquer Egypt—the Queen cannot trust him.'

'The Queen must trust him!'

'He will take Egypt by force.'

'The Roman Senate would never allow it.'

'The Roman Senate does not matter any more!'

The clashing voices rose to a crescendo, then a woman's voice sang out above them all. 'Peace, now, friends,' she said. 'There are many ways to be bold.'

Wen drew a breath, then slipped into the shadows.

She could see very little at first. The torches and braziers were clustered at the centre of the room, illuminating a handful of nobles gathered around a wide wooden throne. On its pillowed seat sat a slight, dark-eyed woman dressed in a simple white tunic and mantle, and wearing the ivory-silk headband of royalty.

Cleopatra Philopator, thought Wen. *The rightful Queen of Egypt.*

The Queen wore no eye colour, no black kohl, and her lips displayed only the faintest orange tinge. Her jewellery consisted of two simple white pearls, which dangled from her ears on golden hooks.

To an Egyptian eye, she was sinfully unadorned, yet she radiated beauty and intelligence. She motioned gracefully to the figure of a man kneeling before her on the carpet. 'Good counsellors,' she sang out, 'before we disagree about what Caesar's messenger has to say, let us first allow him to say it.'

Laughter split the air, morphing into more discussion, all of which the Queen summarily ignored. 'Rise, Messenger,' she said, 'and tell us your name.'

'I am, ah, Titus Tillius Fortis,' the young man said, rising to his feet, 'son of Lucius Tillius Cimber.' The room quieted as the counsellors observed the young messenger. He wore a diplomat's *toga virilis*, though he appeared uncertain of how to position its arm folds.

'The name is familiar,' said the Queen. 'Is your father not a Roman Senator?'

'He is, Queen Cleopatra.'

'I believe I met him many years ago. I was in Rome with my own father, begging the Senate to end their designs on our great kingdom.'

The Roman appeared at a loss for words. There was a long silence, which Cleopatra carefully filled. 'Your father said that one of his sons served in Caesar's Sixth.'

'That is I, Goddess,' the man said, taking the prompt. 'I command that legion now. I am their tribune, though I appear before you in a messenger's robes.'

'Caesar sends his highest-ranking officer to deliver his message?' Cleopatra gazed out at the crowded sea of advisors. 'That is promising, is it not, Counsellors?'

Someone shouted, 'Is he not very young to command a legion?' There were several grunts of assent and the Queen looked doubtfully at Titus.

'I have only recently been promoted,' Titus said. 'I took the place of General Maximus Severus, who died defeating Pompey at Pharsalus.'

The Queen gave a crisp nod. 'You may rise, young Titus,' she said. 'This council will hear your message.'

Titus demonstrated the seal on his scroll to a nearby scribe, who gave an approving nod. The young commander broke the wax and cleared his voice.

'Before you begin,' interrupted the Queen, 'will you not also introduce your companion?'

Titus paused.

'The one who lurks at the edge of the tent there,'

said the Queen, pointing to the very shadows in which Wen hid.

'My Queen?' asked Titus.

Wen prepared to step forward, certain that the Queen had noticed her.

'Do not play the fool, Titus,' said the Queen, craning her neck in Wen's direction. 'He is as big as a Theban bull.'

There was a sudden movement near Wen and a towering figure stepped out of the shadows beside her.

'Ah, you refer to my guard,' said Titus. 'Apologies, Queen. That is, ah, Clodius.'

Wen's heart skipped with the realisation that a Roman soldier had been standing beside her all the while, as quiet as a *kheft*. 'He accompanied me from Alexandria for my protection,' Titus continued. 'He is one of our legion's most decorated soldiers.'

Wen sank farther into the shadows as the Roman guard made his way through the crowd. He wore no sleeves and his chainmail cuirass fit tightly around his sprawling chest, as if at any moment he might burst from it. The red kilt that extended beneath his steely shell was too short for him, exposing most of his well-muscled legs. He held a helmet against his waist and walked in measured strides that seemed to radiate discipline. Wen wondered how she had not noticed him.

'You may stop where you are, Clodius,' said Cleopatra, holding up her hand as her own guards gripped their swords.

The towering Roman turned to his young compatriot in apparent confusion.

'You heard her, Comm—ah—Clodius,' he said in a rough soldier's Latin.

The guard dropped to his knee and bowed. The torches flashed on the muscled contours of his arms, giving Wen a chill. She feared such arms. They were Roman arms, designed to destroy lives.

'Apologies, Queen Cleopatra,' said Titus. 'My guard does not speak the Greek tongue.'

'Of course he does not,' said Cleopatra, regarding the man's arms as Wen had done, 'for his realm is obviously the battlefield, not the halls of learning.'

'Shall I dismiss him?'

A buxom young woman standing beside the Queen bent and whispered something into her ear. 'Do not fear, dear Charmion,' Cleopatra answered aloud. 'He will not harm me. As you know, the Romans value glory over all else. There would be no glory in assassinating a queen on the eve of her military defeat now, would there?'

'You heard her, ah—Clodius,' said Titus in Latin. 'Please, return to your post.'

There was something curious about the way Titus spoke to Clodius. Something in the tone of his voice, perhaps, or in his choice of words. The High Priestess would have sensed it right away and known exactly what was amiss. But Wen could not identify it and was soon distracted by the sight of Clodius himself striding back towards the shadows in which she stood.

Time slowed as he took his position beside her and she perceived the long exhale of his breaths. She braved a glance at him, but his brow was too heavy to see his eyes and the rest of his expression was a mask of shadowy stone. 'General Gaius Julius Caesar,' Titus began, reading from his scroll, 'Protector of the Roman Republic, Defeater of Pompey the Great, Conqueror of Gaul…'

The Queen held up her hand. 'We do not have time for scrolls, good Titus. Please speak Caesar's message in your own words.'

The Roman looked up. 'My Goddess?'

'What does General Caesar ask of me?'

Titus cast his gaze about the room, as if searching for Clodius. 'Well?' asked Cleopatra.

'Ah, General Caesar begs an audience with Your Divine Person,' he said at last.

Cleopatra's expression betrayed no sentiment, yet Wen sensed her careful choice of words. 'What does Caesar hope to gain by summoning me? He allies himself with my husband-brother, Ptolemy, after all, and occupies our very palaces.'

'He has made no alliance with Ptolemy,' answered Titus. 'He wishes to reunite the Lord and Lady of the Two Lands.'

There was a collective gasp and then the room went quiet. 'Reunite me with Ptolemy? For what motive?'

'Your Divinity…ah…to please the gods.'

'He wishes to collect the money my late father owed him,' Cleopatra said to a flood of laughter.

A bald man in a green robe bent to whisper something into Cleopatra's ear. The Queen gave a resigned nod, then set her flickering gaze upon the crowd.

'This priest of Osiris believes that Caesar and my husband-brother conspire to kill me. Who here agrees that Caesar summons me to my death?'

A chorus of voices sang out in agreement, and Wen thought to herself how mistaken they all were.

'You there,' the Queen called out. 'Why do you shake your head in dissent?'

The room went silent. Wen looked around, but she could not discern which of the men had been addressed. 'Do you disagree with the Osiris priest and these other distinguished men?' asked the Queen. She was staring directly at Wen.

She had addressed *Wen*.

Wen felt heat rising in her cheeks. 'Ah, yes, My Queen,' she sputtered.

'Come forward,' said Cleopatra.

Wen willed her quaking legs through the crowd of advisors, imagining what her head would look like on a spike. When she arrived before the Living Goddess and kneeled, her hands were trembling like a thief's.

'You may rise,' said Cleopatra. 'Who are you and by whose permission do you appear in my presence?'

'This is Wen of Alexandria,' offered an ancient man with long white hair. 'She is the woman you requested, Goddess. Egyptian by birth, but speaks a commoners' Latin.'

'Ah, yes, the…translator,' Cleopatra said. 'Thank you, Mardion.' Cleopatra studied Wen with interest and Wen became painfully aware of her bare feet on the Queen's fine Persian carpet. 'Tell me, Translator, why would Caesar not kill me if I go to him now?'

Wen felt every eye in the room upon her and her courage flickered with the braziers.

'Speak,' Cleopatra commanded. 'The fate of Egypt is at stake!'

'I have heard that Caesar has a taste for h-high-born women,' Wen blurted, instantly aware of the veiled insult she had made.

But the Queen only nodded. 'I have heard this rumour as well. Go on.'

'Th-the Gabiniani of Alexandria say that he has conquered as many women as he has kingdoms. The wives of Crassus and Pompey—even Lollia, the wife of the Gabiniani's own beloved General. I do not think Caesar will kill you, Goddess. Instead he will seek to conquer you as he does all women of power and beauty. In order to prove his worth.'

Cleopatra wore a puzzled expression. She narrowed her eyes. 'Do you support my brother Ptolemy's claim to the Horus Throne?'

'No, my Goddess!'

'Then why do you mingle with the Gabiniani?'

'They frequent the brew house where I toil. Toiled. In Alexandria.'

'In other words, you were bound to serve Roman soldiers and speak to them in their tongue?'

'I did not speak, my Queen. I only listened.'

'An Egyptian woman fluent in the Latin of Rome, yet wise enough not to use it,' the Queen said. She sat back in her throne. 'You are a rare coin, Wen of Alexandria.'

Wen exhaled, feeling that she had passed some sort of test.

A beautiful woman with a halo of black hair bent and whispered something in the Queen's ear. The Queen nodded. 'Speak your question, Iras.'

The woman stepped forward and fixed her thick-lidded gaze on Wen. 'You say that Roman soldiers value conquest above all else. How come you by such knowledge?'

'The Roman men I serve often brag of it, Mistress. They seek to conquer foreign women as a kind of sport.

I know this to be true because I—' she began, but her mind filled with a hot fog and she could not continue.

The Queen and Iras exchanged a knowing glance. 'You do not love Roman soldiers, I presume?' asked Cleopatra.

'You presume correctly, Goddess.'

'What is your name again, Translator?'

'Wen-Nefer, my Queen. Wen.'

'Wen, do you believe I can conquer this Caesar of Rome?'

'I do.'

'Tell me how you would have it done.'

'You must make him believe that he has conquered you.'

'And you know this to be the best way possible, based on your knowledge of Roman soldiers?'

'Yes, and because you are cleverer than he.'

'You seek to flatter me?'

'I seek… I seek only to avow that Egypt is cleverer than Rome. And you are Egypt.'

The Queen sat still for several long moments. She motioned to her advisor Mardion and whispered something in his ear. He studied Wen closely, then whispered something back.

She glanced at her two handmaids, both of whom gave solemn nods. 'It is decided,' she said at last. 'I shall heed Caesar's call. I shall travel to Alexandria in secret and meet him in my palace. I shall trick him into conquering me and thus shall conquer him. And you, Wen, will come with me.'

It trespassed the boundaries of reason. A Queen of Egypt relying on the political advice of a simple slave woman? Madness. Either the witty Queen Cleopatra had lost her wits, or the woman who called herself Wen was not who she appeared to be.

Who was she, then? The question gnawed at him. He studied her from his position at the tent's periphery, hoping to discover a clue.

She was a disaster of a woman, in truth. She stood rigid before the Queen in that sack of a dress, staring at her grubby toes. Her hair was a tangle of dirty locks that cascaded over her bronze shoulders in wild black tongues. He could not discern her shape, but her bare arms displayed the unfeminine musculature of a hard-toiling slave. He might have pitied her, if he were not so totally perplexed.

How could an Egyptian slave woman have such profound insights into Rome's greatest General? Her assessment of Caesar had been brilliant—something a military officer or political advisor might have given. It seemed impossible that she could have gleaned such knowledge by simply pouring beer for Roman soldiers.

Perhaps she does more than pour beer, he thought. Perhaps she served as a *hetaira*, a learned prostitute for high-born men. He watched how she held herself, searching for clues. Impossible. Her posture alone suggested a kind of defeat and her chapped, calloused hands told the story of a life of washing dishes and scrubbing floors.

Nay, she was no *hetaira*. She was about as far from such a role as a woman could get. He scanned her body and noticed the pink stain of a scar rising up from the small of her leg. He followed the scar's intriguing path, wondering where it led, but it quickly disappeared beneath the ragged hem of her tunic.

She was an enigma: the only thing about this tedious war council that he did not understand.

Yet she already seemed to understand him, or at least to suspect his ruse.

He had given her no reason to suspect him of anything. He had played the role of soldier flawlessly, had approached the Queen with a single-minded militancy and correctly feigned ignorance of her royal Greek. If there had been a weakness in the performance, it had been in the fumbling commands of his guard Clodius, though none in the Queen's audience seemed to have noticed.

None except—what had she called herself?

Wen.

She seemed to be the only one to suspect anything, for as he, the real Titus, had returned to the shadows beside her, she had flashed him a suspicious glance— one that had rattled him to his bones. Even if she did not know that he and his guard had switched places, she obviously suspected something. And if she could tease out that secret so easily, what other, more serious secrets might she be capable of discovering?

He shook off a shiver and directed his attention to the discussion at hand. The advisors were debating how the Queen might travel to Alexandria without detection by Ptolemy's spies.

'The Queen must make the journey by the River,' one of the priests was saying. 'She can take the Pelusiac branch of the Delta up to Memphis, then back down the Canopic branch to Alexandria.'

'That would take five days or more,' said one advisor.

'And the river boatmen gossip like wives,' said another. 'She would be discovered and Ptolemy would send out his assassins.'

'To go by land would also be unwise,' called another. 'Ptolemy has offered a reward in gold for the Queen's capture. There will be men in every village looking to profit from her head.'

'Then she must go by sea!' someone called. 'It is the only way.'

'Ptah's foot!' barked the advisor Mardion. He wagged a knobby finger at them all. 'Her vessel would be seized the moment it entered the Great Harbour.'

The room erupted in another spate of discussion—one to which even young Clodius did not appear immune. Wen appeared to be the only one in the room not engaged in the debate. She remained eerily still and silent against the din.

At length, Cleopatra stood and raised her hands. 'Gentlemen, it is late. Decisions made in the hours of Seth are never good ones. Tomorrow afternoon we shall reconvene and make our decision.'

There was a collective sigh of relief as the council turned to await the Queen's exit. Titus felt himself relax. They had succeeded in their ruse. None seemed to guess that the two Romans had switched places—that he, the elder and the stronger, was the true son of a senator and the real commander of Caesar's Sixth.

None except, possibly, Wen. She remained still and unmoving as the Queen's entourage of women bustled about their beloved monarch. She had become invisible, it seemed, to everyone but him.

Chapter Three

Wen kept her head bowed as the war council concluded and the Queen and her entourage exited the tent. The advisors followed after, streaming out of the tent in a garrulous mass. Someone pushed Wen forward and she became swept up in the exodus.

She recalled Sol's words—*one of the Queen's attendants will find you*—and realised that she needed to get herself to a place where she could be found. Outside the tent, she headed towards the only torch she saw, then bumped squarely into a wall.

A human wall. Of muscle and bone.

The Roman guard.

His titanic figure bent over her, as if trying to make out the features of her face. 'You,' he breathed in Latin.

Her heart raced. She turned to retreat, but he took her by the arm. 'Who are you?'

'Who are *you*?' she returned, yanking herself free. There was little light and they were surrounded by bodies. He encircled her in his arms, creating a cocoon of protection against the jostling crowd. Her head pressed against his chest.

Poon-poon. Poon-poon.

She had never heard such a sound.

Poon-poon. Poon-poon. Poon-poon.

It was the sound of his heart, she realised—loud enough to perceive, even through the hard metal of his chainmail, like a small but mighty drum.

Poon-poon. Poon-poon. Poon-poon. Poon-poon.

The night wind swirled around them.

'Who are you?' he whispered huskily. He brushed her tangled hair out of her eyes. 'Who?'

She pushed against his embrace, testing his intentions. 'Why does it matter?'

He slackened his hold, but did not release her. 'I wish to know you better.'

Know me better? In her experience, the only thing Roman soldiers wanted to know was how she planned to serve them. Still, there was something unusual about this Roman soldier. When he had cleared the hair from her face, it was as if he had been handling fine lace.

'Why do you wish to know me better?' she asked.

'I sense that you are not as you seem.'

'Is anybody?'

He chuckled. 'I supposed you have a point.'

The crowd had cleared. There was no longer any reason for him to be holding her, though he pulled her closer still, and she could feel the twin columns of his legs pressing against her own.

He uttered something resembling a sigh and she felt the upheaval of his stomach against hers. He moved his large hand down her back, forcing her hips closer and manoeuvring one of his legs between her thighs.

Her stomach turned over on itself and a strange

thrill rippled across her skin. It occurred to her that she was straddling his massive leg as if it were a horse.

'Curses,' he groaned. He took a deep breath and buried his nose in her hair.

What was he doing? More importantly, why was she not stopping him?

'Why do you feel so good?' he asked with genuine surprise, moving his hands in tandem up her back.

She wanted to pull away from him, but she could not bring herself to do it. It was as if his body was having a private conversation with hers and cared not what her mind might think. He pressed his leg more firmly between hers, sending pangs of unfamiliar pleasure into her limbs.

He thrust his hips towards her and she felt the hardened thickness of his desire press against her stomach.

'Enough!' she gasped. She wrenched herself backwards, stumbling to keep her balance.

'Apologies,' he said. 'I do not know what overcame me.'

'I must go,' she said, stepping backwards.

'Answer my question.'

'What question?'

'Tell me who you are.'

'I am nobody.'

'You do not understand my meaning,' said the Roman. 'I am Clodius of the *familia* Livinius. My kin have lived in the same house in the Aventine neighbourhood of Rome for over three hundred years. My father was a soldier and so am I. A soldier and a son. That is who I am.'

'Is that it?'

'Do you doubt me?'

She held her tongue.

'I am not a liar.'

She took one more step backwards. 'I have not called you a liar.'

'But you suspect that I am one.'

'I suspect nothing.'

'You cannot hide from me,' he said. His voice grew in menace. 'You have been trained in the art of suspicion and I want to know who trained you.'

Suddenly, it all became clear. She threatened him: that was the reason he had held her so close. He wished to gain some advantage over her, to redirect her doubt of his own dubious identity. He did not care for her or desire her at all.

'I am nobody,' said Wen, turning away in stealth. 'I am a slave.'

She heard him take another step closer, but she had already tiptoed beyond his sights. She spied a large tent at the perimeter of camp and began to make her way towards it, glad she knew better than to trust a Roman.

'They cannot stand the sight of us,' Clodius observed. He and Titus were sitting together on the beach, watching a group of Egyptian soldiers launch a fishing boat into the sea.

'Can you blame them? Cleopatra's father owed Rome over four thousand talents. Our presence here is like the appearance of wolves at a picnic.'

'So why were we commanded to come?'

Only I was commanded to come, thought Titus. He had been awoken by Cleopatra's advisor Mardion in the middle of the night. The old man had told Titus to gather his belongings. He was to make haste to the beach, by orders of the Queen.

'I believe I was meant to help those fishermen,' said Titus.

'It seems a little early for fishing, does it not?'

Titus gazed at the sky. The stars were fading, but the light of dawn had yet to arrive. A realization struck him.

'That is not a fishing boat at all,' Titus said. 'That is the Queen's ship, man. It is bound for Alexandria.'

'But her route is not yet decided,' said Clodius.

Titus studied the unassuming, double-oared boat, its two young oarsman rowing out past the waves. 'I think Queen Cleopatra is cleverer than we thought. Look there.'

A jewelled hand was reaching around the curtains of the deck cabin, tugging them closed. Clodius gasped. 'She is already aboard?'

'I fear we will soon be parted, Clodius,' said Titus urgently. 'You must remember our ruse. You are the son of a Roman senator now. You must comport yourself with *dignitas* at all times.'

But Clodius was not listening. His attention had been captured by two elegantly dressed women who appeared at the far end of the beach.

The first walked with smooth grace, her limbs long, her hair a wide cascade of tight curls. Her beautiful dark skin shone like polished obsidian and her appealing slim figure was enhanced by the snug Egyptian tunic she wore. In her arms she carried a medium-sized chest that Titus guessed contained belongings of the Queen.

'Venus's rose,' said Clodius.

'I believe she is called Iras,' said Titus. 'She stood behind Cleopatra at the war council. I believe she is the Queen's first handmaid.'

Next to Iras walked the woman the Queen had called Charmion, her Greekness evident in the wreath of flowers adorning her hair. She walked with an energetic bounce, exaggerating the sway of her lovely hips. Charmion, too, carried a small chest, but it was propped on her side, resulting in the favourable display of her abundant breasts.

'Forget Venus—I should like to worship one of those two. Which do you choose, Commander?'

'Remember your *dignitas*, Clodius. You must—'

'But there is a third,' Clodius interrupted. 'Do you not see her?'

It was true. There was another woman walking half a pace behind the other two. She carried a chest that was of much greater size and apparent weight than the other women's, though she was plainly the smallest of the three. Still, she appeared quite equal to her burden and she walked with an almost comical determination.

'That is the Queen's translator,' Titus said. 'Wen.'

'She is not quite as grand as the first two, but pretty in her way,' said Clodius.

Titus swallowed hard. To him, she was more than pretty, though he was unsure what it was about her that made him admire her so.

She had clearly bathed and oiled herself, and her skin shone bronze in the increasing light. Her long black hair had been braided, then pinned in a neat spiral around her head, revealing the alluring column of her neck.

But he had admired many such necks.

Perhaps it was her eyes. The already large, dark lamps had been made larger with the liberal application of kohl, giving her a feline quality that was compounded by her unnerving alertness. She made Titus's blood run hot.

'Well, which do you choose?' asked Clodius. 'Commander Titus?'

Titus cringed. 'You must not address me as Commander Titus!' He dropped his voice to a whisper. '*You* are Titus now, remember? You must play the part.'

What happened next was one of the strangest things Titus had ever seen. The handmaids hurried to join the men loading the shore boat. They placed their chests in the boat and removed their sandals. Then the whole group dropped to their knees in prayer.

'What are they doing, Commander—I mean, ah, Clodius?'

'I believe they are asking their sea god for his good will.'

'The women are allowed to pray alongside the men?'

'In Egypt it is so.'

Suddenly, Mardion and two guards appeared at the edge of the beach. They were towing a large sheep.

'And what now?' asked Clodius.

'I believe they are going to sacrifice that sheep.'

'Does that mean there will be mutton to eat?'

'A son of a senator would never ask such a question.'

'About mutton?'

Titus shook his head in vexation, grateful they were out of earshot of anyone else.

The sheep's death was mercifully swift, though Mardion took his time studying the animal's entrails. When his examination was complete, he took a bowl of the sheep's blood and offered it to the waves. When he returned, he handed the empty bowl to Iras, and bowed to her.

'Did I just see what I think I saw?' asked Clodius.

'An elder statesman bowing to a young woman—yes, you did.'

Clodius shook his head in vexation. 'It is as if the women here are—'

'Equal to the men. No, but they are certainly more equal than in Rome. Did I not warn you about Egypt's backwardness?'

The strange ceremony was not yet over. The men and women gathered at the edge of the surf and, one by one, they dived into the waves, then emerged and headed back towards the fire.

'Jove's balls,' said Clodius, staring at the saturated figures of Iras and Charmion. Their white garments had become transparent as a result of their watery inundation, revealing the dark round shadows of their pointed nipples. 'Just look at those Venus mounts!'

'Watch your language,' Titus scolded. 'And stop gawking. *Dignitas!*'

If Titus had been in his right mind, he might have explained that Egyptian tradition held unusual ideas about female nudity. Visible breasts were common in Egypt and an educated Roman nobleman knew better than to gape at them. Still, when he caught sight of Wen, Titus became culpable of the very behaviour he was trying to prevent.

Her long, dark tunic clung tightly to her flesh, leaving none of her soft curves undefined. It was as if his own body held a memory of those curves and he yearned to pull her against him once again.

Wen's breasts were not as visible as the other women's. The taut peaks of her nipples remained concealed by her tunic's dark hue, but he was inspired to imagine them: succulent dark olives that begged to be tasted.

Curses on his wretched soul. He was trying to teach his young charge *dignitas*, yet he could not seem to peel his eyes away from the vision of some inconsequential slave woman drenched in seawater.

In his frustration, he reached for his guard's arm and squeezed it. 'You have listened to me, but you have not heard me, so let me put it plainly: if your true identity is discovered, you will likely suffer a flogging, or you may be dragged through the camp behind a chariot. Do you understand?'

'Yes,' Clodius replied absently.

'Do you really understand?' Titus repeated, yanking the young man to face him. 'It is your life I am talking about.'

'I understand.'

Titus released Clodius's arm. Chastened, the young soldier remained silent for so long that Titus feared that he had hurt his pride. 'The Egyptian,' Titus said at length.

'What?'

'You asked me whom I choose—of the three handmaids. I choose the small Egyptian.'

A roguish grin returned to Clodius's face. 'Then you are as mad as I suspected.'

The sun peeked over the horizon and the three soaking maidens turned like sunflowers towards its warm rays while the men—the men!—butchered and cooked the sheep. Soon chunks of cooked mutton were being passed around on knives and everyone ate while Titus and Clodius looked on hungrily.

'Mutton or maiden?' asked Clodius with a smirk.

Titus's stomach rumbled. 'Certainly mutton,' he said.

Clodius rolled his eyes. 'I would starve for a week if only I could have just a single taste of maiden.'

'If we stay any longer, I fear we will begin to howl like wolves,' Titus said, stepping from the shade. 'Let us depart.'

But it was too late. Mardion and his guards were already running up the beach towards them, their swords drawn. 'What is happening?' asked Clodius, reaching for his *gladius* sword. 'Why do they attack?'

'They do not attack, so do not fight back!' whispered Titus. 'We are at their mercy now. Remember the ruse.'

The guards seized Clodius's arms and Mardion spoke. 'Titus Tillius Fortis, son of Senator Lucius Tillius Cimber, you are now a royal hostage of Queen Cleopatra.'

Clodius froze. For the first time all morning, the young soldier appeared at a loss for words. 'Your guard will accompany the Queen to Alexandria and guide her to Caesar,' explained Mardion. 'You will stay here at camp. As long as Cleopatra remains alive, so will you.'

'*Dignitas,*' Titus whispered, and the guards dragged Clodius away.

Titus drew a breath. It had not been the most graceful of partings, but they had managed to sustain their ruse. And it had been worth the effort, for the Queen and her advisors had taken Clodius, believing him to be Titus. As a result, the real Titus was now headed back to Alexandria—back to his post at General Caesar's side. There, he could resume his command of the Sixth, as well as his other, more important work.

Relief washed over him as he followed Mardion towards the fire. When he finally looked up, he noticed that Wen was watching him, her large dark eyes as steady as stones. She shook her head slightly, as if in disapproval, then cocked her head at him like a kitten.

Did she suspect him of something? Impossible. He had done nothing to warrant her suspicion. And even if he had, she could not produce any proof of his deception.

Besides, she was just a woman, with a woman's limitations of intellect. He had no reason to worry, though he admitted that in that moment he felt stripped naked by her gaze, as if she were the priest and he the sheep.

They set off at dawn across a glassy sea. Wen stood against the starboard rail, staring out at the vastness, but all she could think of was *his* crocodilian grin and the *poon-poon-poon* of his beating heart.

'The water is beautiful in the morning, is it not?' said Apollodorus, one of the rowers heaving backwards on the row bench.

'A more beautiful sight I have never seen,' said Wen, tossing the Sicilian a friendly grin.

She deliberately ignored the Roman, though he occupied the bench directly behind Apollodorus and his gaze seemed to follow her beneath his heavy lids. She did not appreciate his watching her, for it prevented her from watching him.

She peeked at him sidelong, pretending to watch a gull. He had removed his chainmail cuirass and as he pulled backwards on the oars his tunic hugged against the deep contours of his chest. She had never seen such a powerful man and he flexed his legs with a languid ease that was unnerving.

Restless, she strode behind the deckhouse to the stern, heralding the two rudder boys and pausing near the deckhouse window. Inside, the Queen and her handmaids dozed, snoring in rhythm with the rocking waves. Wen whispered a prayer to Hathor for their peace and safety and another prayer to Isis to give thanks.

Because of Queen Cleopatra, Wen would never again stare at the mud-brick walls and wonder what lay beyond them. Nor would she ever have to endure the stares of drunken Romans, or defend herself against violent lechers, or feel her life slipping away with each pour of beer. Never again—for the Queen had saved her.

In return, she vowed to save the Queen. Wen could not stand up to invading armies, of course, but she could protect Cleopatra from hidden plots and reckless advice. Wen had been trained in such matters, after all—by the High Priestess of Hathor herself. And she would use that training as best she could to support Cleopatra's reign.

Wen stared out at the placid sea once again, hardly able to believe it was real. She had always known the sea was there—somewhere beyond the brew-house walls. It had been close enough to smell, to hear, yet never close enough to touch.

Once, when she was much younger, she had been determined to know the sea. She had begged her master for permission to visit the harbour, hoping to find her way beyond it. Just once in her life, she wanted to gaze out at the open ocean, to witness the tempestuous realm that the soldiers and sailors spoke of with such awe. To see what lay beyond.

Her master said he would consider her request and, as the months passed, she developed a plan. She would follow the shoreline promenade to Heptastadion Bridge, where she would cross to Pharos Island. There, she would make her way to the base of the Lighthouse, sneak past the toll taker and climb to the middle platform. Upon that high perch, she would gaze out at the endless sea and the meaning of her life would be revealed.

It was a beautiful dream, and Wen clung to it fiercely, even as the months passed, and then, slowly, the years. She reminded her master of the request several times, but he only nodded without hearing.

Then, one evening, a fight broke out in the brew house and, in the chaos, Wen was dragged to the rooftop where she struggled against a man twice her size. There were blows and blood, and a terrifying jump. As she wallowed unaided on the stony ground, she became fully aware of how little her dreams mattered. How little *she* mattered.

After her wounds had healed, her master finally granted her wish. 'You may take a day of rest and visit the Lighthouse,' he had told her. He had even given her money—a small round coin for the toll taker: an apology cast in bronze.

But it was too late. 'Thank you, Master, but I would rather stay here,' she had said, returning the coin to his wrinkled hand. She no longer wanted to visit the har-

bour, or the Lighthouse, or gaze out at the Big Green
Sea. Such dreams were not for women like her.

Or so she had believed, until the Queen had saved
her.

Wen returned to the stern and stared at Titus, daring
him to meet her gaze. She resolved to do everything
in her power to be worthy of the Queen's kindness,
even if it meant appointing herself as a royal spy. If
Titus was a snake hiding in the grass, then Wen would
be the hawk. She would not rest until she discovered
his secret.

Titus was grateful for his post at the oars, for it
gave his body purpose. His mind, unfortunately, was
as restless as the sea.

He wanted her and it was a problem. She was not
his to want. She was a slave, a bonded soul. Her body
was the property of another—in this case the exiled
Queen of Egypt.

In truth Titus pitied her, as he did all slaves. There
were so many in Rome now. They represented almost
a third of Rome's population and their numbers grew
with each military conquest. They were a tragic people, so stripped of their own will that they relinquished
it entirely. Not since the time of Spartacus had slaves
risen up and he doubted they would do it again. They
were a passive, miserable lot, resigned to the injustice
of their lives.

Titus pitied slave women: he did not desire them.

That is what he reminded himself as she strolled
about the deck.

That afternoon, a wind came up, a strong northerly
that allowed Titus and Apollodorus to rest their arms

while the rudder boys hoisted the sails. Titus closed
his eyes and tried to rest as their small ship began to
make speed.

They made camp at the mouth of a small river that
evening and enjoyed a simple meal of flatbread, dried
fish and grapes. Apollodorus made a fire and soon they
were staring into its flames.

Titus must have fallen asleep, for he awoke to the
rhythm of Apollodorus's snores. There was a softer
sound, as well—the sound of women's laughter.

'I think he is quite handsome,' whispered a voice
that he recognised as Charmion's. It was coming from
directly behind him, as he lay on his side, his back to
the flames. 'Look at how his hair stands upon its ends.
I would like to run my fingers through it.'

'I, too, am partial to the Roman,' whispered another woman.

Iras, he thought.

'He is so very like a tree. I would like to climb his
branches.'

'I would like to wander the marshes with him,' whispered Charmion. There was a conspiracy of laughter
that made him wonder if 'wander the marshes' really
meant exploring Egypt's prodigious wetlands.

He was sure that it did not. These were women, after
all—silly creatures who enjoyed gossiping and making mischief. He was not wholly against their kind, of
course. He loved their soft, curvy bodies and found it
enjoyable to give them pleasure, though his military
career had afforded him little time for such pursuits.

In the camps of Britannia and Gaul he had learned
everything he needed to know about women, for they
would often visit him in his tent. Mostly they were

working women—Roman and barbarian harlots who followed the legions to earn their bread. They never had much to say, though they were always happy to see Titus and seemed to enjoy the pleasures he offered. Still, he was careful not to flatter himself that they actually enjoyed his company and he always paid them well for theirs.

When he finally returned to Rome he quickly learned that not all women were like the harlots he patronised in the camps. High-born noblewomen were another breed entirely. They were boundless in their ambition—greedy and ruthless as any general. And as the highest-ranking bachelor in Caesar's army, Titus was apparently a territory worth conquering. The mothers of Palatine Hill had made it their business to find Titus a good patrician wife and they presented their daughters to him in a never-ending series of banquets.

But the women were like shells—beautiful, alluring and disappointingly empty. Their desire for wealth and status ranged far beyond their intellect. They were easily bored and seemed unable to participate in even the most basic discussions of philosophy or politics. The women of Rome vexed him, and though he disagreed with Caesar's bloody civil war, he was happy to be called away to duty.

'We must be quiet,' whispered Iras. 'He is probably listening to us right now.'

'I do not think he can understand us,' said Charmion. 'He does not speak Greek.'

'Ah! I had forgotten,' said Iras. 'Do you think if I lay down beside him he would speak Latin into my ear?'

'Senatus Populusque Romanus,' mocked Charmion.

'*E pluribus unum,*' added Iras, snickering.

Women.

Still, these women of Egypt seemed a different breed. Unlike Roman women, they were allowed to study trades and conduct business, as if they were men's equals. They could even divorce and inherit property—backwards notions if ever he had heard them. Indeed, it seemed that Egyptian women said and did whatever they wished, with no consideration for the men who were their natural superiors.

'What say you, Wen?' asked Iras. 'Which of our two oarsmen do you choose?'

Titus held his breath.

'Mistress?' said Wen.

'Do you also prefer the Roman?'

'In truth, Mistress, I prefer Apollodorus,' said Wen.

Titus could not believe his ears.

'Really?' said Iras, in surprised delight. 'How interesting. Well, I suppose the Sicilian has his merits. His loyalty to the Queen is certainly apparent.'

'Almost as apparent as his pot belly,' Charmion giggled.

'Shush yourself,' snipped Iras. 'But tell us, Wen, for what reason do you favour the Sicilian?'

Wen's voice was barely audible. 'He seems loyal to the Queen and his motives are clear.'

There was a pause, then both Charmion and Iras burst into laughter.

'That is quite philosophical of you, Wen,' said Charmion at last. 'Are you sure you do not prefer a man who can throw boulders?'

Wen gave a polite laugh. 'Loyalty is more important than strength.'

Something in the tone of her voice pricked at Titus's mind. It was as if she were speaking to him indirectly, as if she were trying to send him a message.

As if she guessed that he was awake.

He slept little the rest of the night. What bothered him most was not that she did not trust him. He had grown accustomed to the idea of her suspicion, much as a gardener might grow accustomed to an unpicked weed. What he could not fathom was her preference for the Sicilian. Apollodorus was a loyal man, to be sure. Even Titus had heard of his efforts in recruiting Queen Cleopatra's army of mercenaries.

But the man was obviously a glutton. He had breath like a stinking beetle and a stomach the size of a cow's. How could she choose such a man? And why, more importantly, had she chosen him over Titus?

Chapter Four

They departed before dawn the next morning. As Titus and Apollodorus found their rhythm at the oars, Wen appeared alone on the deck. She gazed out at the sea, her arms tight around her chest.

He could have said that his trouble began when his thigh grazed her arm, or moments after that instant, when she stood beside him at the Queen's war council—though that would not have been entirely true. When she slipped into the shadows beside him, he had regarded her as a mere mouse, probably sent from the gossip-hungry soldiers to steal a bit of cheese.

He could have said that his trouble began when he held her against him, trying to protect her from the crowd, but that would have also been a lie. His reaction to her had not been unusual. Women were women after all. Their bodies were designed to give pleasure, though he had to admit that her body had felt better than most.

No, his trouble began that second morning at sea, as she strolled about the deck. She had unfastened her braid from its fixed circle around her head the day before and had failed to refasten it since. The result was a maddening distraction, for its delicate tips brushed back and forth across her bottom as she moved. When she finally spoke to him he was not in full possession of his wits.

'It is a lovely morning, is it not?' she asked.

He opened his mouth to reply, then stopped himself.

She knew that he claimed ignorance of Greek, yet she had asked the question in that language. And in his distraction, he had opened his mouth to respond.

'It is not my place to pry,' she began in Latin, 'or to insert myself in the affairs of those greater than me. I am a slave and you are a soldier, and your life of course is more important than my own. But since we both now find ourselves in service to Egypt's rightful Queen, I wondered if you might forgive my boldness in asking you a question?'

For a moment he wondered if he was not listening to the questions of a simple slave woman, but to the rhetorical machinations of Cicero himself. 'Ah, yes, of course,' he managed.

'Why did you not bow to him?'

'Bow to whom? I'm sorry, I do not understand.'

'Why did you not bow to your commander Titus yesterday when he was taken by the guards?'

'I did not bow to him? Well, that is uncharacteristic of me. I shall apologise to him when I see him next. He must have been quite affronted.'

Her fix on him was so steady, he began to feel unnerved.

'Then he must have been doubly offended when you seized his arm.'

Titus ceased his efforts at the oars. 'I seized his arm? Are you certain?'

'You do not remember? You held it very tightly.'

For all his rhetorical training, he was uncertain as to how to respond. He coughed out a laugh. 'Ah! Look there,' he said, pointing over her shoulder at the rising sun.

She turned. 'Ra is reborn,' she said. She looked at him expectantly.

'I'm sorry, but I do not adhere to the cult of Ra.'

'May I ask what cult do you subscribe to?'

'The cult of logic. It is mostly unknown here in Egypt, but in Rome we Stoics revere it.'

'May I ask what is a Stoic?'

'One who believes that kings and gods should not steer men's fates.'

He saw her blink and was satisfied. Egyptians were quite unreasonable when it came to the subject of their gods and he was certain that he had offended her enough to put her off the subject. He noticed the tiny black blades of her lashes.

'Does the cult of logic have duplicity as its requisite?' she asked, batting those blades.

'Excuse me?'

'You heard me, good Clodius.'

He was stunned into silence. Had she just accused him of lying? But she was a slave. She was not allowed to accuse anyone of anything. 'I'm sorry, Wen, but you are mistaken. I have known the tribune Titus since he was a boy. I am his guard and sometimes his mentor, though I should not be required to explain any of this to you.'

She shook her head, having none of it. 'Forgive me, but I was valued by my former master for my ability to detect dishonesty and I cannot help but notice that your mouth twitches when you say your commander's name. I am compelled by my position in service to the Queen—to whom I owe everything—to request from you an honest answer. Whoever you are, I know that you are neither guard, nor mentor, nor simple soldier.'

He was appalled. 'And whoever you believe yourself to be, it is quite clear that you are just a slave.'

He watched her swallow hard, instantly regretting his words. He had wounded her for certain. She turned back towards the rising sun. When she spoke again, her voice was barely a whisper.

'It is true that I am low,' she began, 'and that I was purchased by the Queen as her slave. As such, I am bound to protect her. But that is not why I do it.'

'Why do you do it, then?' he asked, but she ignored his question.

'You speak of logic. Well, logic tells me not to believe you, for you are a Roman and I have never known a Roman I could trust.'

'You are a woman for certain, for you are ruled by humours and whims,' he growled, aware that his own humours were mixing quite dangerously.

A wave hit the side of the boat, causing it to tilt. To steady herself, she placed her hand over his, igniting an invisible spark.

She glared at him before snapping her hand away and stepping backwards. 'Good Clodius—though I know that is not your name—I would ask that you please not insult my intelligence.'

Her sunny words seemed to grow in their menace. 'I may not be as big as you, or as smart as you, or as sly as you, but believe me when I tell you that I know how to handle Roman men.' She flung her braid behind her as

if brandishing a whip. 'If you do anything to endanger
the Queen, or our quest to restore her rightful reign, or
if your deception results in harm to either the Queen
or either of her handmaids, you will be very sorry.'

Her audacity was stunning. No woman had ever
spoken to him in such a way.

He refused to give her the satisfaction of revealing
his discomposure, however, so he placidly resumed
his efforts at the oars, taking care to stay in rhythm
with Apollodorus.

Still, his troops were in retreat; they had lost the
battle. His unlikely adversary had utilised all the tricks
of rhetoric, along with the full force of her personal-
ity, to enrage him, then confuse him, and then finally
to leave him speechless.

Nor was she yet finished. As the great yellow globe
shone out over the shimmering sea, he felt her warm
breath in his ear. 'Just remember that I have my eye
on you, Roman.'

He turned his head and there were her lips, so near
to his, near enough to touch.

And in that moment, despite everything, he wanted
nothing more in the world than to kiss them.

And that was when his real trouble began.

She could not focus her thoughts. They were like
tiny grains of sand, endless in their number, impossible to gather. She told herself that her inattention was
the result of her worry about the Queen, but she knew
that was not true.

It was because of him.

She had pretended his words could not harm her,
but in truth they had split her in two. *Whoever you be-*

lieve yourself to be, it is quite clear that you are just a slave. That was what he had said to her. *Just a slave.*

And it was true. She *was* just a slave. She was nothing. No one. Her thoughts mattered little, her suspicions even less. To a man like him, she was simply a piece of property, like a tunic or a sword. Her only worth was in her ability to stay out of his way.

Well, she was not going to stay out of his way.

She might have been just a slave, but she was the Queen's slave now. She would do whatever she had to do to protect Cleopatra. She might have mattered little, but now she mattered a little more. She was not fragile, or vacuous, or irrational, as he had so sweepingly suggested. She was…intelligent and strong, and she would prove it to him.

She would prove it to herself.

She walked to the water's edge and stared out at the sparkling white caps, wondering at their beauty. It was the second and final day of their journey and they had made an early camp upon the sands of a small azure bay. Just down the beach from her, the men and boys were fishing from the shore—casting their lines into the gentle waves as if they had not a care in the world.

In truth, it was the beginning of the most dangerous night of all their lives. Their plan was to depart after nightfall and travel the final stretch into Alexandria's harbour under the cover of darkness. They would tie off at the royal fishing dock in the deepest part of night, and travel in silence, avoiding any of Ptolemy's night patrols as they made their way towards Caesar's villa.

And prayed they were not walking into a trap.

Wen watched Clodius from the corner of her eye. He stood knee-deep in the water, casting his line clumsily into the gentle waves. He seemed incapable of trapping anything—at least in this light. Clearly he was not a fisherman. Nor was he a simple soldier. What was he, then?

He was certainly strong. He had removed his armour and stood amidst the waves wearing only a loincloth. His large, muscular chest stretched with his breaths and the long flanks of his back moved like oars as he cast and recast his line into the waves.

She hated herself for staring, but she could not help it. His stomach was a ripple of large, defined muscles, as if they had been shaped by a sculptor from clay. He looked rather like a statue of Heracles she had once seen—that powerful Greek hero with divine blood. She did not blame Charmion and Iras for admiring him. If he did not pose such a threat, she might have done the same.

She had lied when she said she preferred the Sicilian. She favoured the Roman—irrationally, maddeningly so. When she had whispered her threat into his ear that morning, a strange feeling had overcome her. She felt a fire deep inside herself, and a powerful desire to kiss his lips.

It was an odd feeling—to desire a man. She had never done so before. There had been many brew-house clients who had noticed her over the years, a few had even pretended to be kind, but she was careful not to encourage them. She knew how men truly felt about slave women. Especially Roman men. They used them and discarded them as they wished.

Which was why she did not understand her body's

strange yearning for this particular Roman. The High Priestess had taught her much, but she had not prepared Wen for a situation such as this—when her body's desires were at war with her better senses.

She was preparing to dive into the waves when Iras's voice rang out, summoning Wen to the Queen's tent.

Moments later, Wen was stepping inside the shadowy space and beheld the Queen staring at herself in a polished copper mirror. She caught sight of Wen in her reflection. 'Tell me, Wen, how does an Alexandrian beer maid learn the art of debate?'

Wen paused. The Queen must have heard her heated words with Clodius that morning.

'A priestess once told me that there is power in words,' Wen said. 'She taught me how to use them.'

Cleopatra looked up from her mirror and turned to face Wen. 'Then your priestess must have had some training in the rhetorical arts.'

Yes, Goddess. She was the High Priestess of Hathor. She was extremely learned. That is what Wen wanted to say, but she could not, because she had not been questioned directly. *No matter what happens, you must never address the Queen directly. You must wait until she speaks to you.* That was Sol's advice and she meant to heed it.

'Here it is, my Queen,' said Iras, holding up Wen's old hemp tunic.

'It will be a brilliant disguise,' said the Queen. 'Do you not think so, Wen?'

I have been questioned directly, thought Wen. *I may respond freely.* 'I—do not think so, my Queen. I think Pharaoh Ptolemy's guards will be more likely to stop and question a beggar, and less likely to believe her.'

Cleopatra shot Iras a look and Iras gave a resigned nod. 'She speaks wisely, Goddess. Let us think of a different disguise.'

'I have it!' burst Charmion. 'We shall disguise her as a man.'

'But look at her,' said Iras. 'She is too small to pass for a man and too womanly to pass for a boy.'

Wen had an idea. She knew that she was not supposed to address the Queen directly, but she also knew that their lives were at risk. She dared to speak. 'The Queen could wear a *hetaira's* robe,' she whispered. 'It would cover her completely. Only her eyes would be visible.'

Wen waited to be scolded for her insolence. 'It is impossible,' Iras said, shaking her head in disagreement.

'No Queen of Egypt would ever debase herself in the costume of a Greek harlot,' added Charmion.

But Cleopatra was nodding her head in a kind of wonder. 'It is a brilliant idea,' she said softly.

Iras and Charmion stood in stunned silence. 'But it would debase you, my Thea,' said Iras.

Charmion buried her face in her hands.

'Do not fear, sisters,' the Queen said. 'It is only a Janus face that I will wear. Besides, the garment is beyond modest. It will cover everything but my eyes. It will be as if I am wearing a carpet!'

The Queen crossed to Charmion and wiped the tears that were now rolling down her handmaiden's cheek. 'Do not despair, my dearest Charmion,' she said. 'I would never bow before any Roman, as my father once did. I will pretend debasement, but I will never suffer it. I am descended from Alexander the Great, after all! Do not fear for my honour. My honour is Egypt's honour. I will keep it, or I will die.'

The Queen's three attendants stood silent—a Greek, a Nubian and an Egyptian—their hearts humming with pride. This was no spoiled young princess, playing at politics. This was a woman on a mission. This was a queen. *Their* Queen.

They were so enthralled by Cleopatra's speech that none of them noticed the visitor standing outside the tent. *'Veniam in me,'* he said, begging their pardons, his large naked chest shading the entrance. In one hand, he held his fishing rod. In another, he held a fish the size of a cat.

'An omen!' exclaimed Charmion.

'It will make a fine meal,' said Cleopatra, her gaze paralyzed by the sight of Clodius's chest. 'Wen, please accept the fish and tell Clodius that we are pleased.'

Wen swallowed her misgivings and thanked Clodius in Latin. She took the fish into her grasp along with a small blade from the cooking chest and stepped outside the tent. Clodius followed after her.

'Would you like me to end its life?' he asked, gripping the hilt of his *pugio* dagger.

'That is not necessary,' she said as she wrestled with the writhing creature. The last thing she wanted was to be indebted to the Roman for anything.

'Are you able to do it?'

'Of course I am able,' she told him. 'Am I not a woman?'

'Yes, and I am a man and thus you are naturally inferior to me,' he paused, regarding her frown. 'In strength, I mean.'

Once again, he had given away his true feelings

and they maddened her. 'If you will forgive me, I must fulfil the command of the most powerful woman in the world.'

He frowned and she took the opportunity to rush past him towards a cluster of nearby boulders. Her effort was for naught, however, for she sensed him watching her backside as she walked. A quick glance behind her confirmed her suspicion and she threw him a scowl. He returned the look with a sheepish grin and settled himself on a rock.

She kept walking, searching for a suitable place to dispatch the fish. Finding nothing, she was forced to double back around to the cluster of rocks where Clodius sat. She placed the slithery fish on a rock not paces from him. He folded his hands in his lap and smiled at her, as if he had just taken his seat at the theatre.

Good, she thought with satisfaction. *Let him observe how skilfully I wield a knife.*

She steadied the poor, magnificent creature upon the rock, then dispatched it with a quick thrust of her blade. Titus's eyes were riveted upon her, so she lifted her knife and severed the fish's head in a show of strength. It was not an easy thing to do, though she tried to make it appear easy.

When she looked up again, he was still watching her closely, as if she were territory he planned to conquer. She returned his gaze in defiance. *I am in service to Queen Cleopatra*, she reminded herself. *You cannot harm me.*

On impulse, she made a swift cut up the fish's belly and pulled out a long strand of its innards. With the innards in one hand and the bloodied knife in the other, she stood and faced the Roman. 'Is this what you want?' she shouted. She held up her handful of innards. 'This is what I do to my enemies!'

As she held the entrails aloft, he suffered a spasm of laughter so profound that the only way to conceal it was to feign a series of violent coughs. If the entrails had belonged to an enemy, she might have been terrifying. As it was, the only thing he feared was that he might burst some internal part of him in his convulsions, or perhaps even die of laughter.

Her boldness was so unexpected—like a splash of seawater upon his face. The slave Spartacus would have liked her for his army, he thought, for she seemed to care not whom she threatened. Women the world over had always seemed to appreciate Titus, but not this little pigeon.

Still, the more she rebuffed him, the more he seemed to want her. He wanted to link her gory hands with his. He wanted to look into her doubting eyes. He wanted to plant a kiss on her sweet, pursing lips. It was an altogether ridiculous notion, made more ridiculous by his awareness that he vexed her mightily.

Titus watched with rapt attention as she gathered small pieces of driftwood, then set to work whittling them with her knife. Her skewers complete, she deftly filleted the fish into eight equal portions and skewered them, then absently wiped the knife on the skirt of her tunic.

She paused, dipping her gaze to the place where she had wiped the knife. Titus watched an expression of horror spread across her face with the realisation that she had stained the fine garment.

She cast him a narrow-eyed glare then, as if she

blamed him for the mistake. Then she hurled the knife into the sand in an adorable huff. He chuckled once more as she dashed to the ocean where she began a Herculean effort to scrub out the stain.

For the first time, he observed her naked legs. She had unknowingly lifted her skirt to above her knees, giving him a tantalising view of them and a dark suggestion of what lay just beyond. His desire stirred. He felt like Odysseus in the presence of Calypso. He could not take his eyes off her dripping legs. He wondered how they might feel wrapped about his middle.

He ran his fingers through his hair. He needed to find some occupation, lest his *dignitas* be lost on this very beach. The sun flashed off the knife where she had thrown it down and an idea came to him.

He walked up the beach to the place beneath a palm where he had laid his tunic. He settled himself in the palm's shade, watching as Wen returned to the Queen's tent. He found a small bone and had soon honed it well enough to serve as a needle with which to weave palm fibres. He became so absorbed in his task that he did not notice her until he spied her bare feet stepping beneath the shade in which he sat.

'The Queen requests your presence once again,' she announced with a sigh.

'Well, that is a relief,' he mocked. 'I feared that you had come to sever my head!'

'The Queen wishes to ask you a question.'

'Let me guess, the Queen will ask me a question, then you will disembowel me and read the answer in the shape of my innards.' It was all he could do to keep from laughing at his own cleverness.

She glanced at his naked chest with irritation. 'You must be fully clothed to appear before the Queen of Egypt,' she said, then turned and began walking away.

'Come now,' he called after her, fumbling into his tunic. He bounded to her side. 'I was only teasing you, you know.'

'Hmm. Like when you feigned sleep the other night? Were you only teasing then?'

'I feigned nothing.'

'Your breaths were uneven. You would not stop flexing your feet.'

'You watched me, then? As I slept?'

'Your stirring drew my attention.'

'You are right that I could not sleep, for you and the Queen's handmaids were gossiping like hens.'

'How would you know we spoke gossip? You do not speak Greek. You could not have understood our words.' There was a long pause and she took the opportunity to stride past him.

He caught up to her effortlessly and resolved to change the subject. 'It is a lovely day, is it not?' he asked. It was, in truth, a lovely day, though she said nothing in response. 'The sun should not be so warm for *Octobris*. Do you not agree?'

'I do not know what *Octobris* is,' she clipped. 'For me it is the first month of *peret*, the beginning of the season of planting and growth. And, no, I do not find it unseasonably warm.'

They walked together in silence, and she seemed satisfied that she had sufficiently frustrated him. Alas, she was mistaken.

'Earlier I saw an eagle flying near the shore,' he offered. 'Did you not see it? It is yet another good omen.'

She glanced up at him, studying his features. 'Why do you groom your brows?' she asked.

'What?'

'Among the Roman Gabiniani whom I served, only officers trim their eyebrows. Infantry soldiers do not.'

'Well, I am an exception then,' he lied. He searched for words to fill the silence. 'We shall see the Lighthouse tonight as we approach Alexandria. Did you know that there are giant copper mirrors at its apex? They send the fire's light much farther than it would otherwise go alone.'

Wen gave him a curious look, but said nothing.

'Well, I am glad the Queen wishes to consult with me about our journey,' he offered.

'She does not wish to consult with you. She wishes to ask you a question.'

'Well, I am grateful to you for retrieving me.'

'I was commanded to retrieve you.'

'I am grateful none the less.'

She stopped suddenly and dug her feet into the sand. 'Stop.'

'Stop what?'

'Stop trying to endear yourself to me so that I will not betray your ruse.'

'That is not what I'm doing.'

'So you admit that there is a ruse?'

'I admit no such thing.'

'Then why are you trying to befriend me? You are a Roman. Therefore, you will never be my friend.'

'I do not wish to be your friend.'

'And why is that, exactly?'

'Because you are beneath me.'

* * *

The response was wholly expected, but it fell upon her like a blow. She felt weak and diminished. She wished that the sands in which she stood would simply swallow her up.

Still, she would not give him the satisfaction of witnessing her shame. 'I think that is the first true thing that has escaped your lips, Roman,' she said. She stepped from his path.

'Apologies, I did not mean——' he began.

'There is no need to apologise. You spoke truth. Now please, stop bothering me. As you said, I am just a slave.'

She walked on.

'I spoke without thinking,' he called to her. 'I did not mean to offend you.'

'You spoke what was in your heart,' she said without turning.

She was nearing the Queen's tent, but he managed to catch up to her once again. He stopped her in her path. 'Listen to me. You have nothing to fear from me. I do not mean you or your Queen any harm.'

He had positioned himself with the sun behind him so that she was able to stand in the shade produced by his shadow. She wondered if he had done so on purpose. His shoulders were slumped, as if he were trying to reduce his size.

She realised suddenly that she did not fear him. She did not trust him, but she did not fear him. On the contrary, standing there in his ample shadow gave her the strange sense of standing inside a cave.

'Tell me the truth,' she said at last. 'Are you or are you not a soldier?'

He took a breath. 'I am.'

'In whose army?'

'I serve Rome.'

'Not General Caesar?'

He paused. 'We both serve Rome.'

The Rome that is preparing to swallow Egypt whole? Her mouth had become dry. 'What is your purpose here in truth?'

Clodius appeared to choose his words carefully. 'My purpose is to serve the best interests of the Roman people. Now please, can we not be friends?'

Conquest, she thought. *That is your purpose. Why can you not just say it?* To conquer was the only thing Roman men wanted. It was the only thing they knew. Clodius and Caesar were of different rank, but they were cut from the same cloth. Whatever lay before them, they wished to bring it under their control— whether a fish, a woman, or the greatest kingdom on earth.

'I am sorry, Clodius, but I do not make friends with Romans.'

He felt like a dog that had just been scolded. He ducked his head beneath the entrance to the Queen's tent, having no idea that his punishment had only just begun.

'Good Clodius!' said the Queen as he stepped into the shadowy space. 'Thank you for returning. I had forgotten the important question I had hoped to ask you.'

Wen translated the Queen's greeting to Titus, and he gave a deep bow. 'I am at your service, Queen Cleopatra,' he said in Latin.

As his eyes adjusted to the low light, he saw Iras

seated on the carpet beside the Queen, searching through a trunkful of clothing. On the other side, Charmion was carefully picking what appeared to be beetles' shells from one of her pastes. The two women looked up from their tasks as Titus stepped forward. Iras raked her eyes up his legs. Charmion gave a polite nod and followed it with an unseemly moistening of her lips.

Women.

He had no choice but to endure their caprices. He bent to his knees at the base of the Queen's stool in the required obeisance.

'My handmaids are just preparing my disguise,' explained the Queen, touching his shoulder. He rose and stood, but his head bumped against the low cloth ceiling, requiring Titus to crouch awkwardly beneath it. 'It seems I shall appear before your great General in a cloak so voluminous, it may as well be a carpet.'

The Queen had spoken in Greek and he did his best to appear confused. Then he heard Wen's voice from behind him.

'I know you understood everything the Queen just said,' Wen said in Latin, 'and that you only pretend not to. So I will not bother to translate it. You should laugh at her jest now, though, as if I have just explained it to you.'

There was nothing he could do but follow Wen's command. He gave a polite laugh, then bowed his head respectfully.

He realised suddenly that he was surrounded by them—one before him, one behind him, and two beside him—a quorum of fatuous maids who had already begun to play with him like a child's doll.

The Queen unfurled a papyrus scroll before his eyes. 'Forgive my crude markings, Clodius, but as you can see, I have made a rough sketch of the palace grounds. Please, study it for a moment.'

'The Queen wants you to look at the map, but you understood that,' Wen translated.

Titus stepped forward and stooped to get a good look at the drawing. 'We will land at this dock here tonight,' said the Queen, 'then make our way past the main palace to the inner gardens and the Athena's Fountain. There we will part. My women will take the boys to the royal Isis Temple up on the cliffs and you will lead me and Apollodorus to Caesar's military pavilion. Can you show me where that is?'

Wen translated the Queen's words, and Titus pointed just south of the main palace. Cleopatra nodded with satisfaction. 'That is where I thought he would be. Can you get me past Caesar's guards?'

Wen faithfully translated her words, though it irked him that she insisted on standing behind him.

'My mission is to deliver you to Caesar, Queen Cleopatra,' he responded in Latin. 'I will fulfil it.'

Wen translated his words while Charmion made a small mark on the place Titus had indicated. 'His confidence is reassuring, at least,' Cleopatra muttered.

'So is the size of his arms,' returned Charmion, shamelessly regarding his limbs.

He struggled to keep his breaths even. He could not give any indication that he had understood their conversation, for it had taken place wholly in Greek. 'I wonder if his mind is as strong as his body,' said the Queen. 'Let us put him to a test. Wen, please ask Clodius to name the Roman conquests of the last three hundred years.'

Wen translated the Queen's question into Latin, giving him precious time to think. 'There was the defeat of the Latin League just over three hundred years ago,' he began. 'That gave us the area around Rome. And the Samnite Wars that brought most of our golden peninsula. By the Third Punic War we had won Hispania and Northern Africa. Then came Macedonia, Greece, and Carthage and finally, with the defeat of Mithridates of Pontus, all the land from Pontus to Syria. And of course you know of Caesar's recent conquest of Gaul.' Needing no translation of the places and names, the Queen nodded thoughtfully. 'Is that all, Clodius?'

Titus nodded with certainty.

'The Roman says that is all,' Wen told the Queen in Greek, 'but the Roman is wrong.'

Wen stepped out from behind him and took her place beside the Queen. Her new position afforded her a clear view of his heaving chest, and the anger boiling beneath his placid gaze. She had refuted him in Greek, however, and so he could not respond without giving himself away.

'How is he wrong, Wen?' asked Cleopatra.

'He has forgotten the war with King Pyrrhus of Epirus, in which the southern part of the Italic peninsula was taken. He has also omitted the First Punic War, in which Sicily, Sardinia and Corsica were acquired.'

'I believe you are right, Wen,' said the Queen.

Wen watched with satisfaction as Titus swallowed bitterness.

'Can you believe it, Charmion?' Iras said in Greek. 'An Egyptian beer maid knows more about Roman history than an actual Roman soldier.'

'It is a credit to Wen,' said Charmion.

'Or a discredit to Clodius,' said Iras.

The Queen sat back in her chair. 'I believe it was Plato who said that a man's capacity for knowledge is inversely proportionate to his capacity for violence.'

Wen watched Titus cringe.

'It is well that he cannot understand us,' said Iras, rising to stand by the Queen's side. 'I think he would be quite offended by our assessment of his intellect.'

'Perhaps he would,' said the Queen. 'But I am going to give him the opportunity to redeem himself.' The Queen turned to Wen. 'Please ask our fine Roman soldier why Rome wishes to conquer the world.'

'You heard the Queen,' Wen said. 'Why does the Roman beast never sleep?'

Clodius cleared his voice. 'It was Consul Marius who awoke the Roman beast, some hundred years ago,' he began. 'He instituted reforms to our military that changed the nature of Roman warfare. Before Marius, only landed citizens could serve in the Roman army and only for the duration of a conflict. They were paid not in money or land, but in *gloria*—honour and admiration.

'But after Marius's reforms, any Roman citizen—landed or landless—could serve in the army and soldiers were guaranteed pay in lands conquered. Since then, a Roman soldier's livelihood has depended upon the lands he captures. Soldiering is a profession in Rome, like farming is in Egypt. That is why the Roman beast never sleeps, Queen Cleopatra. A Roman soldier must conquer, or die.'

As Wen concluded her translation, the Queen sat back in her throne. 'I have never understood the Roman bloodlust better than I do at this moment,' she said. 'Clodius, you are redeemed.'

'You heard what she said,' said Wen in Latin, feigning uninterest, but she had heard the passion in his words. It was as if Clodius had been reading from a history of the Roman Republic penned by someone who wished to save it.

Clodius gave the Queen a deep, relieved bow.

'Now what can you tell me about General Caesar?'

And there it is, Wen thought, *the real reason Cleopatra wished to speak to him.*

'About his character, I mean,' Cleopatra clarified. 'I know that you are just a soldier, but surely there is talk about him in the ranks. What kind of man is he?'

Wen translated and Clodius seemed to choose his words carefully.

'A Roman soldier never opines on his General's character,' he began. 'But I can say this: the Senate is considering bestowing the title of Dictator upon Caesar for a second time.' Wen noted a grave quality to his voice. 'The Dictatorship would of course be a great honour for General Caesar.'

'A Roman dictator is something like an Egyptian pharaoh, is he not?' asked Cleopatra.

'Yes, but only for a period of time and it must be a time of crisis,' said Clodius.

'What this Roman lacks in historical knowledge he seems to make up for in political expertise,' observed Charmion. She dipped a small quill into a pestle of kohl paste and began to trace a path of black along the Queen's eye.

'It is strange for a soldier to know so much about the

workings of his government,' commented Iras, taking her place beside Charmion.

'He dons little clothing,' said the Queen, 'but I have it in my mind that our good Clodius is wearing a disguise.'

'I am inclined to agree,' said Iras. 'He has far too many opinions for a soldier, and his manners are too refined.'

'I wonder if he understands what we are saying right now,' said the Queen.

Women.

Curses on them and the four representatives of their race who now stood before him. They were staring up at him as if trying to determine which limb would best flavour their soup.

But he was keen to women's wiles. They could poke and prod him all they liked, they would not break his nerve. He kept his head bowed and his expression blank.

'Wen, I have admired your skill in the art of debate,' said Cleopatra. 'Do you think you can discover the truth about this supposed soldier?'

'I do, my Queen,' said Wen.

'Please, go ahead.'

Clodius steeled himself. He was no stranger to interrogations. He had performed them when necessary for Caesar and was always successful. The key to a good interrogation was to endear yourself to the person you probed, then use that feigned confidence to catch him off his guard. Titus almost pitied Wen, for she had no idea who she was dealing with.

'Would you say that Caesar is merciful, Clodius?' Wen asked in Latin.

'Yes, I would say so. He often forgives his enemies, though not always.'

Wen sighed, as if she were settling in for a long conversation. She took a step in his direction. 'Would you say that he is impulsive?'

'I would not say that.'

'Would you say he is excessive?' She reached for her braid and began studying it.

'No, not excessive.'

'But he is ambitious, correct?' She brushed her braid's tail back and forth across her tunic, letting it graze her chest. 'I will ask again, is Caesar ambitious?'

'In Rome, ambition is considered a virtue.' Now she was making small, sensuous circles with the braid, but she was a fool to believe she could divert his attention in such a way.

'In your opinion, is Caesar ambitious?'

'Yes.'

'But I thought that a Roman soldier never opines about his General's character?' He rolled his eyes. *She is going about it all wrong*, he thought smugly. *She should not be putting me on the offensive*.

'What is your true mission?'

'To serve Caesar.'

She stepped closer. Now she stood just inches from his chest. He felt the nearness of her and the warmth of her breath on his skin. She took the tip of her braid and traced it across his naked chest, making his heart thump unexpectedly.

'You told me before that you served the Roman people,' she said.

'What?'

Curse the gods—she was having an effect on him. He could feel the unmistakable swelling beneath his loincloth.

He took a long breath. 'I serve Caesar, who serves the Roman people.'

She spoke softly, as if it were just the two of them alone together. 'Do you view Queen Cleopatra as the rightful ruler of Egypt?'

'I do.'

'Does Caesar?'

'I… I do not know.'

Wen glanced back at the other women, giving Titus a view of the long, taut sinew of her neck. It stretched to the base of her delicate ear, where the sharp angle of her jaw descended to a small, rounded chin. Just above that chin, those beautiful, shapely lips stretched into an irresistible frown.

Nothing had changed. He still wanted to kiss them.

She turned to him in that instant, and the black coals of her eyes smouldered. 'Titus?' she asked.

'Yes?'

The Queen gasped.

He had revealed himself. He had responded to his own name.

'Titus Tillius Fortis, son of the Roman Senator Lucius Tillius Cimber and tribune commander of Caesar's Sixth Legion?'

It was too late to deny it now. To do so would only bring him dishonour. 'That is I.'

The Queen gasped. Her two handmaids stared incredulously at Titus, mouths agape, while Wen appeared to study the floor.

It was not his most important secret, but it was a secret none the less and the four little hens had pecked it from him. The Queen and her handmaids began to chatter in excitement, while Wen continued staring at the ground, her shoulders slumped. He recognised the posture, for he had assumed it himself quite often. He could not remember how many times he had done things he did not wish to do in the course of carrying out Caesar's orders. He was certain that she had not meant to steal his *dignitas*.

Though she must have harboured some small measure of pride. She had used the power of her loveliness to weaken him—had set him afire like a candle, then simply harvested the soft wax.

He had never met any woman like her.

And had never wanted any woman more.

Chapter Five

She watched his shoulders in the milky moonlight. They moved like twin machines, their small gears of muscle flexing with each subtlety of stroke. He was so finely made. It was difficult to discover a part of him that was not taut muscle or ropy sinew or hardened bone.

His heart, perhaps.

Though surely she would never know. If he had wished for her friendship once, she was certain that he did not wish it any more.

After his confession inside the Queen's tent, he had bowed, then returned to his place beneath the palm's shade. He had politely declined to join them for dinner that evening, though there had been plenty of the fish he had caught. Instead, he had huddled beneath his palm and seemed consumed with some busywork involving a needle and thread.

Regret had sneaked up on her like the stars. Though the Queen had seemed pleased with their discovery of Titus's ruse, it had not given Wen the satisfaction she had hoped it would. It was one thing to coax a confession, it was another to lead them into a trap.

And it had been something of a needless trap, after all. According to the Queen, it was common for highborn messengers to create false identities. 'I should have suspected it,' she had told Wen after his exit. 'Disguise is a common way for men of rank to protect themselves against murderous kings.'

Now Wen paced the deck, traversing his field of vision. She wanted to catch his attention so that she might attempt to apologise. She crossed her arms and sighed, standing in full view of the oar bench. She made a fuss of her braid. Not once did he look up from his strokes.

She studied his mighty arms, remembering how he had embraced her outside the Queen's war-council tent. How oddly safe she had felt in that moment, how unexpectedly content. And he had been so earnest in their conversation that afternoon that she had almost believed he was speaking truth. *I did not mean to offend you*, he had said, and when she had stopped in the sand to confront him, he had angled his body in such a way as to shade her from the sun.

It occurred to her that the gesture had also resulted in a kind of embrace: an embrace of shadows.

Why had she been so very unkind to him? Why had she insisted on pointing out his errors, stripping him of both his *dignitas* and his disguise? Why?

But she already knew the answer. Even now, his words twisted in her stomach like knives. *You are nothing but a lowly slave. You are beneath me.* They revealed what was truly in his heart and he could never take them back.

She stopped her pacing and gazed out across the sea. Just above the western horizon an unfamiliar star on the horizon had appeared. It seemed to be growing in size, flickering like a torch's flame.

'Apollodorus, do you see that unusual star?' she asked over her shoulder. 'It is just above the horizon there.'

'That is no star, my dear,' said Apollodorus. 'It is the Pharos.'

Wen gasped. 'The Lighthouse?'

'We shall head for its flame and thus we shall not be lost,' said Apollodorus.

Tears pooled in Wen's eyes. 'It is more beautiful than I remember.' The grand structure was still many *stades* away from them, but its three sections made dark profiles against the night and its bright flame beckoned.

'When did you see it last?' asked Apollodorus.

'When I was a small child,' Wen said. 'I beheld it from the city's Eastern Harbour.'

'And how did you find yourself there?'

'That is a long story, I am afraid.'

'A long story?' Apollodorus said, brightening. He patted the bench between him and Titus. 'Would you not come and tell it in my ear? A distraction would be most welcome on this unnerving night.'

She stared at the open seat and felt her heart beat a little faster. She knew that she could not politely refuse such a request. She also knew that sitting behind Apollodorus would put her exactly half an arm's length away from Titus. She took a deep breath and settled herself between the two rowers.

'I first beheld the Lighthouse the night after I was taken by the slavers,' she began.

She could feel Titus's breath on her neck.

'How came you to be captured by slavers?' asked Apollodorus. 'Tell all that you remember.'

'I remember sitting inside a row boat piloted by a bearded man with eyes the colour of coins. I will never forget those eyes, though my memory of the rest of him has grown cloudy.'

'What then?' asked Apollodorus.

'It was the middle of the night when he and his men took us from the temple. They explained that our mothers were being sent to meet Osiris, by order of Pharaoh Ptolemy the Twelfth.'

'Ptolemy's purges,' mused Apollodorus. 'I remember them well. Cleopatra's father returned from Rome to discover his daughter Berenice sitting on his throne.'

'So he slaughtered Berenice and everyone she knew,' finished Titus.

Wen shivered at the sound of Titus's voice and seized the opportunity to catch his gaze. When she turned, his dark eyes smouldered in the moonlight, though in anger or interest she could not tell.

'Please, continue,' he urged.

'When the bearded man told us that our mothers were gone, one of the smaller girls explained that we did not have mothers, that we were children of the gods. But the man only patted her head and told her that we were going somewhere wonderful.'

'Slavers are wretched men,' said Apollodorus. Titus was still gazing into her eyes. It took all of her will to turn away from him and return to her story.

'The thought of adventure cheered our hearts,' she continued, 'and we floated down the river in a wonderstruck silence—a caravan of innocents who believed themselves bound for some fantastic place. The man smiled beneath his beard and told us to sleep. He fed us salted bread and a cloudy liquid that was not milk.'

'By the gods,' whispered Apollodorus.

'The children ate and drank without question, but I only pretended to drink. I did not trust the man, though I could not guess his purpose. I did not even know what a slave was, then. Labourers would often come to the temple to perform tasks, but they toiled out of love, not obligation.'

Apollodorus sighed and it occurred to Wen that the loyal Sicilian had much in common with those labourers of love.

'We floated downriver beneath a waxing moon,' Wen continued, 'and I remember searching the passing landscape for signs from the High Priestess. I believed that she would not enter the Underworld without first telling me goodbye. I searched and searched for her, but there were only the endless grape plantations, their ancient vines hanging like corpses in the terrible moonlight.'

Wen turned to glance at the moon behind her and became aware of Titus's eyes on her face. She wondered if he was fixing a curse upon her head, or perhaps fantasising about wringing her neck. Still, she did not wish to turn away from him.

'Well, go on,' prodded Apollodorus.

'I asked the bearded man why Pharaoh ordered the priestesses killed, but he did not answer. "Please, Uncle," I begged him. "My heart will not rest. I must know why."

'He held out a small blue bottle. "If you will drink all of this, I will tell you, little calf," he said. When I had finished the contents of the bottle, he reduced his voice to a whisper. "The High Priestess of Hathor loved Pharaoh's usurper."

"What is a 'usurper'? I asked, feeling my lids grow heavier.

"Shush," he said.

"Where are we going?" As my world faded to black, I remember hearing a single word: "Alexandria".'

'Alexandria…' echoed Apollodorus.

'I had never visited Alexandria,' explained Wen, 'though the Hathor Temple was not far from the city and the High Priestess went there constantly. She said that it was the most glorious city in all the world, a city with theatres and libraries, parks and promenades, and a lighthouse to rival the pyramids themselves.'

'I believe she spoke truth,' whispered Titus.

Surprised to hear Titus's deep voice once again, Wen turned to see him heaving away from her, his legs flexing in the moonlight. But it was not moonlight, she realised at length, for the moon had been eclipsed by the Pharos, whose eternal flame grew ever closer, illuminating everything.

She could see Titus so clearly now—and she studied his legs—from their sinuous mounds to their bulging flanks, to the dark flecks of fortune that peppered them.

When he came forward in his stroke, he wore an amused grin. 'Do I have something on my legs?'

Mortified, she went on the defence. 'And I suppose you have seen much of the world, Commander Titus? To be able to say that Alexandria is its most glorious city?'

'Much more than you have, I would guess,' he said.

She let the insult burn her cheeks. She supposed that she had earned it.

'I have seen a good deal of the world myself and would have to agree,' said Apollodorus. 'But please, go on with your story.'

Wen faced forward and continued. 'When I finally awoke from my milky slumber, it was nightfall once again and we had entered a canal, its still waters choked with reeds. It became difficult to breathe. Instead of a glorious city, I saw endless rows of mud-brick buildings, and smelled the grim reek of their waste. I felt my spirit sinking into the canal's murky depths.'

'The Rhakotis Canal,' Apollodorus said, shaking his head. 'The late Ptolemy never had it dredged.'

'I thought that perhaps we were entering the Underworld ourselves, for I had no idea that the Rhakotis Canal opened out into the Eastern Harbour. And when all at once that great expanse of water spread out before us I gasped. There it was, right before my eyes— its eternal flame a-flicker. The Lighthouse.'

Titus's rowing ceased.

'I remember staring in wonder at the towering edifice,' she continued, 'just as we are doing now. I marvelled at its converging shapes—first a rectangle, then an octagon—'

'Then a cylindrical spire held up by columns,' said Titus, 'and topped by a statue—'

'Of Zeus,' they said as one.

Wen paused. She turned to Titus and gazed at his arms, wishing suddenly that they were around her. 'The Lighthouse was my sign,' she told him. 'It was the High Priestess, signalling to me, telling me to be brave, and that she would shine her light on me always.'

Now Apollodorus had also stopped rowing and all was quiet. The ship was moving through the gates of the Great Harbour, pulled by its own momentum, and they passed beneath the foot of the Lighthouse in hallowed silence.

Wen faced forward once again. But she could feel Titus's breath on her neck—small, rapid exhales that seemed to move in time with her beating heart.

Chapter Six

Wen could feel the danger increasing with each heave of the oars.

In the deckhouse, the handmaids were letting the braziers burn themselves out and there was just enough light to observe the Queen beneath her ghostly disguise.

'You do not think that I will be recognised?' she was asking Iras in a whisper, her words muffled further by the fabric of her robe.

'No, my Goddess,' Iras reassured her. 'It would be impossible.'

The Queen pulled the fabric away from her mouth. 'Not even my eyes?'

'They are not your eyes,' said Charmion, 'for they are shaded with red and only lightly kohled. You do not look like yourself.'

'That is a comfort,' the Queen said, though she seemed far from comforted. 'Still, I wonder if Ptolemy's guards will stop us.'

'If they do then Apollodorus and Clodius will speak to them,' said Iras.

'You mean Apollodorus and Titus,' Charmion corrected, sliding Wen a look.

'What if the guard dogs find me?' asked Cleopatra.

'If they do they will only wag their tails,' said Iras, 'for they are all fond of you.'

And so the conversation went. The Queen fussed and fretted while Iras and Charmion did their best to calm her nerves. To Wen's ears, it was like a song in which each woman took a verse, though none dared recite the chorus: that the Queen could very likely be sneaking into a trap.

A death trap.

Wen prayed that it would not be so, though she held little faith in prayer. In her life she had learned that the gods were fickle and often unkind. It was better to expect the worst from them and to prepare one's defences accordingly.

The more defences the better.

An army if possible.

The boat swayed as it touched against the dock, and the four women reached out to steady each other. It occurred to Wen then that they were the Queen's army. Their strange, unlikely group represented her troops—her only protection against the forces of fate. And soon they would be diminished, for only Titus and Apollodorus would be accompanying the Queen into her next battle.

'It is time to disembark,' Titus called to them in his excellent Greek.

The discovery of Titus's true identity had buoyed the Queen's spirits. She seemed to believe that if she and her attendants could push and prod a Roman commander into a confession, there was hope of influencing the other Roman commander the Queen would soon face. 'And you were the reason he spoke, Wen,' the Queen lauded. 'You unmasked him.'

Unmasked. It sounded horrible—like some violent ritual practiced by merciless priests. Wen did not feel deserving of the Queen's praise. She had been similarly pushed and prodded in her life and it had never felt good.

Now Wen pulled back the deckhouse curtain to discover Titus's outstretched hand. It was a gesture of courtesy that she did not deserve.

'Allow me to help you,' he said softly, though he did not meet her gaze. And why should he? She had told him that she did not wish to be his friend. Then she had deceived him into revealing something he did not wish to reveal. It was a wonder he was still willing to help her at all.

Guiltily, she took his hand.

She stepped out on to the dock, squinting for a better view. The moon was setting and the palace complex was hardly visible in the diminishing light. The only thing Wen could plainly distinguish was the shoreline promenade—a wide tile path illuminated by the light of dying torches. It snaked along the shoreline for many cubits before branching off into a lavish canopy of roses. *The entrance to the Royal Quarter*, thought Wen.

The High Priestess had once told her that the Royal Quarter of Alexandria was as grand as its Lighthouse. Surrounded by a high, protective wall, every ruler since Alexander had added to the complex, resulting in a network of interlocking palaces, theatres, temples, fountains, labyrinths, menageries, baths and gardens without end: a paradise on earth.

Soon Wen would be crossing into that storeyed landscape, for it had been decided that they would make their way on to the royal grounds as a group, parting when they reached Athena's Fountain.

There, the Queen, Apollodorus and Titus would go on towards Caesar's villa, and Wen, the handmaids and the rudder boys would make for the royal Temple of Isis for sanctuary.

If Cleopatra's meeting with Caesar was successful, the Queen would send for the women and the boys by the following afternoon. If the Queen did not send for them, then they were to assume that she had been killed or captured.

In that case, they were to run for their lives. The Queen's handmaids were considered extensions of the Queen's *ka* on earth. They knew the Queen's allies, along with her secrets. If the Queen were assassinated, they would be considered threats and would be hunted like gazelles.

Now the Queen emerged from the deckhouse, and took Titus's hand. There was only the light of the Lighthouse to see by and, as the Queen stepped towards his strong arms, she stumbled on the folds of her dress.

'Do you see what I mean, Titus?' she whispered with nervous gaiety. 'I am a living carpet.'

'I will fetch a fold clip,' said Wen, stepping back aboard the boat and ducking into the deckhouse.

She was bending over a chest and did not even hear Titus step beside her in the darkness.

'Where is your knife?'

She nearly jumped. 'What?'

'Your kitchen knife. The one you used to kill the fish.'

'I do not know. I must have left it in one of the trunks.'

He gave a half-smile. 'No, it is here.' He held out the small knife, its blade glinting in a shaft of moonlight.

Wen jumped backwards in fear, searching the floor for something she might use as a weapon. She seized a small pillow, as if it might shield her from the blows she was certain would come.

'Shhh,' he said. He reached out for the pillow she held tightly in her grasp.

'You may try to kill me,' she said, 'and you may succeed. But I warn you that I will scream and my voice will warn the others, and the only person you will succeed in killing is a worthless slave.'

'Wen,' he whispered. 'I do not wish to kill you.' He squeezed the pillow, pulling her towards him. 'On the contrary.'

He pulled her closer still, then put his lips on hers.

Her body grew stiff with the surprise of his touch, but quickly relaxed beneath it. He was kissing her. Kissing her! What was she to do? She did not know how to tilt her head, or where to put her hands, or even when to breathe. But something about his lips felt exactly right.

Just as soon as it had begun, it was over. He wrenched himself away and staggered backwards, pushing the knife handle into her palm. 'Please, take it,' he whispered, trying to gather his wits. 'Forgive me.'

'Gratitude,' she muttered. She did not know why she was thanking him exactly. She did not remember quite where she was.

'It was not my intention to frighten you,' he said.

'Frighten me?' He had done more than frighten

her. He had taken her mind and kneaded it into a soft, lumpy dough.

'It was as if you were expecting me to attack,' he said.

'I was,' Wen whispered. 'And I feared for you.'

'Feared *for* me?'

'Yes, for I would have defended myself most ferociously and you would have ended up as food for the fishes.'

He seemed to choke on something deep in his throat. 'Gratitude, I shall remember that for the future.'

'As well you should,' said Wen. 'As I have told you, I do not—that is, it is difficult for me to trust Roman men.'

'We have that in common, then, for now I find it difficult to trust Egyptian women.'

Wen could see very little in the shadowy deckhouse and she wondered if he smiled. She perceived him reaching beneath his chainmail. 'None the less,' he continued, 'I made this for you.' He pressed a leather object into her other hand.

'What is this?' Wen whispered.

'Your weapon should be hidden from sight.'

'Of course,' she said in puzzlement.

He gave an impatient sigh, then gently guided her arms together until the naked blade slid gently into the leather object.

'Do you see? It's a sheath.'

'I'm sorry. You're…helping me?'

'I'm arming you.'

'But when did you—?'

'I began to fashion it for you after I watched you eviscerate my fish. I finished it later, after you eviscerated me.'

She felt herself blush. She wished she could tell if he wore a frown or a grin.

He touched her hands again, sending a shiver through her. He traced the length of her folded fingers to the sheath, taking hold of two long leather straps that had been dangling from either side of it. 'These straps should be cross-tied around your lower leg and knotted inwardly, so that the sheath is concealed beneath your tunic.'

'Ah,' Wen said, but she could not concentrate on his words. Not when his fingers had just left a trail of fire on her hands. She continued to hold the sheathed knife in her grasp. 'I am grateful,' she managed finally. She was supposed to be doing something, though she could not think of what. The boat thudded against the dock.

'Would you like me to show you how to tie on the sheath?' he asked at last.

'No, no, that will not be necessary,' she said, her heart pounding. 'We must join the others.' She stepped around Titus and headed for the deckhouse door.

'Wait,' Titus said. 'Are you not going to wear it?'

Before she could answer, he was kneeling at her feet. He moved his hands up under the skirt of her tunic and felt for her leg.

His fingers skittered across her flesh. No man had ever touched her in such a way and as he worked she found herself wondering how such powerful hands could be so gentle.

'To be undetectable, the sheath must hang on the inside of your leg. Do you see what I mean?'

He lifted the hem of her tunic, then guided her hand

to where he had tied the sheath to the inside of her lower leg. He did not remove his hand from the top of hers. It was so large and warm. She could not see his eyes, but it was as if she could feel them staring back at her across the darkness.

'Yes,' she said at last, though she had forgotten the question he had asked.

'Knots,' he muttered.

'What?'

'The, ah, knots. Can you find them? You might need to adjust them.'

She realised that he had guided her hand to the knots that he had tied to secure the sheath. She bent lower as if to inspect them. She sensed that her face was on level with his. She breathed in his delicious scent.

'If only we could untie this boat and float away from here together,' he said huskily.

Yes, she thought. *If only we could.*

'Wen?' a voice called. It was soft, barely audible, but Wen knew it well.

'It is the Queen. She calls for me. I must go.'

Wen stood and let down her skirt. 'Gratitude,' she said, 'for the knife and sheath.' She gave a deep bow, then climbed off the boat and disappeared down the dock.

He straightened his cuirass and took a breath. He needed to remember his mission. And what was that, exactly? Oh, yes, to escort Cleopatra safely to Caesar's chambers. And then? To prevent Caesar from making himself a king. It was all very simple, really. He strapped on his *gladius*, and tightened the belt of his *pugio*. Ptolemy's guards would be patrolling the Royal

Quarter and he needed to be ready for them. But all he could think about was the softness of Wen's lips.

When he finally stepped off the boat, the Queen and Wen were already halfway down the dock. He closed the distance between them in four long steps and was soon hovering in the shadows behind the two women, quiet as a thief.

'The gods will have their way tonight, as every night,' Cleopatra was saying. 'But if we are not meant to meet again, Wen, I wish to tell you that you have served me well. It is as if I have known you my whole life. Do you feel the same?'

'I do, my Queen. I do,' said Wen.

'Remind me now of what I must do.'

'You must make yourself into Egypt.'

'Go on.'

'First, you must become Alexandria. She is a woman of wit and education, a woman who recites poetry in one language and teases in another. A woman of the present and of the future.'

'And the second woman?'

'The second woman is Thebes. A woman of the past. Mysterious, beautiful, a woman of otherworldly power and inconceivable wealth.'

'Wealth that Caesar is here to collect.'

'But you will not allow him to collect it—not immediately. You must make him long for it first, then work hard to earn it. Therefore, put it on display. Give him a taste. Remember that you are worth more than he can even conceive. You are Queen of Egypt!'

Titus smiled to himself. She was magnificent— not the Queen, but Wen. She was advisor, counsellor, coach and friend, all in one. Titus had never known any woman like her and feared he never would again.

'Wen, I…I am afraid,' said the Queen. 'I do not want to die.'

There was a long silence and Titus wondered what Wen could possibly say to console the Queen's heart.

'Forgive my boldness, Queen. I know that I am not permitted to address you directly, but I have a story for your ears that I believe will help you.'

'I am listening,' said the Queen.

'It is about a woman I once knew. In her nineteenth summer something terrible happened that made her feel afraid. This woman was…a slave in the brew house where I toiled. One night, a fight arose and, in the chaos of it, a Gabiniani soldier grabbed her by the wrists and pulled her up the stairs on to the rooftop.'

Titus heard Wen's voice crack with emotion. 'This woman, this…slave was accustomed to defending herself against drunkards. She knew where to kick and when to bite, and how to scream loud enough for her master to hear. She had made herself important to him, you see, and she was certain that he would not let anything happen to her.

'That is why she screamed as loudly as she could and fought the Roman with all her strength as he ripped off her tunic and then her loincloth. Somehow, she got free of him. She ran to the far side of the roof. The side that looked out over the Serapic Way.'

The Queen had stopped walking. She was gripping Wen's arm. 'The woman began to scream, but as I said, there was a fight in the brew house that night and nobody could hear her.

'The man punched her in the stomach, then again in

her face. She knew the man who beat her, for he often bragged about the men he had killed in battle. He spoke of killing women, too, as if he had enjoyed it.

'In other words, my Queen, she feared that she would lose her life up there on that roof. That is why she jumped.'

The Queen gasped.

'There was an iron bar protruding from the roof and it tore down the side of her leg, slowing her fall. If it had not been for that iron bar, she probably would have fallen to her death. Instead, she fell into a clump of donkey droppings. She was naked, her leg was bleeding, and her ankle was badly broken, though nobody attempted to help her. Just before her world faded to black, she saw the man who had attacked her. He was standing with several other Romans, laughing at her shame.'

Wen's voice wavered. Titus could not see her face, but he imagined it covered in tears. She was not speaking of some unfortunate companion, he understood suddenly. She was speaking of herself.

'It took a long time for my friend's ankle to heal,' Wen continued, 'but when she was finally able to walk, she found it difficult to resume her duties. She could not eat. She could not sleep. She could no longer climb the small set of stairs that led to the roof. She could not look at the men she served, because each one of them reminded her of the man who had humiliated her and made her afraid. She no longer found any reward in life. She was lost.'

'Oh, Wen,' said the Queen.

'But this story has a happy ending, my Queen,' said Wen. 'One day, my friend was staring at a table full of crumbs, when two Egyptian men came into the brew house. They were speaking to each other of the newly crowned Queen Cleopatra. They said that she had gone to Thebes to perform the last rites for the Buchis bull and had toured the countryside making gifts of grain. They said that she had fought with her brother's advisors against raising taxes and had purchased wheat from abroad to avoid a famine. She had even learned the Egyptian tongue.'

Wen turned to face the Queen. 'Their voices were full of awe, Queen. They said that you were a queen for the people—not just the people of Alexandria, but all Egyptians. They marvelled that you had only seen eighteen summers, the same number that I—that my friend had seen. They called you Isis Incarnate, come to save the Land of Osiris from ruin.'

Titus could see that the Queen was at the edge of tears.

'My friend decided that if a woman of her own age could rule the greatest kingdom in the world, then she could endure whatever difficulties occurred in hers. She decided that she would not let her fear and shame destroy her. And it was because of you. You see, Queen Cleopatra, you had inspired her.'

Titus caught a glimpse of Cleopatra's eyes. They were glassy in the torchlight.

'Wen?' the Queen whispered.

'Yes, Queen Cleopatra?'

'I shall not be afraid.'

Chapter Seven

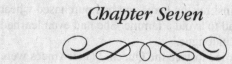

They sneaked into the Royal Quarter, as quiet as crocodiles, and followed the perimeter of its high wall. Nearing a complex of large buildings, they hurried around the small, columned palace where Cleopatra had resided before her exile. 'It is there I shall return,' Cleopatra vowed in a whisper.

Titus kept the group moving and they rushed across the main promenade and soon stood in the bushes near the statue of Athena, her torchlight spilling on to the grassy glade and the small fountain in which she stood.

Everyone was out of breath. Before they could even begin their goodbyes, Wen noticed that the rudder boys had disappeared. She looked out from the bushes and saw them running across the glade to Athena's Fountain, seeking a drink.

One of the rudder boys tripped and let out a loud yelp.

'Look there,' called a man's voice from beyond the light. 'Trespassers!' Soon five of Ptolemy's guards emerged from the shadows.

Titus unsheathed his *gladius* and tossed it to Apollodorus.

'You take the tall one,' Titus told him, stepping from the bushes and drawing his own small *pugio* blade.

'Two men cannot defeat five,' cried the Queen. 'Follow me now. That is an order.'

The rudder boys dashed in terror back to the bushes and soon their group was sprinting across another green with five guards in pursuit.

'They are gaining on us,' said Charmion, stumbling on her tunic.

'I know a way to escape them,' cried the Queen. 'Follow me!' Soon they arrived before an opening in a tall black hedge.

'It is the labyrinth,' breathed Iras.

'Take each other's hands and follow me,' commanded the Queen and she started to the left.

But Titus did not follow. He turned and ran in the opposite direction, back towards the guards.

'Oh, how I wish for a cup of beer!' he sang loudly. 'And one and two and three!'

He is drawing them away from the Queen, Wen thought. *He is going to his death.*

She wrenched her hand free of the Queen's and followed his bellows, rushing past the entrance to the labyrinth just as the guards arrived. 'Did you see that woman?' one of them shouted. 'Follow her!'

She ran forward into the blackness, trying to follow Titus's croons. 'For when I ask for a cup of beer,' he sang, 'the beer maid comes to me—'

She hit a wall of dense bushes and fell to the ground. Recovering herself, she saw several shadowy figures coming towards her. She heard the hard swish of blades being pulled from their sheaths. 'Titus!' she shrieked. She groped with her arms, trying to find an opening in the hedge. *These are the final moments of my life*, she thought suddenly.

Then she felt four fingers link with hers and heard a faint but unmistakable whisper, 'Follow me. Hurry.' She ran in the direction in which she was being pulled, first right, then left, then right again, until the hedge surrounded them on all sides.

'A dead end,' Titus whispered in defeat.

'Do not say that.'

They stood together for a long while, just listening. There was no sound at all, not even the snap of a twig.

'Down here,' Titus whispered at last. He was crouched at the base of the hedge. 'There is a hollow in which we may hide.'

Wen bent to his side, feeling along the ground until it gave way, and she felt a small hollow area, just big enough for a body.

'Where will you hide?' Wen asked. He appeared to be cutting off small branches from the adjacent hedge.

'I will lie with you.'

'But only one person can fit in the hollow.'

'We will lie closely.'

She lay down in the hollow facing outwards and he lay down beside her, arranging the cut branches atop his body in a thick layer. Of necessity, he was lying very close. She could feel his hard legs against hers. Her breasts pressed against his chest.

This is what it is like, she thought. *When a man and a woman lie together*. It was something she had imagined often, never believing she would experience it herself. Yet here they were, like two halves of a whole. The only difference was that they lay not in a bed, but in a hollow in the ground. And they were not man and wife, but Roman and Egyptian. Commander and slave. Born enemies.

'They are searching the labyrinth now,' he whispered. His face was so very close to hers. His lips. 'But they will not find us—not unless they have dogs.'

'Or torches.'

'Do not fear. I will keep you safe.'

Wen did not know how to respond. *Gratitude* did not seem sufficient. No one had ever vowed to keep her safe—not in all her adult life. She had never been worth keeping safe.

'But why did you follow me?' Titus asked in barely a whisper. Her ear was just inches from his lips.

'You gave your sword to Apollodorus,' whispered Wen. 'You had no defence.'

'And you thought you could help me?'

'I did not think.'

'No, you did not,' he said. They lay in silence for many moments. 'You could have been killed.'

'So could you.'

'Forgive me,' Titus breathed.

'There is nothing to forgive. You were trying to save the Queen.'

'No, I mean… I was not referring to my recent actions, but rather…my former words.'

'Your speech is like this labyrinth,' she said with amusement.

'What I mean to say is that I have underestimated the women of Egypt and you most of all.'

Was he mocking her? She knew how he felt about women and slaves. Or did she? It was difficult to think clearly. He was too close. The solid expanse of him filled her awareness. Then she felt it. It was a growing hardness against her thigh. The hardness of him. Reflexively, she jerked backwards.

'I am very sorry about that,' he said. 'I am afraid I cannot help it.'

Her heart throbbed, though it was not entirely fear that moved her. 'I promise not to touch you,' he continued solemnly. He reached down and adjusted himself away from her.

'Thank you,' she said, exhaling. She could not believe this was the same man whom she had suspected of treachery.

'It is I who should be asking forgiveness of you,' she whispered.

'You owe me no apology.'

'I treated you without respect before the Queen. You did not deserve to be tricked in such a way. I beg your forgiveness, Titus Tillius Fortis,' she whispered. 'Will you grant it?'

'You remembered my whole name,' he muttered softly.

'If we are to die this night, I must know that there is peace between us,' she said.

'I am sorry, but I cannot accept your apology, for you were not disrespectful. You were only…magnificent.'

She stiffened. 'Do you mock me, Commander?'

'Mock you? Is it so hard to believe that I admire you?'

'I thought I was benea—'

But she could not finish, because a hand burst over Titus's shoulder and grabbed her throat.

In a single motion, Titus unsheathed Wen's kitchen knife and sliced it across the guard's hand, producing a torrent of blood. He jumped to his feet. 'Stay behind me, Wen,' he commanded. 'There are many.'

Torches. They had brought torches, just as she thought they would, and must have caught sight of Titus's shape beneath the branches.

Now the guards rushed towards them. She saw Titus kick one in the gut, sending the man and his torch to the ground. A third guard lunged forward, brandishing a sword. Titus landed a hard blow to his jaw, knocking him backwards and relieving him of his weapon. Titus turned and thrust the kitchen knife into Wen's grasp. 'Defend yourself,' he commanded.

He stepped towards the third guard, going on the offence. She could hear the clanking of their swords as she watched their shadowy movements just beyond the view of the flames of the fallen torch. Titus was landing thunderous blows, but he was not fighting to kill. 'Stand down,' he ordered. He sent their third attacker to the ground with a slice to the leg, then moved on to the fourth.

She was so entranced by Titus's efforts that she did not see the fumbling movements of their second attacker lying at her feet. By the time she noticed him, he was standing before her, his grasping hands stretched outward.

Suddenly, she was no longer in the labyrinth, but on the roof of her master's brewery. The man was walking, groping at her, speaking all the horrible things he planned to do to her. *'You think someone will come to your rescue, girl? Well, you are mistaken, for you are nobody.'*

Wen stepped backwards, searching for an escape route. But this time, there was no escape. There was no ledge to jump from. There was only an impenetrable hedge. She was trapped.

The man stepped closer, his eyes watching the blade of her knife. Titus's words echoed in her head. *Defend yourself.* She realised that she was not trapped. She had a knife. She was Wen of Alexandria, Advisor to the Queen, and she had a knife! She did not need anyone to rescue her. She could rescue herself.

She lunged at him, slicing her knife across his arm and causing him to recoil. And in that half-second she lunged forward with all her strength and tackled him to the ground.

'Do not even think of reaching for your weapon,' she hissed in his ear. She held her blade to his neck. 'Do you think I will not use this knife?' she growled. Her hands were trembling.

'Do not kill me, please,' the man begged.

'Stay still and I will not have to,' she said. Time slowed as she listened to the fighting beyond her view. She could hear every blow, every groan of effort. 'Still,' she reminded the man, though her words were unnecessary. He was utterly frozen beneath the threat of her blade.

After many moments, she heard a loud grunt and the shuffling of footsteps. 'Wen?' Titus said somewhere beyond the flames' reach. 'Wen?'

'Titus?'

'By the gods,' Titus gasped as he stepped back into the light. He paused for a moment as he beheld Wen holding the guard at knifepoint. He rushed to Wen's side. 'You have done well, Wen of Alexandria.'

He took the man by the throat. 'You will lie down and stay put, do you hear me?'

The man gurgled his assent, and Titus turned to Wen. 'Come now, we must find the Queen.'

He helped her past the attackers' writhing, groaning figures. 'Did you kill any of them?' Wen asked.

'Not a one,' Titus replied. 'They shall all have headaches tomorrow morning. Now come.'

Wen wanted to ask him why he did not kill the guards, but there was no time. He had taken her by the hand and was leading her out of the labyrinth at a fast run.

When they arrived beneath Athena's torch, Wen heard a small gasp, then beheld a ghostly figure running towards her. 'You brave, foolish woman,' said the Queen, embracing her. 'I feared I had lost you for ever.'

'We have lost only time,' said Wen.

'She is right,' said Titus. 'We must part now, before more guards discover us.' He turned to Wen. 'Wen, give me your knife.'

Wen handed Titus the knife and he bent to her feet to sheath it. 'Will I see you again?' she whispered, fearing his answer.

'You will,' he said. 'Though I fear that things will change between us.' He pushed her knife back into its sheath and stood.

'We must go now,' said Apollodorus. The Queen stepped between the two strong men and linked her arms in theirs.

'Yes, let us go,' said the Queen to Titus. 'Take me to your leader.'

Chapter Eight

Wen stared out of the western windows of the Temple of Isis, keeping watch. *I fear that things will change between us*, Titus had told her, and she turned the words over and over in her mind, trying to make sense of them.

Did he mean that when he returned to his duties, he would be obliged to treat her like a slave? Or was he suggesting that there would be more moments like the one they had shared in the deckhouse, when he had pressed his lips to hers? She did not even dare to hope.

Then, as the pale dawn began to illuminate the white buildings of the Royal Quarter, Wen spied an escort of twenty Roman soldiers.

For a moment, Wen's heart leapt in the hopes that Titus was among them—he had come to rescue them, as she had secretly hoped he would. But she could not make out his face amongst the mail-clad, helmeted men, who all looked alike.

The entourage came to a halt at the entrance to the temple and demanded to speak with the Queen's hand-maids. Fearing a trap, Iras and Charmion hid in one of the inner sanctums while Wen went out to receive their leader.

'We have come for Cleopatra's women—to return them to their rightful place at the Queen's side,' the leader said.

'I am one of those women,' said Wen. 'How can we be sure this is not a trap?'

'The Queen told me to tell you that the carpet was a success. Does that mean anything to you?'

Soon they were walking amidst the entourage phalanx of soldiers, past dozens of Ptolemy's guards.

Wen's heart hammered in fear. Their mission, apparently, had succeeded, but they appeared to be in more danger than ever. The armoured men delivered them to the entrance of the Queen's palace, where they hastened up the stairs to the Queen's living chamber.

'Oh, sisters, how glad I am to see your faces!' Cleopatra exclaimed, embracing them each in turn. 'I am happy to tell you that we are now under the protection of Julius Caesar.'

Wen was glad, though she also noticed what the Queen did not say: *We are safe. I have been restored as Queen. Caesar does not intend to conquer Egypt.*

'Tell us everything!' asked Charmion, taking a seat on the couch opposite the Queen.

'What did you say to him?' Iras asked, collapsing next to Charmion.

Wen stepped quietly to a servant's position, standing at Cleopatra's shoulder. 'He did not recognise me,' the Queen said, 'so I asked him to guess who I was.'

'You did not!' gasped Charmion.

'Indeed I did. I walked about the room and told him that I felt like an actor in a satyr play.'

'And what did he say to that?' asked Iras breath-lessly.

'He laughed at me,' said the Queen. 'He said that if that were the case, I should have been hiding a flight of doves beneath my skirts.'

'Rome's greatest general said that?' asked Iras.

'Hercule!' exclaimed Charmion. 'What then?'

'I reached into my bag and pulled out my cobra bracelet.'

The Queen glanced up at Wen. 'Then I walked around the room slowly,' she continued, 'letting him see me push the bracelet into place. I watched him notice its lapis eyes and study its carnelian-studded tongue.'

'He is known as a collector of fine things,' offered Iras.

'What then?' cried Charmion.

Cleopatra grinned. 'He offered me a goblet of wine, which I accepted, though of course I did not drink.'

'Very wise, Goddess,' said Iras.

'Then I reached into my bag and placed each of my rings upon my fingers, one by one.'

'He must have guessed your identity then,' said Charmion.

'If he did, he said nothing. He only raised his gob-let and asked me why I hesitated. "Only princesses and queens needed to worry about poison," he said.'

'And what did you say to that?' asked Charmion.

'I did not say anything at all,' said the Queen. 'I only gave a little smile with my eyes.'

'Oh, but it must have been a moment!' exclaimed Charmion, clapping her hands together.

'I believe I caught him quite by surprise,' the Queen

laughed, 'for his cheeks turned the very colour of the wine! Still, I was careful not to make too much of it. These Roman men have their pride, do they not?' The Queen cast Wen another glance and smiled.

'What then, Queen?' asked Charmion.

'He asked me if I was going to try to seduce him. I told him that I would never presume to such a thing. We spoke of the flood, the price of olive oil and other quotidian things. Soon we were both yawning.'

Cleopatra shook her head in amusement. That was all she ever said about her first meeting with General Caesar—a story that was sure to be embellished over time. There had been no instant attraction, no grand seduction—at least not the way the Queen told it.

Still, Wen sensed a small change in her. The anxiety that she had expressed on the dock had disappeared, though her circumstances had changed only a little. It was enough to give Wen reason to hope.

'Come now,' said the Queen. 'Tell me about your journey to the Temple.'

As Charmion and Iras described their nervous trek to the Isis Temple, Wen ceased to listen. She stepped towards the window and glanced down at the group of Roman soldiers protecting the entrance to the Queen's palace. It seemed to Wen that there were not enough of them.

Ptolemy had surely learned of his sister-wife's arrival by now. He was probably only a few cubits away, in fact, occupying the main palace closest to the sea. If he sent enough of his guards, they could quickly overcome the Queen's defences. What then?

'Where is Apollodorus?' asked Iras suddenly.

'He is keeping watch just there,' said Cleopatra, motioning to the balcony.

'Apollodorus,' called Iras. 'Come inside for just a moment so that we may congratulate you.'

Apollodorus stepped inside and the two handmaids embraced him. 'You are well met,' said Charmion. 'Thank you for protecting our Queen.'

'It was an honour,' said Apollodorus. 'Though we are not out of danger yet.'

There was an angry shout from somewhere below, and Apollodorus dashed back out on to the balcony. 'Who goes there?' he called down.

'By order of Ptolemy the Thirteenth, we demand entry!' shouted a voice.

Ptolemy's soldiers, Wen thought. *They have come to kill the Queen.*

The Queen rushed on to the balcony and stood behind Apollodorus.

'You may not pass,' one of the Roman guards was shouting, 'by order of General Julius Caesar.'

Charmion and Iras rushed out on to the balcony and stood flanking the Queen. Wen tried to step out to join them, but she could not bring her feet to cross on to the high perch.

She knew that, at any moment, Ptolemy's soldiers could come rushing up the stairs to the Queen's living chamber and would likely slaughter them all.

She ran to the chamber door and bolted it shut, as if a single bolt could possibly hold off a battery of armed men. She searched the room for weapons, remembering the small knife she carried around her ankle.

Titus, she thought. If only he were here. If only he could help them.

Instead, she heard the soft slapping of what sounded like a hundred pairs of sandals on the courtyard below. 'They have come!' Charmion exclaimed. 'Caesar's soldiers have come! Two centuries of them at least!'

'Look how Ptolemy's guards retreat from them!' cried Iras. 'We are saved!'

'Look, there!' said Charmion suddenly. 'It is Titus! Do you see the blue-crested helmet he wears? He commands them.'

Wen gasped, though she should not have been surprised. Titus had admitted that he commanded Caesar's Sixth. She simply had never dreamed that she would see him do it.

But she wasn't *seeing* him, not really, for she remained trembling just inside the balcony.

'You need not fear, Wen,' said the Queen. 'The balcony is perfectly sound and you will be rewarded by the sight below it.'

Fighting her fear, Wen stepped out on to the balcony and craned her neck to get a glimpse of him. He was not difficult to find. He towered above the other soldiers, his blue-crested helmet fluttering in the breeze. A long red cape further distinguished him from his men. He wore it tossed over his shoulder, revealing the contours of his dark leather cuirass, which had been moulded to the muscles of his formidable chest.

He was every inch a commander, and Wen was awed by the sight of him.

He is still Titus, she told herself. *He is just a man.* But he seemed more than just a man. He was a leader, a commander, a model of discipline, strength and no small measure of ambition.

The Roman soldiers whom she had served at the

brew house had often spoken of the *Cursus Honou-rum*—the steps taken by a Roman patrician who aspired to rule.

First he received tutoring in the rhetorical arts, then distinguished himself as a military leader. Upon his return from conquest, he used his spoils to acquire both a wife and a clientele. Finally, through an elaborate system of choosing that the Romans called 'elections', the man acquired a series of ruling positions, culminating in the office of Roman consul.

Clearly, Titus had already completed the most difficult part of that path to glory—he had distinguished himself as a leader. It seemed clear that he aspired to much more. He had said it himself—he feared things would change between them and now Wen knew why. He did not care about her. He *could* not care about her. Not with a century to command, and a ladder of glory to climb back in Rome. What did she expect? She was just a slave, after all. She mattered not.

Wen saw Titus glance at the balcony and she dared to raise her hand in a wave. But he quickly looked away from her.

Of course he did. He was a Roman commander and she was an Egyptian slave.

'Wen, why are you laughing?' asked Charmion.

'Because I am a fool.'

All week, he thought about that wave. It was so very small, so very exposed—like a leaf floating in the air.

He should have returned it. He should have given her that small reassurance. But he could not. He was a Roman commander and had been in full view of his troops. A commander did not wave at women on balconies. A Roman was the pillar of *dignitas* for his legion. As soon as that *dignitas* was lost, so was all discipline and order. And if all discipline and order was lost, then so would be the Queen's life.

And Wen's.

Neither of the women realised how fortunate they were. Instead of eliminating the Queen, Caesar had decided to reinstate her. For days he had been working to reconcile her with Ptolemy and the time had finally come for him to announce their truce. Caesar did not mean to conquer Egypt after all, or so it seemed, and Titus rested knowing the great General's ambitions were in check.

To announce the reconciliation of Ptolemy and Cleopatra, Caesar had chosen the balcony of the Library of Alexandria, reasoning that the high buildings surrounding it would allow his voice to carry far. For protection from the mob, he had ordered that Titus place two hundred of his men around the Library and two hundred more to escort Caesar, the Pharaohs and their entourages to the site.

Now, as those royal assemblages made their way through the crowd, Titus worried that he had not stationed enough men to protect them. The citizens of Alexandria were rowdy and anxious. Their hate for Caesar seemed even stronger than their love for their young Pharaoh, and they booed the great General even as they applauded the royals who followed him.

Titus did not notice Wen until he was well inside the Library. He had not expected her to come, for she was only a slave and not an official advisor of the court, though he admitted that her function was more difficult to describe.

What was not difficult to describe was her loveliness. She wore a fitted white tunic, glorious in its simplicity, and her skin shone a rosy bronze amidst the dusty shelves. The paint upon her eyes had rendered them both larger and more exquisite than he remembered and her silken black hair had been arranged to fall around her cheeks in a feathery frame.

He wanted to speak with her—nay, he wanted to embrace her—but he knew he could do neither. He laboured in his official capacity once again and needed to remain aloof.

Still, he lingered at the back of Caesar's entourage as they headed to the second-floor balcony, hoping to keep Wen in his sights. Titus did not see the fireball until it was falling towards Caesar's head. The General had stepped out on to the balcony impulsively, with little protection, and Titus lunged in front of the burning missile with his shield, sending a cascade of sparks into the air.

'Move back!' he urged Caesar and his men. 'Get off the balcony!'

A burning coal followed close behind and he batted it away with his arm. He searched for Wen, trying to make sure she was out of danger.

'If we were in Rome, those would have only been melons,' remarked Caesar with a wry grin.

Titus escorted Caesar back into the Library and spied Wen huddled between two shelves of scrolls. 'Stay near me,' he told her. 'You and the Queen's handmaids, I mean.'

And to think that earlier that morning, he had resisted Caesar's suggestion to bring his shield. 'How much worse can an Alexandrian mob be than a Roman one?' Titus had asked.

'You'll see,' Caesar had replied.

Now Titus watched in horror as a boat anchor was hurled over the balcony, followed by a rain of stones. 'The stones are meant to fix the anchor in place,' explained Caesar, his tone rich with admiration.

The anchor was being pulled from below and Titus watched in alarm as the anchor itself held fast. Imagining a stream of murderous scholars travelling up its taut chords, Titus ran to the edge of the balcony and severed it with his dagger. He was rewarded for his efforts with several more flying hot coals. He shot a glance at Caesar, who only continued to laugh.

He found Apollodorus standing near the Queen. 'Is there a third-floor balcony?' Titus asked.

'No, but we can go to the roof,' Apollodorus said.

'Lead them there,' Titus commanded, and the royal entourages of both Cleopatra and Ptolemy, along with Caesar and his military guard, fell in line behind Apollodorus and headed for the roof.

Meanwhile, Titus fetched several guards and placed them on the second-floor balcony. 'Do not allow anyone to reach this balcony,' he commanded.

He was hurrying to catch up to Caesar when he found Wen. She had fallen in line at the rear of the group and was doubled over in the stairwell, trying to catch her breath. Titus knew that he was supposed to be protecting Caesar, but he could not abide the idea of Wen suffering in fear. He watched her struggle upright and attempt to climb. With each step, she appeared to turn a darker shade of green.

'Wen, are you well?' Titus asked.

'I fear high places,' she mumbled, slowing her pace. 'Please, just leave me. Do your duty.'

But he did not want to do his duty.

In the week since they had parted, he had found it maddeningly difficult to think of anything but Wen. He could not concentrate on his physical training, his correspondence, even his advice to Caesar. He had paced among the lavish furnishings of his chamber, past trays of food, shelves of scrolls, and mosaics more beautiful than anything in Rome, seeing none of them.

It was as if he had caught a fever—some terrible malaise that brought thirst and shivers and visions of an Egyptian woman with her toes buried in the sand. She had weakened him, the black-braided nymph.

He yearned for her body, but also for her mind, for she wielded it like a secret knife. How could she know so much about Roman history? Or political strategy? Or human nature? No simple slave could possibly have gleaned that kind of knowledge by tilting beer into cups. Nor could a mere child of a temple, if that was what she really was. She was brilliant in the way of a scholar.

But she was a woman. A woman! Women were not scholars. They were mothers and wives, maidservants and harlots. Besides, she was too desirable to be a scholar. Even now, he felt slightly unnerved as he followed behind her. The way her hips moved on her way up the stairs made it impossible to consider her a threat to anything but his self-control.

She was like a scroll whose text he thought he understood, but upon rereading could no longer decipher. How could he solve this difficult puzzle, he wondered, so that he might again sleep at night? How could he comprehend her mysterious hold on him so that he might be free of it?

They arrived on the stairwell landing, and she doubled over again.

'Are you well, Wen?' he asked.

'Please go on,' she said between breaths. 'Your General needs you now.'

'Caesar is capable of deflecting his own fireballs,' Titus said and thought he saw the hint of a smile traverse her face. She pressed her back against the stairwell wall. 'I shall accompany you back to the street,' he insisted. 'I will take you to a healer.'

'No, no!' she gasped. 'I must rejoin the Queen!' She lunged up the stairs. 'I cannot fail her—'

In her rush up the stairs, she stumbled, and he watched her ankle twist beneath her.

'Wen!' he shouted. She rolled over, holding her ankle and cringing in pain. Titus bent to help her, but she held up her hand. 'Please, just go away!'

'You have injured yourself. I will take you to the healer. Come.' He bent and grasped her by the wrists.

'No!' she shouted, wrenching herself free of him. She appeared to be on the verge of tears. She took a long, slow breath. 'Apologies, but I do not like to be held by the wrists.'

'You are injured. You must allow me to help you.'

'Please just go,' said Wen. 'It does not matter. I do not matter.'

'You matter to me,' he whispered.

There was a loud thudding sound from the street, followed by a haunting chant. 'Go home, Roman! Go home, Roman!' sang the crowd.

'Curses,' he said. Caesar needed him, but Titus did not wish to leave her alone. She was injured and in pain.

'Go!' she urged.

Hating himself, he bounded up the stairs and arrived on the rooftop. There, Caesar was opening his arms out to the angry Alexandrians as if in a grand embrace. 'I was told that the only thing the men of Alexandria love more than knowledge is justice,' Caesar called.

The crowd flailed in a riot of energy and movement.

Titus took his place behind the purple-caped General and put on his helmet. He wondered if Wen was all right. He pictured her limping down the stairs, or collapsing in despair.

'But what do Alexandrians love more than justice?' Caesar asked the crowd. Receiving no response, he smiled. 'Why, beer, of course!'

There was a smattering of laughter, followed by a flood of angry hisses. 'Wise men of Alexandria,' Caesar continued, 'I have come to your fair city to present you with a gift.'

Upon hearing the word *gift*, the mob quieted.

She is probably down the stairs by now, Titus thought.

'I was told that the men of Alexandria are the most intelligent men in the world,' continued Caesar. 'I was told that they invent great machines and cure diseases and build monuments that stretch to the heavens.'

There was an upwelling of cheers as Caesar motioned to the Lighthouse, then to the giant hilltop temple of Alexandria's patron god. Finally, he turned and pointed to the building upon which they stood. The Great Library of Alexandria, the shining jewel of the modern world.

She is sitting down near one of the scroll shelves, Titus thought.

'Now that I am here, wise men of Alexandria, I see that it is true what they say about you. Your rich, fair city reflects your union with the natural order. I believe that here in Egypt you have a name for that union. What do you call that?'

'Ma'at!' someone yelled.

'Ma'at,' echoed Caesar. Your city reflects your love of wisdom and of *ma'at*, of heavenly balance.' With this last serving of flattery, a great hurrah rose up from the crowd.

She is collapsing in pain, he thought. *She is all alone*.

'Well, then, wise men of Alexandria, I am sure it must pain your hearts to see that the *ma'at* of this great city has lately been lost, for the last wishes of your late Pharaoh have gone unfulfilled.'

There was a collective groan.

'It pains me, as well,' said Caesar. 'To see a brother and sister at war with each other is a breach in the natural order. The Ptolemies are descended from Alexander the Great, after all. It is the will of the gods that the greatest bloodline in history reign over the greatest kingdom in the world.'

'Let Ptolemy rule!' cried someone.

'Let Ptolemy rule indeed,' repeated Caesar. 'But he cannot rule alone. That is not the will of his father, nor of the gods themselves. Even in Rome, our consuls do not rule alone. There are always two. Thus the scales of justice remain balanced. It is the natural way of things. It is *ma'at*.'

Discussion pulsed through the crowd. *She is sitting all alone in despair*, he thought.

'The *ma'at* must be restored,' said Caesar.

* * *

She reached the bottom of the stairs and took a breath. Her ankle felt better, but she felt unsteady. She found a bench just below the high window and listened closely as Caesar continued his speech.

'Wise men of Alexandria,' he was saying, 'do not think that I have come here to plunder, or that I wish to seize the greatest kingdom in the world for Rome. Egypt? Ha!' Caesar laughed. 'That would be like a dog trying to seize an elephant!'

There was strident laughter and more cheering, and Wen wondered if Caesar spoke truth. Did he really have no intention of conquest? *Listen to what he is not saying*, the High Priestess would have said. *Read the actions behind his words.*

'No, wise men of Alexandria,' continued Caesar, 'I come here to set right what has been wrong, to honour the late Ptolemy's wishes, to restore *ma'at* to this great land. This brings me to your gift. I give you your two divine sovereigns. Reconciled!'

As Wen listened to the storm of cheers, a realisation washed over her. That applause had been his intention all along—to stand before the Alexandrian crowd and receive their gratitude. He had given Alexandria back its warring monarchs—a great gift indeed. But the real power lay with the giver.

Caesar wants something, she thought. *But what exactly? Egypt? The Queen?*

'He wants the world.'

Wen jumped as his deep, throaty voice settled over her, followed by a strange feeling of comfort.

Titus stepped out from behind a shelf.

'Titus? You mean that he wishes to be King?' Wen asked.

'That is what I fear,' said Titus.

'Why would you fear such a thing? As commander of his legion, would you not also wish it?'

She watched the muscles of his jaw flex. 'You have injured yourself,' he said, glancing at her ankle. 'What I wish is to come to your aid.'

He sat beside her on the bench, and the hairs rose up on her skin. 'Should you not be with Caesar now?'

'He has won the crowd. I am no longer needed.'

Wen gazed up at the window, wishing her heart would stop beating.

'Come, let me see your ankle.' Wen shook her head vigorously. She pulled her whole foot beneath her tunic. She could not allow him to touch her again. Strange things happened to her body when he did.

'Why will you not allow me to help you?'

'You are a commander and I am a slave. It is not your place to help me.' She reminded herself of their last conversation: *I fear that things will change between us.* The words were proof of his indifference to her and she needed to remember them well.

Titus removed his helmet. 'What if I were just a man?'

'But you are not just a man. That is what you meant when you said that things would change between us. I see that now.'

'That is not what I meant.'

'For a man of your rank to even sit beside a woman such as me is an affront to the natural order. It is a violation of *ma'at.*'

'Do you really believe that?'

'I do not know what to believe.'

'You can believe this.'

His lips found hers and suddenly he was kissing her right there, amidst the knowledge of the ages. His soft lips pressed against hers with the force of some strange propulsion. She stiffened with the shock of it, then found her surprise quickly convert into joy.

She kissed him back, drinking in his desire, swilling it, afraid that this was the last time she would ever taste a drop.

His odour alone seemed to alter her mind—so much salt and lavender and musk—like a potion that would either kill her or save her life.

She only hoped she smelled half as good, tasted half as rich, felt half as wonderful to him. She knew that she was just a slave and that they had no future. Still, none of it seemed to matter when her lips were locked with his.

'Let us rejoice,' said Caesar triumphantly. 'And tomorrow, let us feast!'

But Wen was no longer listening.

Chapter Nine

Queen Cleopatra swept into the Reception Hall, her sandals snapping across the tiles like whips. 'Who does Caesar think he is ordering a feast?'

Iras and Charmion followed closely behind her, along with a company of Roman guards. The Queen was almost to the base of her throne when she noticed Wen standing at its edge.

'Where have you been, Wen?'

Wen collapsed in obeisance.

'Apologies, my Queen, I could not ascend the Library stairs.'

'Oh, rise by the goddess, Wen, we are far beyond that now.'

Wen jumped to her feet as Cleopatra sent a flurry of expletives echoing through the hall. 'If Caesar thinks he can simply reconcile me with the brother who put a price on my head, he is gravely mistaken.'

Cleopatra arrived at the base of her throne and scratched her head. 'And now this cursed feast!' she exclaimed. 'Who does Caesar think he is ordering a hundred cattle slaughtered by tomorrow evening?' She paced back and forth between the marble sphinxes that guarded her throne, too distraught to ascend. 'The audacity of it!'

Wen suspected that the Queen was not angered by Caesar's announcement itself, but by the fact that she had not been the one to make it. 'And free beer in the temples? That will require significant purchasing. Where does he think it all comes from, I wonder?'

'I suspect Caesar wishes to placate the Alexandrians,' Wen said without thinking, 'for they are violent and prone to riots.'

Iras and Charmion looked at Wen in shock, for she had not been invited to speak.

But the Queen did not reproach her. 'The people of Alexandria are indeed prone to riots!' she exclaimed. 'They are violent, dangerous agitators! By the gods, they may as well be Romans!'

At that, the four women broke down into something resembling the laughter of hyenas.

The Queen crossed to a nearby table and poured herself a goblet of wine. 'The royal treasury will be empty by morning thanks to Caesar.' She held up the goblet as if to make a toast.

'Has that wine been tasted?' Iras asked Charmion.

'I believe so,' said Iras, 'but we should ask Apollodorus just to be—'

The Queen did not wait for Iras to finish. She drank down the goblet's contents in a single gulp. 'If I die now, at least I shall be remembered as the Queen who would not submit to Caesar's extravagances.'

She took three more goblets from a shelf and poured wine into each. 'There you are, my sisters,' she said, motioning to the vessels. 'If you dare. I assure you that we have nothing left to lose.'

Iras gave Charmion a glance and they both reached for their goblets. Then all three turned to look at Wen, who walked to the table and raised her goblet high.

Wen remembered that moment upon her tongue as much as she did in her memory, for it was the first time she had ever tasted wine.

'Well done, *ka* sisters!' exclaimed Cleopatra. 'Now let us get to work, for we have only a single day to arrange a banquet for the history scrolls. Charmion, would you call my scribe? There are requisitions to be written.' Charmion gave a bow and scuttled out of the chamber.

'Iras, would you please find my Steward Hemut? I would like to see his expression when I tell him we have one day to arrange a royal banquet.'

'Yes, Goddess,' said Iras and she was soon rushing after Charmion.

'And, Wen...?'

'Yes, my Queen?' said Wen, the powerful tartness still exploding on her tongue.

'Oh, Wen, there is so much to be done! I can hardly think.'

'Shall I advise the temples about the beer and bread distributions?' Wen asked, remembering how much she had appreciated such distributions herself.

'Ah, yes! Go to the Isis Temple and tell the head priestess. She will send word to the other temples. Tell them the rations will arrive this afternoon.'

'Yes, my Queen.'

'And would you find Apollodorus? I need a bodyguard. Pothinus was so enraged after Caesar's speech that I fear he might try to kill me himself.'

'Pothinus, my Queen?'

'My brother's advisor. The brains behind his unfortunate reign.' Cleopatra sighed. 'I cannot beat Pothinus without Caesar, but I fear that Caesar has outmanoeuvred me.'

'I do not think so,' Wen said.

'I want to believe you.'

'He may appear as Alexandria's saviour today, but Alexandrians are cynical. They know better than to trust him.'

'I fear they are enamoured of him.'

'Hunger motivates love of a passing nature only. After the belly is filled, it disappears.'

'If he leaves Alexandria now I am as good as dead.'

Wen dared not look at the Queen directly. 'You still hold fast to what is most precious?' She had spoken without being questioned, though in truth she did not care. The Queen's only hope against Ptolemy and his wicked advisors was to win Caesar to her side. Indeed, she needed to make him her champion.

'I do,' said the Queen. 'Though I cannot say if he is even interested in me.'

'He is interested.'

'How do you know?'

'How could he not be? You are utterly magnificent,' Wen pronounced grandly, as Charmion might have done. The Queen laughed. 'Also, the two of you are much alike.'

'Yes, we both wish to rule Egypt.' Cleopatra laughed bitterly.

'Apologies, my Queen. I did not mean—'

'There is no need to apologise for speaking the truth, Wen.'

Cleopatra poured herself another goblet of wine.

'Caesar could call his legions to Egypt at any moment. He could make us a province at his whim. That is what Ptolemy—and the Alexandrians themselves—do not understand. The Romans are as inevitable as the tears of Isis.'

'It is true,' Wen said, speaking freely now.

'Though I understand that hunger better now,' the Queen added. 'It is a hunger born of poverty. Titus explained it well.'

'That he did,' said Wen, remembering the taste of his lips. She had stopped their kiss after only a few moments, fearful of being seen. Now she wished she had let it go on.

'It makes me wonder what Egyptian soldiers would do if they had to fight for their bread.'

'Conquer the world,' Wen offered cheerfully, 'in the name of their Queen.'

Cleopatra smiled sadly. 'All I want is the kingdom my father left me. I know I can serve its people well—and not just these wretched Alexandrians, but *all* Egyptians. There is a glory and a grace in our way of life that a Roman governor could never understand.'

'Yet some kind of relationship with a Roman is inevitable,' Wen said. 'You are fortunate, for you stand in a position to dictate the terms.'

The Queen flashed a beguiling grin. 'You fortify me, Wen.'

'You must call upon every persuasive tactic you know, Goddess. Though you remain firmly rooted, you must bend like a reed. For every effort of resistance your brother presents to Caesar, you must present an effort of alliance. Or there will be a Roman fort in every town from Thebes to Alexandria.'

'A covenant with Seth Incarnate.'

'To save your Egypt's life as well as your own.'

'Would you do such a thing, Wen? Attempt to seduce a stranger? A Roman? Speak truthfully.'

A vision invaded her memory: a man with a pitted nose and hair that smelled of rancid oil. He was saying something in Latin—something ugly and perverse—and pulling Wen by the wrists up a flight of stairs.

'My Queen,' Wen said, blinking the vision away, 'I do not know if I could seduce a Roman.'

'But you already have.' she said. 'Do you not see it?'

'Goddess?'

'Titus. He looks at you as if you were a sculptor and he a lump of clay. And do not tell me that he did not try to kiss you that night in the labyrinth.' Wen tried to conceal her surprise. How had the Queen known about the kiss? 'Queens are trained to observe,' Cleopatra said. 'If I did not know better, I would say that you had kissed him again quite recently.'

Was Wen so very transparent? Perhaps so, for even now, she could not stop her blush. 'My Queen is wise,' she said. She touched her fingers to her lips, remembering.

'Let us hope not too wise. These Romans like their women vacuous and pliable, I fear.'

'Caesar can have any woman he wishes. You must show him that you are different. You are a prize worth fighting for.'

The Queen sighed. 'And what if I am successful? I fear I will not be able to sustain the ruse.'

'If a ruse it is. Perhaps you will grow to like him.'

'There is little to recommend him. They say he is fifty-two years old!'

'Well, he is almost bald,' Wen offered.

'How is that a recommendation?'

'Does it not make him almost Egyptian?'

The Queen gave a mighty laugh, then buried her head in her hands.

'Do not despair,' Wen said, 'but fortify yourself. And no matter what you do, do not give him your heart.'

There was a sudden pounding on the entrance doors. Startled, Wen hastened across the long chamber and heaved back a thick, ebony door. There, standing before her, was Caesar himself, accompanied by Titus.

He had not expected to see her face again so soon. She inhaled when she saw him and her cheeks turned a lovely shade of crimson.

'Greetings, General Caesar,' she told Caesar. She gave a deep bow, then quieted her voice. 'Greetings, Tribune Titus.'

'Greetings, Wen.'

She did not look at him and her shyness sent a pang of lust through his limbs.

'Since it appears you have struck my advisor dumb,' said Caesar, 'I will say that I have come for an audience with the Queen.'

'As you wish, General,' replied Wen. 'Please follow me.'

As Wen led them down the long, empty chamber towards the elegant green throne stationed at its end, Caesar slowed his stride.

'Is this the one you were telling me about?' he whispered in Latin.

Titus felt his skin prickle. Earlier, he had explained

to Caesar that one of the Queen's women had discovered his identity.

He had not mentioned that Wen was a slave, or that she could speak their Latin tongue. Still, there was no way to correct the General now. 'Well, is this the woman?' he prodded in Latin and Titus managed a small nod.

'She is nice,' Caesar said, taking her measure from behind.

Titus tried to remain calm. He was not supposed to interfere with Caesar's activities, whatever their nature. 'Observe and report, Titus!' Those were Cicero's orders. 'Do not disrupt the course of events until absolutely necessary. Remember that you are just a spy.' He had even made Titus swear an oath.

But now, as Titus watched Caesar's eyes range across Wen's lovely backside, he knew that he would break that oath a hundred times if it meant keeping her away from him. The Roman Republic be damned—he would not hesitate to stick a knife in the old lecher if he ever set a finger on Wen.

Fortunately, as they neared Cleopatra's throne, Caesar's gaze was quickly diverted from the lovely servile backside moving before them to the royal one stepping up the dais to the throne.

'Greetings, Caesar,' said the Queen in her light, musical tone. She glanced over her shoulder in an offhanded way, then completed her ascent with an exaggerated sway of her hips. 'I am honoured that you have come to visit me in my humble Reception Hall.'

Titus glanced around the towering space and wondered just what was humble about it. Behind the massive stone throne stretched a wall-sized mosaic of the

Egyptian goddess Isis, her breasts bared above her tree-sized red sheath, her headdress itself a throne.

On either side of the mosaic stood two massive columns that supported the richly painted ceiling. Careful not to stare, Titus stole a glance at the painting overhead and beheld a river scene populated by innumerable deadly animals and as many naked children playing together in impossible harmony.

But that was only a passing wonder in comparison to the massive marble statues that had been erected on either side of the Queen's high throne.

They were giant sphinxes.

They stood two heads taller than Titus and twice as wide. *How old are you?* he asked the feline noblemen. *From what fantastic quarry were you hewn?* The chimeras gave no answers, yet seemed to carry the wisdom of the ages in their emerald eyes.

'Greetings, Titus,' the Queen said, catching his attention. 'I see you are fond of my little cats.'

He bowed low, trying to conceal the rush of blood in his cheeks. 'Greetings, Queen Cleopatra.'

Titus noticed that Wen had taken her position at the foot of the dais. She appeared to be trying to suppress a rather sphinx-like grin.

'You may touch them, if you wish,' Cleopatra told Titus. 'The sphinxes, I mean.'

'Gratitude, Queen, but I find them too beautiful to sully with my brutish hands.'

At that, the Queen let out a laugh. 'Well, they are the hands that brought me safely to this throne, and for that I shall always be grateful.'

He bowed again, at a loss for words.

'Titus, you are not the only man here to whom I owe

my gratitude,' the Queen continued, shifting her gaze to Caesar. 'Your performance today was magnificent, General. I have never seen the Alexandrian horde so moved. Under whom did you study the rhetorical arts?'

Caesar did not answer the Queen's question. He only stared at her in wonder. 'You look radiant, Queen,' he said at last.

'If I am radiant then it is you who has made me so. By reuniting me with my husband-brother you have restored me to my throne.'

'I have merely followed your father's wishes. In Egypt, a late pharaoh's will is the law, is it not?'

'It is.'

'You are fortunate in that. In Rome the law is much more complicated.'

If Titus had been listening closely to Caesar's words, he would have recognised the shadow of Caesar's ambition and the threat to come. But he was thoroughly distracted by Wen. She remained standing at the base of the Queen's throne only a few arms' lengths away, her eyes fixed forward in a maddening show of duty.

'Your father's will is why I am here,' said Caesar. 'I will read it today before the Royal Council of Advisors. It is a formality, but as the executor I wish your restoration to be seen as legal.'

The Queen shifted in her throne, crossing one leg over another and exposing some of the skin of her thigh. 'You are very thorough, General.'

From the corner of his eye, Titus noticed Caesar swallow hard. 'I try to be.'

'You also act with great haste. I was rather shocked when you announced the feasts.'

'Can you blame me for wanting to experience the pleasures of the Ptolemaic court?'

'No, I cannot,' said the Queen. She lowered her voice. 'And I promise you that they are not to be missed.' Cleopatra raised her chin to a more regal angle. 'But it will be no small feat to organise a city-wide festival in a single day.'

'The way in which one confronts the unexpected reveals one's character,' Caesar replied. 'I am sure you will pass the test.'

'The staging of feasts? As a test?'

'Why not?' replied Caesar. 'It would amuse me to observe if you can organise them. It is not a person's birth, but a person's merit that impresses me most.'

'Is that so? Then in that sense we are the same,' said the Queen, sliding Wen a look. 'I have heard that you find your greatest supporters among the common people.'

'That is true,' said Caesar.

'I, too, am supported by commoners. What is it that they are called in Rome, Wen?'

'The plebeians, my Queen,' Wen said.

Titus wished she would look at him—just give him a small glance. He needed to know that she felt it, too—this strange force pulling them together, despite themselves. In the Library, she had pulled away from his kiss and stood before him, her cheeks flush, her eyes glowing. She had commanded him to return to his duty and said something about hers. Then she simply opened the door to the Library and slipped past the guards.

By the time he had got past the guards himself, she was already gone—disappeared into the common crowd. But she was not common, not at all. She was advisor to the world's greatest Queen. *Who are you, Wen of Alexandria?* he wondered. *Who?*

'Ah, yes, the Roman plebeians,' said Cleopatra. 'They are like our Egyptian fellahin, yes?'

'Only in their poverty,' said Caesar. 'They are much closer to the Alexandrian mob in their humour.'

'It is no wonder they favour you, then, for you are able to manipulate their passions.'

Caesar gave a vain toss of his head. He seemed unaware that his own passions were being manipulated quite handily.

'General Caesar, what is your purpose here?' she asked suddenly.

Caesar stiffened. 'I wish to solidify Rome's alliance with Egypt.'

The Queen smiled tightly. She studied her knees, as if trying to think. 'You must forgive us,' she said at last. 'We have failed to offer you and Tribune Titus any refreshment!'

She glanced at Wen, who retreated to a corner of the corridor and emerged bearing a silver tray laden with an amphora and four golden goblets. She placed the tray upon a high table at the base of the throne.

In a blur of nubile grace, the Queen stepped down the stairs of the dais and stood beside Wen.

For a moment the four of them stood looking at each other—like two pairs of opponents meeting before a contest.

The Queen lifted the wine vessel with two hands and began to pour, while Wen held a cloth beneath the lip to catch the drips. As the Queen filled each goblet, she spoke gently and intimately to Caesar, as if she were confessing to her closest maid. 'You must think me terribly naive to ask you why you are here, General—especially since I already know. You are here to recover my father's debt.'

Caesar watched Cleopatra carefully but said not a word. She handed him his goblet.

'You may be sure that as long as I sit upon the throne I will labour to pay that debt in full, and with interest.' She handed a goblet to Titus and one to Wen, then took the fourth into her own hands. 'I will always remember that you restored me to my rightful throne. The problem is that the moment you leave Egypt, I am as good as dead.'

She raised her goblet and Caesar raised a brow. 'Your insight surprises me, Queen.'

'Please, call me Cleopatra.'

Caesar grinned. 'Let us drink to you, then…Cleopatra.' Caesar raised his goblet, then emptied its contents in a single gulp. Titus did the same, feeling more at ease as he watched Wen take a tentative sip.

'I may be young and inexperienced,' continued Cleopatra, 'but I assure you that I understand the challenges and responsibilities of being Queen.'

'Do you?' said Caesar, smirking. 'It requires more than just pouring wine.'

The Queen's eyes flickered with the delight of a challenge. 'I know that my brother's advisor Pothinus would much rather go to war with Rome than see your debt paid. And of course every leather-shod noble in Alexandria is behind him.' The Queen refilled their goblets. 'I also know that Rome cannot afford another long war.'

'Nor does it wish for one.' Caesar gave Titus a look, then drained his cup once again. 'I am tired of battle.'

It was a lie, of course. Caesar was never tired of battle because he was never tired of glory. It was the difference between Caesar and Titus. Caesar fought for his own glory, while Titus fought to defend the Republic.

Titus shuddered, feeling the sudden burn of Wen's gaze upon his skin. It was as if she had heard Titus speak his thoughts aloud.

Titus kept his face taut and expressionless, though he feared Wen could see his doubt of Caesar like a halo around his head.

'And, of course, the city of Rome becomes a starving hamlet without reliable exports of Egyptian grain,' continued the Queen. 'With me dead, my brother will ban that trade, for his advisor Pothinus hates Romans even more than he loves beer. I fear it is in your interests to keep me alive, General.'

'You speak like a politician,' said Caesar. 'How is it possible that one so young and lovely should have a mind so seasoned and sharp?'

The Queen only laughed. 'And now we have delivered our best flattery to each other and are similar in that, as well,' she said.

'I am many things, but a flatterer I am not.'

'Ha! Then I am bested, General, for I have just admitted that I am.'

They both drank at once, never taking their eyes off one another, while Titus stole another glance at Wen. The hint of a smile traversed her lips.

'Pothinus and General Achillas hold the Egyptian

army at Pelousion,' the Queen said. 'I fear they will begin their march to Alexandria any day.'

'I see the net you are weaving,' said Caesar carefully. 'I wonder if the thread will hold.'

'You have everything to gain from helping me defend my throne. Think of it as a test of merit.'

'A test?'

'And if you pass, you shall be handsomely rewarded.' The Queen ran her finger across the lip of her goblet.

There was a long pause, and Wen held her breath. Cleopatra had just asked the most powerful man in the world to fight for her, with herself as the prize for victory. All of the Queen's hopes and ambitions—along with both of their lives—depended on Caesar's answer.

'*If* we achieve victory,' Caesar growled. He appeared angry and energised all at once. He set down his goblet and began to pace. 'I travel with little more than a legion. They are Roman soldiers, but they are not invincible.'

'Send for more,' said the Queen. 'Does Rome not have legions stationed in every province?'

'It is not that simple.' Caesar turned to Titus. 'Who would send men?'

'Mithridates of Pergamon would do it, if only to spite his late father,' said Titus. 'And ambition alone might motivate Antipater of Judea…'

As Titus spoke, it became clear that he possessed a vast political knowledge—not just of the Roman troops stationed near Egypt, but of their leaders' proclivities and motivations.

It should have been no surprise to Wen. He was a commander of a legion and an advisor to a general. It was his job to know such things. Still, Wen sensed some deeper purpose beneath his words. She wondered what it could be. *Who are you, Titus of Rome?* she wondered. *Who?*

'Atticus of Crete is close,' Titus was saying, 'but he would require some incentive.'

'Incentive?' asked the Queen.

'You must reach into your coffers, Cleopatra,' said Caesar. 'Can you do that?'

Cleopatra laughed. 'I have no choice. Without your help, I will be dead by the Festival of Osiris.' Caesar gave her a doubting look, but the Queen only smiled. 'Do not fear, General. I will find the gold to pay the legions. I will melt Alexander's golden sandals if I have to.'

'Do not do that!' Caesar exclaimed. 'I mean, let us hope it does not come to that.'

'Then you will help me defeat my brother?' asked the Queen.

'Before I agree, I have a request.' Caesar gazed up at the Queen's magnificent throne. 'Allow me to sit on your throne for a few moments, then join me upon it.'

'What?'

'I wish to sit upon your throne, then I want you to sit on my lap. That is my request. If you will fulfil it, I will help you in your cause.'

A wickedness had seeped into Caesar's expression, making Wen's skin prickle. *Here he is at last,* she thought, *the dissolute womaniser, the famous seducer of other men's wives.*

She stole a glance at Titus, but his face was a mask

of stone. Was he shocked by what the General had said, or merely bored by it? She sensed it was the former, and that there was something Titus continued to hide from her. From everyone.

'Think of it as my…incentive,' said Caesar.

To her credit, Cleopatra betrayed no emotion. 'It appears that we have run out of wine,' she said. 'Come Wen.'

Before Caesar was able to respond, they had disappeared through a servant's exit and into a small anteroom. The Queen collapsed into a chair. 'Oh, Wen! Will the debasement ever end?'

'It is an unusual request.'

'Do you not think it unusually *depraved*?'

'I think that he is a Roman man and thus he is by nature depraved.'

'Hem! Well, I do not believe Titus to be depraved. You hesitate to agree—why?'

'It is just…a feeling that I have about him. He is obviously one of Caesar's closest advisors, yet there is something about Caesar that disagrees with him.'

'Caesar's depravity!' cried the Queen, laughing. 'If only it were Titus I was obliged to seduce.'

'Perhaps it is well that you find Caesar depraved. It will enable you to keep your…honour from him as long as possible.

'My honour? He wants me to sit on his lap, by the gods!'

An idea struck Wen. 'You must ask for something in return.'

'Beyond his promise to defend my throne?'

'He must know that he cannot trifle with your honour. If he pushes, you will push back.' It was a strange thing to say, especially for a slave, though Wen believed it with all her heart.

The Queen jumped out of her seat. 'Gratitude, Wen! You have saved me once again.' She lifted the amphora of wine and handed it to Wen.

'We must first refill it, yes?' Wen asked.

'That is not necessary,' said Cleopatra. 'It is still quite full.'

Titus saw Wen re-emerge from the shadows and tried not to stare. She followed behind the Queen with quiet grace, the large amphora balanced effortlessly in her arms, her expression full of secrets.

'Apologies for the delay,' the Queen said, and Wen placed the large jar upon the table as Cleopatra met Caesar's gaze. 'Of course I will allow you to sit on my throne, General. And I will join you there, as you have requested. But you must give me a small token in return, so that I may preserve my honour.'

'And what might that be?' Caesar asked, swallowing his wine.

'Cyprus.'

Caesar almost choked. 'What did you say?'

'I want the island of Cyprus. Rome took it from my grandfather. Now I want it back.'

'An entire island?'

'Return Cyprus to Egypt and I will allow you to sit upon my throne.'

Caesar shook his head. 'It is impossible. Even if it were in my power to grant, I could not appear to favour you over your husband-brother. The Alexandrian mob would murder me in my sleep.'

'Give it to my younger siblings, then,' she said at

last. 'Give it to Arsinoe and Ptolemy the Younger. In your career, you have doubled Rome's territory. Are you not allowed to do as you like with a small island? Return Cyprus, and let the Alexandrians marvel once again at your generosity.'

Titus could see the flattery at work on the great General's resolve. 'Did you know that this particular throne belonged to Rameses the Great?' the Queen continued. 'It is true. My great-grandfather, Ptolemy the Third, had it transported from Thebes. It is said that Rameses launched his campaign against the Hittites from that throne.'

Titus wondered if it was true, though it did not matter. Upon hearing the name Rameses the Great, Caesar grew misty-eyed and he walked to the base of the throne like one entranced.

'Cyprus, then,' he said. If Caesar had not been so distracted by the invocation of Egypt's greatest King, along with the idea of his own largess, he might have realised that he had been outwitted.

By a woman.

'Cyprus it is,' said Cleopatra, grinning in triumph.

And so it was that Caesar made the short journey to the top of Cleopatra's throne and settled himself into its wide marble seat. He took several deep breaths of the rarefied air and cast his gaze out across his imagined audience. 'This is how it should be.'

Titus glanced at Wen. Her head was bowed, but she was watching Caesar out of the corner of her eye and her lips twisted in the beginning of a grin. *Cyprus was her idea*, Titus realised.

It was Wen who had encouraged the Queen to heed Caesar's call and counselled her in how to seduce him.

And now, thanks to Wen, Caesar had postponed his ambition. Whatever designs he had on Egypt would have to wait, for he had agreed to be the champion of its lovely Queen. It occurred to Titus that by neutralising the Roman Republic's greatest threat, Wen might have singlehandedly saved it.

When he returned his attention back to Caesar, he noticed that the General's face had twisted into a mischievous grin. Caesar motioned to the Queen. 'Come, Cleopatra,' he commanded.

Obediently, Queen Cleopatra ascended the stairs and sat down upon the great General's lap. Titus's impulse was to look away. For reasons unknown to him, he did not wish to see Cleopatra in a state of debasement.

But then something quite unexpected occurred. The Queen began to laugh. He glanced up at the throne—there she was, her mouth agape, lost in a flurry of giggles.

She had placed the loose ribbon of her diadem over the top of Caesar's head. It fell over his long forehead, between his eyes and down the long sweep of his aquiline nose. The great General was blowing at the ribbon like a child might do, and it was fluttering in the air above his nostrils.

It was the most undignified thing Titus had ever seen. Gaius Julius Caesar, Roman General, Senator, Imperator and Consul of Rome, was acting a fool. And Cleopatra Philopator, Queen of Egypt, was baiting him.

Had the two gone mad? Had they been struck dumb by the gods? Had they simply drunk too much wine?

Wen stood silently beside Titus, her head still bowed, pretending not to watch. As Cleopatra pulled

her ribbon off Caesar's head and the General moved
his arm more tightly around the Queen's waist, Titus
realised that their antics were not wholly innocent: they
were expressing what appeared to be real affection.

Out of respect, he looked away and, in that same
moment, so did Wen. Her gaze collided with his and
he felt a pulse of warmth vibrate into his bones. On
impulse, he reached out his hand.

Incredibly, she took it and let him pull her next to
him. They stood shoulder to shoulder and watched
Cleopatra and Caesar share a kiss.

'Congratulations to us both, Titus,' Caesar said in
Latin, peering down from his high seat. 'You have your
woman and now I have mine, though I am certain that
yours will not ask you for an island.'

Titus squeezed Wen's hand, then smiled and nodded
at Caesar, struggling to remain composed. And as the
drunken General bent to plant another kiss on Cleopatra's lips, Titus kissed the top of Wen's head. 'He does
not know you speak Latin,' he whispered into her ear.

'But he knows of me, for you told him,' Wen whispered back.

'Do you find that so hard to believe?' Titus asked,
letting his lips linger in her hair.

'What is this?' clucked the Queen. 'Do our two closest advisors conspire against us?'

Startled, Wen stepped away from Titus.

'They conspire for certain, though I fear only Venus
knows their aim,' said Caesar.

The Queen and Caesar raised their goblets. 'I salute
you, Wen and Titus,' said Cleopatra, 'for there are no
two people better matched.'

Titus reached for Wen's goblet, and offered it to her

with a wink. They had witnessed the bargaining and shared in the revelry of these strange, secret alliances. Their fates were tied together, in victory or in defeat.

Titus and Wen raised their goblets high.

And they drank.

Chapter Ten

The next morning, Wen stood in attendance at the base of Cleopatra's throne and willed herself to focus. While the Queen distributed her commands to a never-ending stream of servants and scribes, Wen studied her own hand, remembering how Titus had held it. It was remarkable how easily their fingers had linked together, like the pattern of an unusual weave.

'Beware the heirs of Romulus and Remus,' the High Priestess had always told her and she tried to recall all the reasons she should not be thinking about him. But when she tried to enumerate them, a vision of his handsome face crowded in on her calculations, and her mind became foggy with desire.

She felt as if he had conquered her somehow, had taken her inside his crimson cape and enveloped her, until all she could feel was his rippling strength and all she could see was red.

She was so lost in her thoughts that she did not notice the small servant boy enter from the side of the hall. Rushing towards the throne, he stumbled on his own two feet.

'Oh, dear,' Cleopatra said as he collapsed on the floor with a pained yelp.

Wen leapt to the boy's side. 'Are you harmed?' she asked.

'I—I am unharmed,' sputtered the boy, trembling with nerves.

'Do not fear,' Wen whispered to him. 'She is a kind queen.' Wen tilted her head up at the Queen. 'He says he is unharmed, Goddess,' Wen reported, though the Queen did not appear interested in the boy. Her attention was instead riveted on Wen's exposed leg.

Wen realised that her tunic had somehow lifted in her efforts to revive the boy, and the length of her pink scar had become fully exposed. She gasped in horror, quickly pulling her skirt over the unsightly mark. The Queen's expression remained frozen.

'Apologies, Goddess Queen,' the boy began, struggling to his feet. 'I was sent by the High Steward. He seeks a trusted servant. For the banquet. To serve the Queen.'

'My apologies, young man,' said the Queen, turning her attention reluctantly to the boy. 'You are?'

'Khu.'

'Will you forgive me, Khu? I did not hear your request.'

'It is of nothing, Goddess Queen,' said the boy, visibly calmed. 'The High Steward sent me to request additional servants to attend you and your entourage at the banquet. He said that you should send women you trust.'

The Queen glanced doubtfully around the hall, fingering her pearl necklace. 'I fear that many of my body servants remain outside Pelousion at present,' she said.

Wen cleared her voice, hoping to catch the Queen's attention.

'I am afraid I can spare no one, Khu,' said Cleopatra.

Wen stepped forward. 'It would be my pleasure to serve at the banquet, my Queen,' she said.

'That is very generous of you, Wen,' said Cleopatra, 'but you are too important to serve at a banquet.'

But I am just a slave, Wen thought.

Khu bowed and began to take his leave. 'Wait,' said Wen. 'Goddess, may I approach?' The Queen gave a nod and Wen bounded up the dais. She bent to the Queen's ear. 'Ptolemy does not know who I am, nor do any of the members of his entourage. If I served at the banquet, I could keep my Horus eye on them—perhaps I might learn something. I am skilled at such work.'

A guileful smile broke across the Queen's face. 'You are indeed, Wen of Alexandria. You are also extremely clever.' She turned to Khu. 'On second thought, I have decided that Wen shall serve. Please escort her to the Banquet Hall and give dear old Hemut my regards.'

Khu nodded many times over, clearly pleased. Cleopatra took Wen's hand and squeezed it.

'Go forth, dear Wen, and play your part. Only do not forget the roles and riches of this life are illusions. They matter not.'

Wen paused. The saying was familiar. If Wen had been in full possession of her wits, she would have realized right then where she had heard it before. But she was too excited to think. Like every young Egyptian girl, she had been raised on stories of the splendour and hospitality of the Ptolemaic court. Now was her chance to experience the stuff of her very dreams.

But there was a deeper reason for her thrill. She believed that Titus would attend the banquet. She could hardly wait for the moment she spied him. She would float up to him and offer him a drink of wine or an edible from her tray. He would look at her with gratitude and perhaps something else, something that would send a sharp pang of warmth down to her toes.

She was practically skipping as her young escort led her down the promenade and through the main gardens. She knew when they had arrived at the Banquet Hall's entrance, for its giant white-marble pillars were legendary. They even had a name: the Gates of Luxury.

The Gates were just the beginning of the opulence of the Ptolemaic court, a lavishness that had been given its own name: *tryphe*. Wen had heard it sung about in songs and lauded in poems. The High Priestess had even spoken of it to her long ago. 'The servants carry tableware made of pure gold,' she had told Wen.

Now Wen was to be one of those servants.

Khu led Wen into a small, crowded room where dozens of servants were laughing and conversing. Some ate hungrily. Others appeared to be stretching and oiling their skin. Still others were openly changing their clothes.

Khu led Wen to the far end of the room. There a tall, handsome woman was putting on an Egyptian wig before a sprawling bronze mirror. 'Only one?' she said to Khu in Egyptian, but he had already disappeared into the chaos of the room.

The woman looked at Wen sidelong, then returned to her task. 'I am Marni,' she said. 'You have been appointed to aid me in serving the Queen's entourage.'

'I am Wen.' Wen gave her most supplicating bow.

'It appears you are gifted with natural beauty and that is well. Still, we have much to do to prepare you for this honour in a very short time. Come with me.'

Wen followed Marni into a large hall that must have stretched to half a *stade* in length. Colourful mosaics adorned three of the walls. The fourth was transparent. Incredibly, Wen could see all the way through it to the Royal Harbour beyond.

'It is colourless glass,' said Marni without giving it so much as a glance. 'The Parthians sent it as a gift to Ptolemy the Tenth.'

Wen could not take her eyes off it and she nearly stumbled on a large marble fountain rising up in the centre of the hall. Inside the fountain were two finely wrought statues. The first statue was the Greek sea god Poseidon. A stream of trickling water flowed from the mouth of a large fish he held in his iron hands.

Just behind Poseidon, the Egyptian god Serapis held his own massive creature: a golden-horned bull. The God of Abundance wore a vessel-shaped hat from which an endless cascade of wheat kernels poured.

It was an incredible sight. Wen had seen fountains in her life, but never one that flowed with both water and wheat.

As if Poseidon and Serapis were not enough, there were numerous large marble statues scattered throughout the hall—each with its own bronze nameplate— Wen could not help but pause before the statue of a strong, well-proportioned man. He looked so familiar. She glanced down at the nameplate. *Heracles*, it read.

'You must never do that in the presence of guests,' said Marni. 'Nor must you ever speak to a guest, or look one in the eye, understood?'

'Understood.'

Marni held out her arms grandly as they reached the far side of the hall. 'As you may have guessed, this is the Hall of Greeting. It is where the guests will arrive and receive their first refreshments.'

Wen noticed servants moving in and out of the great hall through small, shadowy openings along its sides. 'You will use the servants' closets to replenish your wine and to refill your tray with small bites. Anything that you serve to the Queen you must taste first, and you must ensure that she sees you do it.'

'I may taste the dishes?' Wen asked in disbelief.

'You *must* taste them,' said Marni.

Wen smiled at her good fortune as she followed Marni to the beginning of the longest mosaic. Marni's eyes raked over her body. 'You are comely enough, but can you walk?'

'What?'

'At a royal banquet, the men and women who serve the guests must reflect the beauty and the grace of our ancient land. As such, they must also be able to walk properly. Walk for me.'

Wen took only a few strides before Marni stopped her.

'Did nobody ever teach you how to walk like an Egyptian?'

'What?'

Marni pointed to the mosaic beside which they now stood. 'Do you see the woman in that image?'

'Yes,' Wen said, studying a picture of a woman carrying a plate full of dates.

'Do you see how erect she stands? How she holds her chin? She is not proud; but neither is she shy. She is one with everything and everyone around her. Tell me how she is walking.'

'Heel to toe?'

'Yes. Now try again. Hold your head with dignity. Keep your upper body straight, but not stiff. And do not rush. Imagine that you are floating just above the floor. Like an Egyptian.'

As Wen practised walking, Marni continued her instruction 'When the Pharaohs arrive, the guests will place their goblets on our trays and then drop to their knees in obeisance. Those of us designated to serve the Pharaohs will make their way to their sides. Understood?'

'Understood,' Wen said, her heels already beginning to ache.

'Our next task is to see if you can wash.'

Wen followed Marni through two large tortoiseshell doors into another banquet hall with a ceiling so high it might have been the sky itself. As she stared up at the amazing structure, she noticed that its tree limb–shaped beams were plated in gold. Amidst those gilded branches soared two massive golden eagles.

She blinked several times to make sure she was not suffering from an illusion. The eagles appeared suspended in the air, their talons flexing, their great wings outstretched. She wondered what it might be like to be as free as such a bird.

To be free at all.

'This is the Hall of Sustenance,' Marni said. 'You may wonder at the sights as much as you like now, but when the guests arrive you must not observe either the food or the furnishings. Nor should you ever lock eyes with anyone. The difference between a servant and a guest is precisely that restraint and you must keep it in the first two halls. Do you understand?'

'I understand,' Wen said, hoping she could remain indifferent to the opulence all around her.

The Hall of Sustenance was lined with a single long table of polished ebony currently being set with golden tableware. *Do not gape*, Wen told herself, though she had never seen so much gold gathered together in one place.

'I assume you know how to wash someone's hands,' said Marni.

'I have never provided that particular courtesy,' Wen answered.

Marni appeared mortally wounded. She demonstrated a golden bowl filled with a floral-smelling paste. 'This is a mixture of rose petals, oil of almond and lye. Pour a little water into it and then stir it with four fingers. Four fingers—remember that! Wait for the Queen to place her hands in the water, then massage her hands in it. When she lifts them out of the bowl, you must place them in the water basin directly to rinse. Then dry them with this cloth. Say, "Bastet bless you", and take the basin away. Do you understand?'

Wen nodded meekly. She had served the Queen throughout their journey to Alexandria in what she had believed to be quiet competence. Now she was questioning her abilities. Would she remember everything Marni was telling her? She did not wish to dishonour the Queen before her guests, but she feared betrayal by her own inexperience. Marni motioned her into the next chamber.

Where the second hall was a towering cavern, the third hall was an inviting cave. It was smaller than the first two and felt slightly warmer. As in the first, a single fountain dominated the middle of the space. This fountain was graced by the figure of Dionysus, god of wine and ecstasy. In the god's left hand was a bunch of grapes. In his right, he cradled a large amphora from which a purplish liquid was continuously poured. Wen gaped in astonishment when she realised what that liquid was: wine.

'This is the Hall of Delights,' said Marni. 'It is the third and final hall, where the guests will rest and be entertained after they have dined.'

The room contained multitudes of couches upon which innumerable pillows had been arranged and were presently being fluffed. There were low tables everywhere and Wen saw all manner of sweet delicacies set upon them. Overhead, long drapes of cloth gave the room a feeling of comfort and intimacy.

'We will remove our guests' sandals here at the entrance and wash their feet following the same custom as for their hands.'

Wen nodded, noticing several unusual couches occupying the centre of the room. Four lions' heads—frozen in eternal snarls—perched at the ends of each of their armrests and real lions' paws graced their posts. 'That is where the Pharaohs and their attendants will repose,' explained Marni. 'At first, we will pour for the royal women and do their bidding.'

'At first?'

Marni studied Wen gravely. 'A Ptolemaic banquet is like a journey and the Hall of Delights is the journey's end. Here, to honour the god Dionysus, guests often seek their own undoing. Through dance, music and wine, they pursue union with the divine. Differences are less important in the Hall of Delights, and boundaries between people may be breached. As the festivities progress, you may begin to receive commands not just from women, but also men.'

Wen felt her stomach tighten. 'What kind of commands?'

'Simple commands, usually. A man may ask you to cool him with a fan, for example, or to help him adjust his repose by retrieving a pillow or two. Such commands should be cheerfully fulfilled. Your primary purpose is to help the guests enjoy themselves, after all. However, later in the evening, a man may ask you to dance for him, or rub his feet or...other things. You may fulfil such requests or refuse them. It is your choice. If you refuse, however, it is customary for you to take your leave.'

Overcome with relief, Wen gave a mighty sigh. She would not have to run in terror from the Hall of Delights! She had heard many stories about the banquets of Cleopatra's father, including rumours of licentious behaviour and indulgences of the flesh. She certainly did not want to participate in such things, though part of her wondered exactly what such indulgences entailed. In truth, she did not wish to leave the hall exactly, only to disappear into the shadows so that she could witness everything.

Her curiosity became worry as she realised that Titus would surely be among the guests, taking his enjoyment. Would he choose to partake of the pleasures offered in the third hall?

Surely he would. He was strong and virile and handsome, and he wore no symbol of commitment to any woman. Surely he partook of Dionysian rituals—or

Bacchanal rituals, as they were called in Rome. She felt a strange pang of displeasure as she imagined him spotting some beautiful servant woman and requesting that she sit upon his lap.

What if that woman is you? she thought hopefully. A warm energy travelled beneath her skin as she imagined Titus lounging upon one of those luxurious couches, motioning to her with his hand. In her vision, he poured Wen a goblet of wine and asked her if she would like to hear a poem.

It was an absurd notion. When would an exalted Roman commander ever stoop to pour wine for a servant? He had stooped to kiss her on two different occasions, that was true. But in both cases, she had been the only woman anywhere near.

Now he would be surrounded by them—women of beauty and breeding, who would surely be competing for the attention of such a handsome, high-ranking man.

'In the Hall of Delights, a guest—man or woman—may ask you to join in the revelry,' Marni was saying. 'They may even wish to serve you in some way.'

It was as if Marni had read Wen's thoughts. 'Yes, in the Hall of Delights, the servants become the guests and sometimes the guests become servants. And that is well, for we are all people, are we not?'

'We are indeed,' Wen replied, deciding that she liked Marni after all.

'That is why it is so important to follow the rules of service in the first two halls. It allows for a greater catharsis when they are undone in the third hall. It is the nature of *tryphe* and also of life.'

So now Wen knew. The Ptolemaic banquets that

were so famous throughout the world were not simple indulgences of the senses. There was a religious principle at work in them: three seasons of the year, three stages of life, three parts to a banquet.

She recalled the Queen's words: *The roles and riches of this world are illusions. They matter not.* It seemed that this was the lesson of the third hall. There was the doing, the being and finally, the undoing.

Wen realised suddenly where she had heard that saying before. It was one of the High Priestess's favourites.

'Come,' Marni said. 'Let us fit your gown.'

They travelled through a dark corridor, then somehow emerged into the same room in which they had first met.

'Try this,' Marni said, presenting Wen with a tubular white linen gown. As she slipped into the fine garment, Wen sighed. The fabric felt like cool breath upon her skin.

'Theban linen,' Marni said when she saw Wen's delight.

'It does not fit,' she said, trying to pull up the tunic's low band.

'Oh, it fits,' said Marni. 'You look—worthy of serving the Queen.'

Wen stared at her naked breasts resting above the tunic's elegant band. 'But I am a slave.'

'You are lovely. You represent the grace and beauty of Egypt.'

Wen wondered what Titus would think of her bared breasts. Would he consider them blessings? She hoped he would and feared he would not. She could think of little else as she joined the other servants in their preparations. They worked the rest of the afternoon—

polishing goblets, folding napkins and spreading rose petals upon the floors. Soon Ra hung above the horizon in an amber haze and it was time to don their gowns.

Arriving in the Hall of Greeting, Wen was relieved to find a hundred other women dressed just like herself, along with a hundred men wearing white pleated kilts and little else. Both the men and women were young and of fine physical form, and Wen observed that many of them looked quite similar to the idealised statues among which they walked.

'Do you see, Wen?' whispered Marni. 'The nobles of Alexandria only wish to walk amongst beauty and admire its form, be it of stone, bronze or flesh.'

Their army of servants had a most unlikely commander—a tall reed of a man with a voice that sounded like a boy's. 'Attention, please!' he sang out from the Greeting Hall's entrance. 'As many of you already know, I am Hemut, the High Steward. Tonight we celebrate a great success—the reconciliation of our beloved Pharaohs.'

There was a wave of loud cheers.

'This banquet must be a celebration like no other. Through it, we will show the noblest men and women of Alexandria that our kingdom is at peace, that our rulers are sound, that our trade is secure. Most importantly, we will show them that Egypt is General Caesar's gracious host and not his supplicating client!'

More cheers.

'Now, it is true that this banquet was hastily arranged, but that does not mean it will be hastily deployed. We will uphold the reputation that we hold dear and our guests will walk away transformed. To achieve this distinction, you know what you must do. You must conduct yourselves in a way that honours your sovereigns. You must be the embodiment of beauty and grace. Tonight, you are like the Nile: you are everything that is beautiful and eternal about this glorious land. Now go forth and flow.'

Chapter Eleven

It did not take long to spy her. She sauntered amongst the other servants like a Pegasus among horses. Still, it was not her gait that caught his attention, but her inappropriately exposed flesh. Her abundant breasts, unclothed and fully visible, swayed gently with her movements, drawing his astonishment, then, might Jupiter strike him down, his desire.

It was profane, the way that she was dressed. He could not believe that the Queen had allowed it. He knew that Egyptians did not follow traditional codes of modesty, but this went far beyond a mere cultural conceit. This was a corruption of decency.

He could not abide it. He was a military commander and a senator's son, after all. He had been gently raised. He had been educated at Rhodes, had been weaned on Pericles and the ideals of self-rule. Who was he if he could not rule his own lust?

She was just a woman, after all. A woman was only as powerful as a man allowed her to become. That was what he had always believed, had been taught since he was a boy. *You have no dominion over me*, he told himself now, as he watched her move amidst the Queen's allies. *You are just like all the other women serving at this banquet.*

But she was not like the other women. She wore the same long white tunic and same black, shoulder-length wig, but her eyes were brighter, her lips redder, her honey skin flush with some greater store of vivacity.

And her mind? Her mind was a mysterious weapon—as elegant and clever as the Trojan Horse.

He wanted her so badly that he felt ill. She had rejected him, mistrusted him, even threatened his life, yet he wanted her more and more each day.

Her lips alone were like medicine. He craved their healing, their soft uncertainty. The feel of her body against his had been a salve for his troubled soul, one that stimulated and soothed all at once. There was a peculiar magic at work for certain—some ancient Egyptian curse that turned educated, honourable men into helpless fools.

He drank down his goblet in the hopes of calming himself, but the wine only increased his ardour. It seemed that every Roman officer in the room had his eyes on her, along with every Alexandrian high-born worthy of his robe. *Who is that gracious Egyptian beauty with breasts like Venus and eyes like a doe's?* they whispered.

She is mine, he wished to say, though it would have been a lie. She had allowed him to kiss her, that was true—both in the boat and in the Library. And the kisses, while chaste, had sent him spinning. But both kisses had been interrupted: the first by the call of duty and the second by Wen herself, leaving him to wonder if she wanted him at all.

He adjusted the folds of his toga and downed another goblet of wine. He would speak with her this very night. He would take her aside and ask her all the questions cluttering his mind. *Who are you? What are you hiding? Would you let me kiss you again?*

And again?

He had just begun to make his way towards her when he felt a large hand gripping his elbow. 'Was it not Aesop who said to be careful what you wish for?'

Titus turned to regard a young cavalry officer whom he barely knew. 'Well met…ah…'

'Gnaeus.'

'Ah, yes,' said Titus, raising his goblet in greetings.

'I do not blame you, Tribune Titus,' Gnaeus said, casting his gaze across the hall. 'She is quite a lotus. Just look at those…blooms.'

'You speak as if your education took place in a corral,' Titus snarled.

'I merely observe where you direct your attention.'

'My attention has been preoccupied with certain affairs of state, if you must know,' Titus said absently, craning to keep Wen in his sights.

'You refer to the reconciliation of the Pharaohs?'

'Indeed,' Titus lied. He wished Gnaeus would find another peer to plague.

'Then why do you wear a frown, Commander? Surely you should be enjoying yourself,' said Gnaeus, gazing admiringly at Wen. 'And if you do not wish to enjoy yourself, then I hope you do not mind if I do.'

Titus was so preoccupied with keeping an eye on Wen that he did not immediately catch Gnaeus's meaning, and, by the time he turned to respond, the young cavalry officer had already begun to make his way towards Wen.

Titus growled at the veiled warning Gnaeus had issued him and growled again when he realised he needed to find a latrine. Soon he was standing impatiently before an elegant marble basin, praying he would reach her before Gnaeus did.

A Roman soldier entered and stood beside Titus, and Titus recognised him instantly. He was one of Caesar's bodyguards.

'Strange to have to do this indoors,' Titus remarked.

'I was just thinking the same,' said the man. 'Though I am happy for the privacy.' He stepped away from the basin suddenly and bent over as if in a bow. Then he caught sight of the tattoo behind the man's ear.

It was a large letter *B*—the unmistakable mark of the Boni. The man was a spy, just like Titus.

Titus's heart began to pound. He dropped his voice to a whisper. 'I thought that I was the only one in Alexandria.'

'You will be soon. I leave for Rome tonight.'

'What will you report?'

'That the bull has allied himself with the rose and that the two aspire to rule together.'

'They have said no such thing.'

'No, but is it not obvious?'

It was. Titus had witnessed it himself. The bull and the rose—Caesar and Cleopatra—were allies now. If they could succeed in defeating Ptolemy's forces, they would emerge the two most powerful people in the world.

'The Roman Republic is at risk,' added the man. 'What more does Caesar plan?'

Titus hesitated. He did not wish to betray Caesar—not when Wen's life was risk. Then again, how many more people would lose their lives if monarchs once again ruled Rome?

Titus sighed. 'If Ptolemy's army marches on Alexandria, Caesar will send me to Pergamon to secure aid from Prince Mithridates. He cannot defeat Ptolemy's army without such aid.'

The man nodded. 'A messenger will contact you soon with your orders.'

Titus bowed his head and tried to collect himself. He feared that he would soon be ordered to kill Caesar, something he did not know if he could do. Or perhaps he would be ordered to simply abandon his duty, allowing Caesar to be butchered by Ptolemy's army. Either way, he would be leaving Wen in grave danger. The thought of it made him ill.

He emerged from the latrine and made his way towards Wen. She was moving among the women she served like flowing water. A pour of wine here, an offer of fruit there. Her long thin arms reached out like a swimmer's.

He pushed his way past stands of bearded scholars and thickets of bejewelled merchants.

As he neared, he noticed several Roman officers clustered near her, including the snivelling Gnaeus. They were observing her, casting lewd glances in her direction and exchanging veiled comments with one another. Titus paused, listening. 'I wonder how those melons would taste with a bit of honey,' said Gnaeus.

Titus knew it was neither the time nor the place for a scene. But it was impossible to see anything but

Gnaeus's covetous gaze, or hear anything other than the roar of anger between his own ears.

She felt Titus's hand upon her arm before she saw him and the simmering cauldron of desire swirling inside her was suddenly set to boil. He was here. He had come. She could not show her delight, though she felt it spreading to every part of her. She could show nothing but placid grace.

'Greetings, Commander,' she said, keeping her gaze on the distant mosaic.

'You must come with me now,' Titus urged.

'Apologies, Commander, but women may not serve men during this part of the banquet. I will find a male servant to attend you straight away.' It took every bit of her will to keep from meeting his gaze. *Beauty and restraint*, she told herself. She was a representative of the Queen. She needed to preserve the *ma'at*.

'I am not your Commander and do not wish for a male servant.' Angling his body around hers, he hustled her into a servants' closet.

'This is not allowed,' she said, stepping deeper into the closet. He was oddly agitated. She feared him and yearned for him all at once.

'I did not like how those men were looking at you.'

'What men?'

'The Roman officers standing near you. They were speaking about you as if you were a piece of fruit.'

'I must return to my duty,' she said. *As a spy for the Queen.* She tried to move around him, but he blocked her path. 'We cannot speak together,' she explained. 'It is against the rules of the first hall.'

'What rules? Am I not a guest at this banquet? Can I not do as I like?'

'I admit that I had hoped to see you,' she said at last. *Had longed for it.*

'And I had hoped to see you, though there is too much of you to see.'

His disappointment in her appearance felt like a blow to her body. 'I had hoped that you would be pleased with the beauty of my gown.'

'Pleased? You have exposed yourself to the base desires of every single man in this hall.'

'Perhaps you do not understand the Egyptian custom of dress.'

He stepped forward, removing the space she had placed between them. 'You have made yourself an object of lust.'

He was so close.

'I am an embodiment of beauty.'

He pressed his chest against hers and she felt an almost painful warmth somewhere deep inside. It was happening again. Their bodies were moving together, doing what they liked. 'You should not be serving at all,' said Titus huskily. 'You are the Queen's closest advisor.'

She tilted her head back, and could almost feel his lips on hers. He pushed his body hard against hers, and she stepped backwards into a shelf. A silver knife clanked to the ground. A bell inside Wen's mind. *You are dishonouring the Queen.* Recovering her senses, she stepped away. 'Of course I should be here. I am a servant—a slave.'

Titus bent over slightly, as if she had wounded him. 'I want you to cover yourself at once,' he breathed.

'I cannot cover myself. I am playing a role and this is my costume. I represent the beauty and grace of Egypt.'

'I do not care what you represent! No Greek or Roman woman would ever be seen in public with her br—' He motioned towards her chest, then looked away.

'But I am not a Greek or a Roman woman. I am an Egyptian woman.'

'You are *my* woman!'

'What?'

'You heard me.'

'I am no man's woman. I belong to the Queen.'

She turned to escape, but he caught her by the arm.

'I am leaving soon,' he said.

'Leaving?' *But you cannot leave.*

'If Ptolemy marches his army on Alexandria, then Caesar will dispatch me to seek aid.'

'But Ptolemy does not march on Alexandria.'

'Not yet.'

'You think that he will?'

'I fear that we have little time left, Wen. Together, I mean.' They were the saddest words she had ever heard.

His fingers found hers and interwove with them. A candle flickered inside her and she swayed forward into him.

'Wen—' he began, but could not finish, because a tall thin figure stepped into the closet beside them.

'If you would be so kind as to unhand the royal servant,' said the High Steward.

Titus released Wen's arm.

'Now if you would be so kind as to explain what you are doing in a servants' closet?'

'I came to cover her. She should not be wearing such a gown,' Titus said.

'Indeed?' said Hemut with mock amusement. 'And why not?'

'It is indiscreet. It exposes what should only be seen by her husband.'

'In Egypt, young women expose their breasts with pride, for they represent their potential as mothers. You must honour our custom.' Hemut gave a loud sniff. 'Roman.'

'I am Titus Tillius Fortis, commander of Caesar's Sixth Legion. You would ignore the wishes of one of your most exalted guests?'

'In this matter, yes.'

'Why?'

Hemut sighed. 'Let me try to explain it in a way a Roman can understand.' His high boyish voice became a kind of blade. 'As the guests at this banquet, you and all the other Romans must adhere to the customs of your hosts, the Ptolemies of Egypt. If you do not, word will spread among the Alexandrian elite that the Romans do not show respect.'

Noticing the knife that had fallen, Hemut lifted it, though he did not put it away.

'I do not know if you have noticed, but the Alexandrians are fickle and quick to revolt. Who knows? They might decide to run your little legion out of the city. Or worse, they might try to start a war with Rome. At the very least, they may decide to stop exporting Egyptian grain, without which half of Rome and its hinterlands would starve. Her breasts stay bare, Commander. Have I made myself clear?'

Suddenly, a trumpet blared and a herald's voice sang

out. 'Lord of the Two Lands, Horus Incarnate, Pharaoh Ptolemy the Thirteenth!'

Wen jumped. If Ptolemy had arrived, Cleopatra would not be far behind. She watched closely as the young Pharaoh Ptolemy stepped into the hall. He was dressed in the Greek style, with a lengthy white chiton and strappy brown sandals he seemed to drag as he walked. A thick golden collar hung heavily around his young neck, causing him to slouch, and the royal diadem tied across his brow had already gone crooked.

The servants held out their trays to receive the guests' goblets. Then all the guests dropped to their knees and the male servants who had been selected to serve Ptolemy made their way through the kneeling crowd.

'You may rise,' the young Pharaoh said at last.

Inside the closet, Wen turned to Titus. 'The Queen will arrive soon. I must go.'

'Yes, you must,' said Hemut, urging Wen out of the closet as the trumpets blared once again.

'Lady of the Two Lands, Isis Incarnate, Queen Cleopatra Philopator the Seventh!' sang the herald.

Queen Cleopatra appeared in the entryway of the great chamber and paused. She wore an expression of cool dignity and, as she stepped forward, the only sound was the soft clinking of her gem-studded sandals upon the ebony floor.

The guests dropped to their knees. As Wen began to make her way towards the Queen, Titus's words sank into her soul. He was leaving soon. They had very little time left.

Wen studied the Queen's long, shimmering black gown, fighting her emotion. *Beauty and grace*, she told herself as she walked. *Heel to toe.*

She had no idea how much time they had. A week? A month? One night? She felt panic sneaking beneath her skin. It was as if the gods had presented her with a table full of food and commanded her to eat it in a single bite.

Heel to toe. Heel to toe.

Wen arrived at Cleopatra's side. 'You may rise,' the Queen told her guests.

Wen slipped into a nearby servants' closet and found a full amphora of wine. She tipped it into an empty goblet and brought it before the Queen, taking a cautionary sip before handing it to the Living Goddess. 'I know you cannot speak to me, or look at me,' Cleopatra whispered to Wen conspiratorially, 'but I wish you to find Pothinus and General Achillas. Try to discover their plan.'

Wen nodded graciously, determined to play her role. She filled the cups of Iras and Charmion next, and they thanked Wen in whispers.

'Pothinus is the portly one,' said Iras.

'General Achillas wears an Egyptian-style kilt.'

Soon the trumpet sounded once again. 'General Gaius Julius Caesar,' announced the herald. There was a smattering of weak applause as Caesar and his large entourage of officers swept into the room. This time, nobody dropped to their knees, though an ominous silence prevailed.

Caesar ignored the affront. He appeared determined to endear himself to the snobbish Alexandrians. He made his way across the hall, sipping the wine, admiring the statues and speaking courteously to anyone willing to converse. Wen searched for Titus, but could no longer find him.

Disappointment weighted her steps. Perhaps Hemut had dismissed him from the banquet altogether and all her secret hopes for the Hall of Delights would come to nothing.

Perhaps she would never see him again.

She was so preoccupied with thoughts of Titus that she almost passed by two men—one short and portly, the other thick and strong—speaking in hushed tones. She slowed her pace.

'We must wait until the right moment,' the first was saying softly, scratching at his fleshy jaw. The strong man stepped closer, but directed his attention at a distant wall.

'No, we must act now. Every day he grows stronger.'

Wen made a slow circle around them and, when she returned, she noticed that the strong man wore an Egyptian military kilt and shirt. 'No more talk,' he was saying. 'We shall begin our march on Alexandria tomorrow. In three days, we will make our attack.'

'How many men do we have?' asked the fat man.

'Twenty thousand.'

Wen arrived at the servants' closet to find Marni squeezing a lemon over a plateful of oysters.

'Who is that man in the kilt and shirt?' Wen asked. 'He does not look like the others.'

'That is General Achillas,' said Marni. 'He is the head of the Pharaoh's army. Will you hand me that cloth?'

Wen could scarcely believe her ears. It appeared that her spying mission had been a success. An alarming, terrifying one. She needed to tell the Queen as soon as she could. Then her own curiosity stirred.

'One more question.' Wen held the cloth in the air.

'How many men do you think Caesar has with him? How many soldiers?'

'I thought you said only one question?' Marni asked. Seeing Wen's expression, she sighed. 'I would say four thousand men—a little more than a legion. Now will you give me the cloth?'

Wen tried to imagine Caesar's four thousand men defending the palace against Achillas's twenty thousand. *It is not a cloth*, she thought. *It is a white flag.*

Chapter Twelve

He watched her wash the Queen's hands—another absurd Egyptian custom, yet there was something wholly sensuous about the way she did it. Her long, thin fingers kneaded and splashed in a quiet rhythm, never spilling a drop.

He imagined her washing his own hands. He wondered how it might feel to have her fingers interlock with his once again, this time immersed in the element of water. He admitted that he wished for much more than that, though he tried to put it out of his mind.

He fingered his coin purse absently. It was much lighter than it had been before his encounter with Hemut. But for everything there was a price and Titus knew he would have given every last *denarius* he owned to the cranky Steward if it meant being allowed to watch Wen for just a few more hours.

Now she patted Cleopatra's hands with a linen towel and appeared to be whispering something in the Queen's ear. What secret was she telling? Probably some trifling, womanly thing, though the Queen shot an urgent glance at Caesar after Wen finished.

Caesar, for his part, was the picture of manners. He sat across the long banquet table from Cleopatra, conversing quietly as his hands were washed by his own attendant.

As Pharaoh Ptolemy's honoured guest, Caesar sat beside the young monarch. The sullen-looking boy slumped at the head of the table, already looking bored. Beside Caesar sat the portly advisor Pothinus, his eyes never resting, then Titus himself, then the younger Ptolemy brother, and so on according to rank.

General Achillas, the head of Ptolemy's army, was conspicuously absent, though that absence did not make Titus feel any safer. Indeed, it was painfully obvious that he and Caesar were surrounded on all sides by men who would very much like to see them dead.

Fortunately, the banquet hall—or Hall of Sustenance as they so ceremoniously called it—was no battle ground, unless they were in a war of the sexes. In another strange proclivity, the Egyptians had arranged the seating so that all the male guests were seated on one side of the table and all the female guests on the other.

Cleopatra sat to Ptolemy's right, directly across from Caesar, then came Cleopatra's younger sister Arsinoe, then Iras and Charmion, and so on. The result was that whenever a male guest looked up, he beheld the female sitting across from him—in Titus's case, Charmion—and the bare-breasted female servant designated to serve that female guest—in his case, Wen.

Pothinus slid Titus a patronising grin. 'Our customs must seem strange to a Roman,' he said.

'Not strange,' Titus lied. 'Only fascinating.'

'Women and men remain separated until after

dinner—that is a Greek tradition. But ritual hand washing goes back to at least the Seventh Dynasty of Egypt,' explained Pothinus. 'We have proof in the form of mosaics.'

'Is that so?' said Caesar. 'I should like to see such ancient works.'

'That would require a trip upriver,' Pothinus remarked. 'I imagine you are anxious to get back to Rome soon.'

'Not necessarily,' said Caesar. 'It is in Roman interests to ensure the security of Egypt, however long that takes.'

'Of course it is,' said Pothinus, his voice like rusted tin.

'It is not necessary to journey upriver to see the sights when we have so many marvels to be witnessed here in Alexandria,' offered Cleopatra.

She leaned forward solicitously. 'General Caesar, will you allow me to give you a tour of our humble Museion tomorrow? As you know, we are quite proud of our Alexandrian scholars. We have manuscripts written by the hands of Aristotle, Eratosthenes, Archimedes and many others.'

'Ah! Eratosthenes,' said Caesar. 'There is a man I would have liked to have met. Calculated the circumference of the world, did he not?'

'We have his maps!' exclaimed the Queen. 'I must show you them tomorrow.'

Caesar gave Cleopatra a devouring look. 'I would very much like to see them.'

Caesar's interest in Eratosthenes's maps was not feigned. It was said that they were the most detailed reflection of the known world—the world Caesar wished to conquer.

'I will give you a tour of our great Hall of Muses,' said Cleopatra. 'It is where Iras, Charmion and I studied.'

'You studied at the Museion?' asked Caesar.

'Yes, of course,' replied Cleopatra.

'Alongside men?'

'Women are equally able to benefit from the enrichment of the mind, are they not?'

Caesar shook his head. 'Plato did not think so.'

'Perhaps he did not, but I am sure his wife disagreed.'

There was hearty laughter.

Caesar leaned forward and studied the Queen closely. 'Do you truly believe that women are equally able to study the mysteries of the world as men?'

'I do,' said the Queen. 'And I can prove it to you, if you would like.'

'How do you propose to do that?'

Now the whole table had gone silent. This was exactly what the bright-minded nobles of Alexandria had come for and they listened with rapt interest as their Queen attempted to prove herself against the world's most conquering General.

'Ask me anything,' said Cleopatra.

'What?'

'Anything. Ask me any question you like, from any discipline—science, rhetoric, history. I vow that I will answer it correctly. And if I cannot, one of my women will. Women are just as able as men to think for ourselves.'

'A test then,' Caesar pronounced, seemingly aware of his audience. He sat back in his chair. 'All right, Queen Cleopatra. Here is a question from the sciences.

You mentioned Archimedes. Explain the principle at work in Archimedes' Screw.'

There was a spate of whispers among the dinner guests followed by a low hush. 'You seek to trick me with your very first question,' said the Queen, her voice ringing across the hall. 'Archimedes is known for his principle of calculating volume, though that is not the principle at work in his screw. The principle you allude to is friction. Aristotle spoke of it in his experiments with inclined planes. The screw minimises the friction of the water, making it easier to lift.'

There was a collective sigh followed by a spate of discussion. The Queen had done well. Very well. Even Caesar was nodding his head, apparently impressed. 'All right then, here is a question that will challenge you in a different way. Where do our thoughts form, in the head or in the heart?'

'Of course you would ask such a question. Visitors to Egypt often do,' said Cleopatra. 'To prepare our mummies for the afterlife, we remove the contents of the head, but not the heart. But Herophilos proved many years ago that the head is where the mind is located and all our thoughts good or ill.'

Another spate of celebratory whispers rippled through the crowd, and Caesar narrowed his eyes. 'What is the best treatment for the sacred disease?' Caesar asked.

'Valerian, of course!' said the Queen. 'And heat around the head.' Caesar cocked his own head in amazement and Titus inwardly did the same. Few people knew that Caesar himself suffered from that ailment.

'Do not look so surprised, General Caesar,' said the

Queen. 'Did Homer not say that the people of Egypt are more skilled in medicine than any of human kind?'

'What are the three modes of persuasion?' he fired back.

'Logos, ethos and pathos. You used them to great effect yesterday when you addressed the Alexandrian mob.'

Caesar shook his head in frustration. He turned to Titus. 'You ask her something, Titus. Let us see if you can give her more of a challenge.'

Titus nearly choked on his fig. He felt the eyes of everyone seated at the table focus on him. His mind raced. Caesar had asked questions in science, medicine and rhetoric. What subject remained? *History.*

'Ah, who was the last Roman King and when did he reign?' Titus asked.

It was a suitable question and Caesar gave him an approving nod. Titus took a sip of water.

'Hmmm,' said the Queen. The guests were frozen in their seats. Even the servants had stopped their work. She craned her neck down the table. 'Women, I must request your aid on this particular matter.'

Charmion and Iras looked at one another, then shook their heads. Arsinoe sighed and gave a nod of resignation. 'Wen?' Wen was standing behind the Queen, holding the Queen's wash water.

'Lucius Tarquinius Superbus, my Queen,' Wen said. 'Five hundred years ago. After Superbus's bloody reign, Rome became a republic.'

There was a collective hum of satisfaction, and Caesar sat back in his chair. 'You are right,' he admitted.

She *was* right—incredibly so. Tarquinus's reign was the most significant in all of Rome's history, for it had motivated the people to abandon monarchy and put a better form of government in its place. The leaders of this change were good men and it was for them that the *Boni* themselves had been named.

The Queen clapped her hands together. 'Are you satisfied, General?' she asked Caesar. 'Have you not witnessed that women are equal in science, rhetoric and history? Or shall we answer more questions?'

Caesar sat back. 'I am persuaded.'

The Queen gave a dazzling smile.

'Though I wonder,' Caesar continued, 'if a woman could be equal to the task of ruling a kingdom?'

The question was breathtaking in its recklessness. Sitting right beside Caesar was the actual ruler of Egypt—a young man. What Caesar was suggesting could easily be construed as a threat.

'Now there is a question for which I am glad I do not have the answer,' said Cleopatra. 'Nor do I ever wish to, for I have my husband-brother. Only together can we carry out that weighty task.'

Now Titus recognised Caesar's aim. The General had deliberately spoken the question at the back of every Alexandrian's mind to give Cleopatra the opportunity to refute it.

News of this exchange would travel around the city faster than the north wind, and surely the exiled Queen would find herself with more sympathisers. Even in the safety and comfort of the Hall of Sustenance, Caesar was preparing his defences.

Still, Titus could not believe that the exchange had been entirely strategic. Caesar appeared genuinely impressed with the Queen's knowledge. Even now, he seemed to marvel at her, his expression a mixture of awe and puzzlement. It was as if she were some strange chimera whose existence he had doubted until now.

In sum, Caesar looked the way Titus had long ago begun to feel—about Wen.

The dinner waxed on and there seemed to be no end to the delicacies placed before them.

'Warblers in plum sauce,' Hemut pronounced. 'Roast piglet stuffed with pomegranates. Baked sturgeon stuffed with goat cheese.' The wine flowed and the conversations became louder and more jovial.

Titus drank more wine and watched Wen with growing boldness. He had to speak to her again—if only to bid her farewell. He feared that at any moment Ptolemy's army would attack Alexandria and Caesar would send Titus to secure aid.

But there was something he feared even more—that the *Boni* would command him not to bring that aid and that he would never see Wen again. Once, he looked up and it seemed that the golden eagles perched in the towering ceiling had begun to flap their wings.

When it seemed that there could not possibly be more feasting, Hemut announced that the Pharaohs would be pleased if their guests would accompany them to the Hall of Delights.

'Let it be done!' exclaimed Cleopatra, clapping her bejewelled hands into the air. The guests stood from their chairs and watched in awe as two large tortoiseshell doors at the back of the hall creaked open, though no servants appeared to be pulling them.

'They are hydraulic doors,' Iras remarked, passing by Titus's side. 'They are powered by a current of water that flows beneath the palace.'

'Really?'

'It is invisible, but it is there,' she said, tossing a glance at Wen. 'Enjoy your evening, Titus.'

The Hall of Delights was a room dressed in finery. Colourful cloths plunged from the ceilings and billowed over thick couches draped in silks. Beneath the couches lay the finest carpets; beside them, tables were overflowing with sweets. Small fires flickered in braziers throughout the room and there was the soft hum of lutes following the beat of a deep-hearted drum.

Wen followed the Queen as she entered, not giving Titus a second glance. Titus was ushered into a chair and a servant began washing his feet. As the young man soberly massaged sweet-smelling oils between his toes, he felt as if he might burst into laughter.

He cast a glance at Caesar, but the General seemed strangely heedless of the absurdity of it all. It gave Titus a chill to watch the General indulge in such extravagances. Every day he seemed less like a general and more like a king.

Titus waved his servant aside and towelled off his own toes. Then he stood and stepped forward into the Hall of Delights—barefoot, a little drunk and smelling of lilies, hoping to declare his interest to a woman forbidden to speak to him.

This is all perfectly normal, he told himself, scanning the room for an innocuous place to sit. He caught a glimpse of a man wearing the hooves and horns of a goat.

He had to blink his eyes. The man was completely and unashamedly unclothed. His manhood stood out from his waist in an obscenely engorged horizontal shaft. His only adornment were his hooves and horns, and a short, goat-like tail that had been fixed to his backside.

He was, Titus realised, a satyr. Titus had read about the mythical beings and seen them depicted in plays—though never so completely exposed. They were the mischievous, lustful goat-men who accompanied the wine god in his adventures. He looked around the luxurious room and discovered many such satyrs, some playing music, others dancing, others playing dice and drinking from large amphorae.

The satyrs were not the only mythical creatures darting about. There were also alarmingly amorous young women wearing deerskin skirts and crowns of ivy. They flounced amongst the guests, playfully caressing the men and herding them on to the couches. Nymphs!

This is no banquet, Titus thought. He had not known it, but the moment that he had stepped through those magically moving doors, he had unwittingly become a character in an illicit satyr play.

He saw Wen push past one of the satyrs. The goat-man tickled her with his tail as she retrieved an amphora of wine. Titus tried to identify the overbold creature, but quickly lost sight of him in a blur of flesh and hooves.

He stumbled aside as the herd headed towards a shallow wooden basin just behind him. The attention of the guests was upon the goat-men as they linked their arms together and broke into a traditional Greek drinking song. They stomped their legs in unison as they sang, and Titus noticed a dark purple liquid staining their hooves.

They were stomping grapes.

A throng of interested onlookers was now heading towards the stomping satyrs, and Titus knew he needed to escape that part of the hall. Spying an empty sofa just beyond the chaos, Titus put his head down and began to trek towards it. He was just reaching it when he felt a tap upon his shoulder. He turned to discover a bare-breasted nymph blinking up at him with a wicked glint in her eyes.

The nubile young woman wore a crown of ivy in her hair and green leaves were painted on her nipples. She tipped a goblet of wine into Titus's mouth, then finished the rest herself.

'You are a handsome man,' she chirped, rubbing her chest. She pushed Titus back on to the couch and began to crawl up his body like a cat. 'Would you like a massage?' she purred, squeezing his legs. 'I can help you off with that heavy toga.'

In his youth, he might have gladly seized upon such an opportunity. Glancing around the room he saw many Roman officers already doing just that. In one illicit corner, a Roman officer was shouting lewd commands to a dancing nymph, who appeared to be obeying him in her provocative movements. In another, several of his countrymen had stripped down to their loincloths and were kissing and petting their own nymphs in a tangle of limbs.

But Titus had no enthusiasm for such indulgences of the flesh. The only nymph he wished to tangle with was Wen and he had already lost sight of her. He leaned his head back as the nymph still seated upon his lap placed a path of warm kisses up his neck. He closed his eyes, imagining she was Wen.

When he opened them, he gave a start. It was Wen. She was staring at him from across the room.

'No, no, no!' cried Titus, sitting up. He felt the moisture of the nymph's wet tongue inside his ear. Seeking rescue, he heralded a roving satyr. The goat-man lifted the amorous nymph to standing, then bent her over the arm of Titus's couch.

This is all perfectly normal, Titus told himself again, preparing to intervene. But as the satyr feigned his act of lewdness upon her, the nymph only laughed and shrieked. At last, the nymph wriggled herself free and ran off towards a group of men in cows' horns.

'Gratitude,' Titus said to the satyr. The satyr bowed, then trotted away towards some new misadventure.

Titus did not even have a chance to breathe before another woman was invading his ear, this time with a whisper. 'Can I fill your goblet or tie you up?' she asked. She was dressed only in tattoos—a human canvas of writhing snakes, beetles and crocodiles. In one hand, she held a deep blue amphora, in the other, a whip.

'Erm, wine, please,' he said, for it seemed that she had offered him a choice between the two. He lifted his empty goblet and accepted the cloudy crimson liquid the woman offered.

'Gratitude,' he said and drank a small sip.

'You are a beautiful man,' she said, raking her eyes up and down his body. 'You deserve a kiss.' Before he could move away she had planted her lips on his.

When he looked up from the strange encounter, he felt many sets of eyes upon him. 'He kissed the maenad,' someone whispered.

'Nay, the maenad kissed him,' said another.

He glanced towards the fountain and noticed that one of his observers was Wen. She was standing just behind the Queen, smiling placidly. All the colour in her cheeks had gone.

Did she think that he had kissed the tattooed woman on purpose? *Curses!* He shooed the maenad away, then stood. He needed to cross the hall and speak to her. But there was Hemut standing at its entrance, shaking his finger at Titus in warning.

Titus slumped back upon the couch.

And that was his front-row seat for the spectacle to come, for in that instant, Gnaeus sidled up to Wen and offered her a goblet of wine. Gnaeus! And she accepted it. She shot Titus an injured glare, then took a hearty sip.

'Yes, drink up, my sweet,' said the Roman. He was a portly young man with a lecherous grin and cheeks red with the effects of drink. He did not look Wen in the eyes. Instead, he appeared to be addressing her breasts directly. 'What fruits are you offering this lovely evening?'

'None, I am afraid,' she said. She had not meant to lead him on. She had been so unnerved by Titus's kiss with the maenad that she had accepted his goblet without thinking. Now she did not know how to escape him.

'Come, let me rub your feet,' he said, leading her to a nearby couch. He was clearly a Roman soldier and his simple chainmail marked him of low rank. He reminded Wen of the men whom she had served at the brew house and, as she gazed into his eyes, she felt a dull loathing.

The Roman took a slice of orange from a nearby tray and blandly held it out to Wen.

'Feed it to me, would you?' he asked. He was sitting far too close. She held it out to him and as he bit into the fruit, a tiny bit of juice dribbled on to her breasts.

'It appears that the oranges you offer are overly juicy,' he slurred, staring at the stain of syrup upon her breasts. 'My apologies, little Venus. Shall I help you clean them?' He opened his mouth and the fire of panic shot through her.

Gnaeus was hovering over Wen like a panting hyena. And Titus could do nothing about it. He glared at Hemut, who glared back at him. *Do not even think of it*, the Steward's expression seemed to say.

Curse Hemut, Titus thought. *And curse Gnaeus. And curse the Hall of Delights.* He fumbled inside his coin purse for a silver coin and motioned to a passing nymph.

'This is yours if you would attend to Steward Hemut for a few moments. I have heard he likes to be tickled with feathers.' A grin stretched across the nymph's face as she plucked the coin from Titus's hands.

Freed from Hemut's watchful gaze, Titus crossed to the couch where Gnaeus and Wen reclined.

'Excuse me, Brother,' said Titus, 'but would you mind if I cut in? I promised this young woman I would oil her feet.'

'This one is taken, Commander,' replied Gnaeus, 'but as you can see, there are many others to choose from.'

Titus closed his eyes, struggling to control his desire to punch the young cavalry officer in the face.

'Apologies, Brother,' he said calmly, 'but I must insist. Priority of rank, you see.'

'But there is no rank in the Hall of Delights,' Gnaeus protested. 'Or is that not the point?' He slid an oily glance at Wen's breasts.

Dignitas, Titus told himself, though he was about to explode. 'I bid you stand, Brother.'

Slowly, Gnaeus stood, his short, portly figure dwarfed by Titus's towering one. 'Let us settle this dispute as men,' Titus said at last.

'That is not necessary,' said Gnaeus. He grabbed Wen by the wrist, yanking her up off the couch. Wen gave a small cry and tried to struggle free.

'That was a mistake,' said Titus, raising his fist to Gnaeus's face. 'You must never, ever grab her by the wrists.' The Hall of Delights went silent.

'You there!' cried Caesar. He was reposing on a nearby couch. 'As your General, I command you to step away from that woman. She belongs to Titus.'

Gnaeus released Wen's arm as if it were a venomous snake, then slunk away into a group of roaming satyrs. Titus gave the General a deep bow and was left standing before Wen without any words at the ready.

'Gratitude,' she said at last. 'It seems that you have saved me once again.'

'That man is a toad.'

'I did not know how to get free of him without disturbing the *ma'at* and dishonouring the Queen.'

'There is very little you could do to dishonour the Queen after your performance in the Hall of Sustenance. Will you sit with me a while? I have taken up residency on that couch over there.'

Titus motioned to the corner where his couch remained thankfully unoccupied. Wen frowned.

'Are you sure you do not wish to sit with another? The maenad, perhaps?' She glanced at the tattooed woman, then studied the floor.

'I would no more want to sit with that kiss-stealing human canvas than I would want to cosy up on a mat with Gnaeus.'

Wen smiled. 'And what of the nymph?'

'What nymph? You are my nymph,' said Titus.

She accepted his hand, and he led her to his small island of sanity at the edge of the hall. 'Drink?' he asked Wen, offering the goblet that had been filled earlier by the maenad.

'Gratitude,' Wen said. 'Though I wish it were water, not wine. All of this washing and drying of limbs has made me quite thirsty.' She looked around to ensure she had no witnesses, then drank down the goblet in a single swill.

'Well done!' Titus remarked. 'I do not think half the men in this Hall could have drunk that as fast as you did.'

'Half the men in this hall have not been on their feet since this morning,' she said. She rubbed her eyes, then sank deeper into the couch.

It was a small miracle. Here she was, the most beautiful woman in the whole of Egypt, sitting beside Titus of her own free will. She leaned her head against his arm and his spirit swelled. Finally, they were together, and they had the rest of the night to converse. First he would find her some water, then begin his inquisition in earnest. He would ask her about her life as a temple child and her experiences at the brew house. With each answer, she would add a detail to the picture of her, until she had sketched a canvas so rich and varied that there would be nothing left to know.

It was an eminently logical scheme and guaranteed to cure the illness of longing that plagued him so that he could be on his way. He watched her close her eyes and a soft blanket of peace suffuse her expression. The problem was that he did not want a cure for his longing, nor did he wish to leave her side. He wanted only to get closer.

'I cannot get you out of my mind, Wen,' he confessed. 'I fear that I am in love with you.'

When he bent to look at her again, he realised that she had fallen into a deep and total slumber.

'Is she all right?' A tall, handsome servant woman approached, a look of concern wrinkling the swirls around her eyes.

'I believe so. She went to sleep rather quickly, though.'

The woman glanced at the empty goblet. 'Who poured the wine, do you remember?'

'The maenad poured it.'

'From a blue bottle?'

Titus nodded.

'Oh, no. The maenads serve only wine mixed with milk of poppy.'

'What? Why did nobody tell me this?'

'Everybody knows that maenads distribute milk of the poppy,' said the woman. 'It is one of our oldest customs.'

He rolled his eyes. 'I will not allow her to recline here all night in a poppy-milk haze,' he said. He glanced around the room at the Roman soldiers. They were circling like hungry jackals.

The woman nodded, then gave a musical whistle. A boy appeared at her side.

'I am Marni and this is Khu. He will lead you to my room in the servants' quarters. You may leave Wen there. It is safe.' She stepped a little closer to Titus. 'And you will *leave* her there, yes?'

'I will not touch her, if that is what you are suggesting,' said Titus. 'But I will stay to watch her breaths and to ensure that the poppy haze lifts. She consumed a dangerous amount.'

The woman seemed satisfied with his answer and gave a deep bow. 'Follow Khu,' she said. 'I will tell the Queen.'

Khu led Titus through a series of low corridors and hidden rooms, arriving at the end of a long hallway, and Khu motioned to a small door.

'This is Mistress Marni's room,' he announced.

Titus thanked the boy, then tossed him a coin.

She was quite light and easy to manoeuvre on to the low mattress—a rather threadbare thing that appeared to have been stuffed with straw. Tucked in a corner was a loosely woven hemp blanket, which he spread over her body as best he could. He wished he had a pillow for her head.

After she was settled, he sat himself down in the corner and studied her face. It appeared even softer in sleep. Her hair shot off in every direction and her black eye makeup spread outward from the corners of her eyes, making them appear like the wings of two soaring birds. Her lips were slack and slightly open, and it was all he could do not to kiss them.

But such kisses were not to be—not on this night, or any other. The next time they kissed—if they ever kissed again—it would be her idea, not his.

Chapter Thirteen

She awoke to the song of a rooster and a throbbing ache inside her head. 'Titus,' she whispered, though she knew not why. She knew very little, for a fog had settled over her mind. She opened her eyes to discover that she lay upon a thin mattress in a room with no light.

Strange pictures flashed behind her eyes—images of sands and seas, of towering white palaces and trays of rich foods and the shadowy profile of a man in a toga walking towards her, making her heart leap. The visions had all the colour and magnificence of a dream—one from which she did not wish to wake.

The rooster called out again, and she pulled the blanket over her eyes. 'Titus,' she said once more, as if whispering a prayer.

'Wen.'

She caught her breath. 'Titus?'

'Wen?'

She sat up. Across the small room sat the man from her dreams, his chiselled face brightening. 'You are awake!'

She blinked her eyes. She was indeed awake, though

she could not say that she had yet recovered her mind. She blinked again. 'The Queen!'

'The Queen knows that you are well and under my protection,' Titus said.

'But, what—?'

'At the banquet last night, I allowed you to drink from my goblet. The wine you drank was not wine. It was a potion of milk of poppy. I brought you here to see you through the night.'

He glanced at her exposed breasts and she gathered the blanket around her. 'To see me through the night?'

'I did not touch you, Wen. I am not that kind of Roman.'

Her head throbbed mightily. She touched her tightly wrapped loincloth. It had not been disturbed.

'I only watched your breathing,' he added with more softness. 'Milk of poppy is a potent potion. I feared you were in danger. I feared for your life.'

'I am grateful for your oversight,' she said, and the silence stretched out between them. There was something she was forgetting, something she needed to tell him, but she could not think of it. She gazed into Titus's handsome face. 'You must be quite tired, having watched me through the night.'

'I do not feel tired,' he said. His eyes flitted over her and the silence between them grew larger still.

'Did I sleep peacefully, or thrash like a crocodile?' she said at last, offering a light-hearted grin.

'You were peaceful. Though at one point you assumed a rather alarming position.'

'What position?'

'You looked like Alexander in his tomb.' He volleyed a laugh and seemed to await its return.

She stayed silent. 'I am sorry. I do not know what you mean.'

'I mean the pose of Alexander the Great in his tomb. Yours was like his for a time.'

She examined the weave of her blanket, uncertain of what to say.

'You do not know the pose, do you?' he asked at last.

'No, I do not.'

'You have never visited the tomb, have you?'

She shook her head, feeling the familiar heat of shame rise to her cheeks. She was a woman of Alexandria who had never visited Alexander's tomb. He could not have done a better job of reminding her of her station had he commanded her to wash his very feet.

'I will take you to it, then,' he said suddenly.

'What?'

'I will take you to the tomb. Today. Now.'

'That is impossible. I... The Queen. I must go to her.'

'Wen, she is probably still at the banquet.'

'The banquet! I had forgotten. I must go now.' She jumped to her feet and he rose to his. He stepped to the side and blocked the door.

'Wen,' he began again. 'There is little time left for us...' He looked around the windowless room in frustration. 'Life is a sprawling palace and in it there are many rooms, some grand and some humble. And...and there is always much to do.'

Wen frowned. She wondered if he had also consumed the milk of poppy. 'And sometimes in the course of one's work in this...this palace of life,' he continued, 'one passes by a window. When one passes by this window, one must not hesitate to look out, do you see? One must gaze out at the view and let the breeze caress one's face, for one never knows when one will pass another window. Perhaps never. Do you understand?'

His deep brown eyes burned bright.

She shook her head, though she feared that she did understand. 'I must return to the Queen.' She moved around him and stepped towards the door.

'You have left your old life, but it has not left you,' said Titus.

The words stung. But they burned through the fog in her mind, and suddenly, she remembered what she needed to tell him.

'Last night at the banquet, I overheard Pothinus speaking with General Achillas. He is going to march on Alexandria. He will arrive in three days' time.'

Titus closed his eyes. 'And so it begins.' He let out a sad sigh. 'Did you advise the Queen?'

'I did.'

'You are an excellent spy,' he said.

Before Wen could respond there was a knock at the door and a rather tired-looking Marni shuffled inside. 'Apologies, friends,' she said, kicking off her sandals. Her wig was crooked and her kohled eyes were smudged and weary. 'I am happy to see you awake, Wen,' she said, taking a seat upon her mattress. 'You have returned to the land of the living.'

'Greetings, Marni,' said Wen, 'I did not realise this is your room.'

'It is indeed,' she said with a small measure of pride. 'Royal servants of a certain age are granted their own rooms.' She nodded at Titus. 'I trust that you slept comfortably and...unbothered?'

Wen answered with a reassuring nod. 'I slept very soundly, yes. But I shall leave you, for you are weary, and I must return to the Queen,' Wen said.

'Go with the goddess,' said Marni, nodding sleepily. 'Though I do not think you will be missed by Queen Cleopatra.'

'What?'

'She has been awake all night speaking with General Caesar. She was awake even as I left the Hall moments ago, though I believe she was preparing to leave. Surely the General will return to his quarters soon, as well. They were both practically collapsing with exhaustion. I am certain they will both sleep through the day.'

Just over Marni's shoulder, Titus was leaning against the side of the door, his thick brows raised.

'Hmmm…' he said, and his breath was like a warm breeze through a window.

'Marni?'

'Yes, Wen?'

'May I borrow one of your tunics?'

'Let us say that we are newlyweds,' Wen proposed, speaking to him in Greek. 'We are farmers from some distant Egyptian *nome*—Abydos, let us say—and we have come to see the sights of our kingdom's great capital.'

They were strolling up Heliopic Street in their plain linen clothes, enjoying the late morning sun on their faces.

'Newlyweds?' he asked and was rewarded with Wen's blush.

'It is the most logical connection between us,' she

reasoned. 'Or if you would rather, we could be father and daughter?'

'Newlyweds it is,' he replied. 'But in that case we must hold hands.' He held out his hand and, in her great logic, she took it.

'You are quite cunning in your way, Titus,' she observed, swinging her arm playfully. 'Are you sure you are not a spy like me?'

His stomach sank and for a moment he thought she meant to trap him.

'I certainly am a spy—for beautiful women.'

To his great relief, she blushed again, then laughed. 'Beautiful? In this?' She held up her plain white tunic, then shook her head. She had no idea that she could make any piece of clothing look as lovely as an autumn day.

And that is what it was—a lovely autumn day. What had she called it? The beginning of *peret*. The season of planting and growth. 'Soon we will have to return to our fields, Wife,' he chided, surprised that the title came so easily to his lips.

'Yes, Husband,' Wen returned gamely. 'And the cows will need milking.'

'And the plough will need fixing.'

'And the weeds will need pulling.'

'When will we find time to do our conjugal duties?'

She let a shocked giggle escape, and he caught her by the waist.

Venus's rose—she was beautiful. Her lips seemed even darker with her exertion, a faint henna paint still tracing them, and the sunlight glittered off the green and gold flecks in her eyes.

He remembered his vow. As much as he wished to

kiss her lips, he would not do it. He did not know if she wanted him at all. If she did, she would have to show it.

Thankfully it did not take long.

She stretched to the tips of her toes, then gave a small jump, landing a juicy peck on one side of his smile. It was enough to send him soaring.

He leaned over, positioning his lips conveniently close to hers. 'That was nice,' he said. 'Wife.'

She gazed into his eyes, as if considering her options.

'Do you know how much I want you?' he breathed, forbidding himself to move closer.

Slowly, she put her lips to his again.

The world around them seemed to fall away. He breathed deeply, following her lead as she parted her lips and then seemed unsure of what to do next. He felt his arousal begin to throb beneath his toga.

Slowly, she stepped back. 'Well, that was a husbandly kiss,' she pronounced, a rush of crimson flooding her cheeks.

He took her hand in his and they resumed their stroll, though he wondered if their feet were actually touching the ground.

Wen gazed at the buildings and temples in wonder, and it occurred to him that she was seeing them for the first time. She was splendid in her wonder—cheerful and joyous as a girl. He wanted to show her everything she had missed, not just in Alexandria, but everywhere.

'Ah, there it is,' he said, leading her to the steps of a massive, many-columned building. 'The tomb of Alexander the Great.'

She twirled with delight before the steps, then dashed up them two at a time. 'Why do you tarry, Husband?' she teased as she reached the top. She accepted his hand and together they scanned the sprawling concrete expanse that marked the outside of the tomb.

It was only midmorning, but the patio was already a hive of activity. Dozens of vendors lined the perimeter. They stood outside their stalls and carts, sizing up the visitors. Outside one stall, several priests spoke reverently as they held up an Alexander-themed doll. A bearded scholar strolled past the food stalls, as if considering which fig he might study. A fat merchant lingered near the florist, inspecting a myrtle wreath for sale.

Old men shouted, children cried and young people huddled in preening packs. As Titus and Wen took their place in the snaking entrance line, Titus could not help but think that the real attraction was not the great General's tomb, but the variety of people gathered to see it.

'Temple or tourist attraction?' he asked Wen, turning to behold the spectacle.

'Both,' she replied. 'Tourists have become like locusts in Egypt. I have heard that Khufu's Pyramid and the Colossi of Memnon are the same. Even the Lighthouse is said to be awash with sightseers. I fear that one day all of Egypt will become a tourist destination.'

He laughed aloud. 'When you are not sniffing out lies or threatening men's lives, you are really quite witty.' He pecked her cheek. 'Keep our place in line and I will fetch us something to eat. What would you like, Wife?'

Her lips had frozen into that charming position they took right before a grin. 'I will eat whatever you present before my lips, Husband,' she said, and as he walked towards the vendors he wondered if he could keep his lust tethered for the day.

He scanned the food stalls, searching for something to delight her. He knew that she was hungry, for she had only tasted small morsels of the feast the night before. He filled his cloth with as many different kind of foods as he could.

'What is all that?' she chimed when he returned.

'These are called meatballs and those are cucumber sandwiches with chickpea paste, and those are slices of melon dusted with an Indian spice called cinnamon.'

He picked up a meatball and held it to her lips. 'Taste it,' he said, and she could not refuse him. She parted her lips and ate.

'I have never tasted anything so delicious in all my life,' she proclaimed. He selected a bite-sized sandwich from the basket and held it up again.

'Do you not want to sample it yourself?' she asked, but he was already pushing it past her lips. A look of ecstasy flashed in her eyes as she chewed, making his own stomach go hungry with lust.

'Now I wish to feed you a sample,' she cooed. She took a slice of melon from the cloth and held it before his lips.

He devoured the small specimen, along with the tip of her slender finger. Her look of excited alarm as she reclaimed the delicate digit was almost too much to bear. *How did you do that?* her big eyes seemed to ask. *How did you make me feel that way?*

Hot molten desire burned through him.

'I wish to show you pleasure, Wen,' he whispered. 'Will you let me?'

She did not answer. She only plucked another slice

of melon. Instead of consuming it, however, she placed the fruit into his hand and opened her mouth wide.

The next moments were a blur of lust. His finger pushing the fruit between her lips. The gentle pressure of her mouth as she consumed it. The feel of her tongue around his finger. His insides turning to barley mash.

They must have finished the food and drunk the jar of beer he had purchased, because soon they were holding hands again and the line into the tomb had begun to move. He could think of nothing but the taste of her finger inside his mouth and hardly noticed when they passed into the central columned hall of the tomb.

He heard Wen gasp as she beheld the floor-to-ceiling mosaics and watched her marvel at the grand tapestries adorning the towering space. Sun shone through the high stained-glass windows, onto the shoulders of acolytes kneeling in prayer beneath a great bronze statue of the conqueror.

Titus hardly noticed any of it. He could only see Wen walking ahead of him through the hall, its colourful light painting her cheeks.

They followed the crowd down a dark corridor. Natural light was replaced by torches and braziers, and soon they found themselves waiting outside the heavily guarded inner sanctum.

Only two people at a time were allowed into the sacred space and Titus could feel Wen's palm begin to sweat as they neared their turn. Finally they were allowed to enter the hallowed burial chamber of the greatest conqueror the world had ever known. Inside, the air was thick and still. Candles wavered in their holders, further heating the stifling space. Titus had to force himself not to plug his nose, for the subtle stench of decay seemed to have permeated the walls.

This was not Titus's first visit to Alexander's resting place. He had come here with Caesar the day they had landed in Alexandria. Caesar had entered the chamber by himself and, when he had re-emerged, Titus had noticed the stains of tears upon his cheeks.

Titus had gone in eagerly after Caesar, wondering what could have moved the great General to such emotion. It was what he did not behold beneath the glass-covered sarcophagus that surprised him the most. Alexander's corpse sunken and leathery, his eyes hollowed-out bowls. His three-hundred-year-old arms were only bones. They rested in a position resembling the expression of thirst.

Titus wondered what Caesar had seen in the tomb that Titus had not. It was not until the following day that he had finally pieced together the puzzle. 'Do you remember how they received me at Ephesus?' Caesar had asked him.

'They called you the son of Venus,' Titus had answered. Caesar gave a satisfied nod.

It was in that moment Titus realised why Caesar had been so moved by Alexander the Great. It was because he wished to *be* Alexander the Great. He wished to be worshipped as a god.

'He is so wrinkly,' whispered Wen. 'Though for three hundred years old, he is remarkably well preserved.'

'Do not think divinity produced that effect.' He bent to her ear. 'Unless you are speaking of the divine workmanship of the Egyptian embalmers.'

It might have been the joke itself, or just the effect

of his breath in her ear, but a delicious, unholy smile spread across her lips. 'And this is how I looked when I slept? As if I was preparing to strangle myself?'

'I fear it is so. You are lucky that I was there to prevent such a thing.'

She gave him a playful punch. 'His breastplate is a wonder, is it not?'

'I heard that it takes six men to lift.'

She walked to the base of the massive alabaster crypt. 'And his sandals appear also to be made of gold.'

He knew what she was thinking: *Just one of those sandals could pay off Egypt's debt to Rome.*

She looked up at him curiously. 'Is this what it is like, Titus?'

'What?'

'To be free? Is this how it feels? To go where one chooses and do what one likes? To wander about as if the world were one's own?'

'Yes,' he said, then paused. 'But freedom is more than that.'

'What more?'

'It is an endeavour.'

'You are speaking politically? You refer to the Roman Republic?'

He nodded gravely. 'It must be guarded from those who would take it.'

'You mean kings.'

And generals, he thought. 'Kings are dangerous, because they can do what they like. It is kings who would have us worship them in this way, as gods.' He gestured to Alexander's corpse. 'But even he was just a man.'

'You will surely be stricken by Alexander's thunderbolt for saying that,' Wen whispered.

'I have already been stricken by a thunderbolt, but not one belonging to Alexander.'

A guard stepped into the chamber. 'Next,' he announced, motioning mechanically to the door. Already, the next two visitors were being ushered into the chamber behind them—a pair of Buddhist monks.

Titus and Wen exited the room in silence, each wrapped in their own thoughts. He had never before had such a stimulating conversation with a woman and the exchange had only made him want her more.

As they stepped into the dappled light of the entrance hall, she flashed him a dazzling smile. 'Husband, will you answer me one question?'

'Anything, Wife.'

'Is our marriage a kingdom, or a republic?'

'I think it is a kingdom, but that we disagree about who rules. Therefore, we both rule.'

'Which makes it something of a republic after all, does it not?'

'Your intellect slays me.'

'You mock me, Husband?'

'I admire your reasoning.'

'And I admire yours, but I fear there are some flaws in it.'

'What flaws?' he responded lightly. He recognised the dangerous look in her eye.

'You were speaking of freedom, but you were referring to the freedom of men only, not women or slaves.' He could see her watching him. Beneath her cheerful facade she was deadly serious. 'Did you not once suggest that women were naturally inferior to men and that slaves were beneath you?'

'I believe I have been recently cured of those particular errors in logic.'

'You refer to Queen Cleopatra? Of her influence on you? A woman ruler equal to men.'

'I refer to you, Wen.' He took her hand and kissed it. 'Me?'

'You have proven it to me beyond refute. You are both a woman and a slave, but you are Cleopatra's equal.'

They stepped out into the sunlight. 'You flatter me,' she said.

'I would never be so foolish as to flatter you, my *cara*.' He directed her down the stairs, and they turned up a quiet street. His body seemed to hum with aliveness.

'Do you believe me to be an exception, then?' she asked innocently. 'Do you think that women and slaves are generally inferior, but that I happen not to be?'

He pulled her down a quiet alley and aimed her for the sloping awning of an abandoned shop. 'I believe that women and slaves are equal to men. You have convinced me of it.'

'I wonder about your sincerity, for you are an educated man, and an educated man would not allow a single anomaly to negate the rule.'

'Not if the rule itself is flawed.' He pulled her beneath the palm leaf shade. 'And the anomaly is so cursedly beautiful.'

'That is not a—' But he would not allow her to finish. He placed his lips upon hers and let his desire tell her the rest. He had spoken the truth, though he knew it would take time to convince her of his sincerity. But now he could not stand any more talk. He needed to feel her body against his. He needed to taste her lips.

Chapter Fourteen

Her retort was at the ready, but he obliterated it with his lips. She was going to say that this was not an exercise in circular logic, but his warm, wet tongue began making circles in her mouth instead.

She felt dizzy. In one moment, she had been strolling down the steps of Alexander's tomb, conversing civilly; the next, she was sneaking up some empty alleyway like a grave robber.

And then this—mad, hot bliss.

He pulled her more firmly against him, stepping backwards until he crashed into a wall and she crashed against him. He guided her hand to touch the fullness of him. 'Do you see, *carissime*?' he said, switching to Latin. 'There is nothing to fear. It is just me wanting you.'

She had some idea of what men did to women out of desire. The Roman man who had tried to harm her had flashed his desire before her like some terrible weapon.

Now, feeling Titus's desire for her, that memory surfaced along with a creeping fear. Her head swam.

She pulled her hand out from beneath his and pulled away.

He let out a long disappointed breath. 'As you wish.'

'Apologies,' she began. 'I just—'

'You just did not wish it,' he finished for her. He stepped away from her, lifted his arms and pressed them against the wall. He looked like Atlas pushing back against the sky. 'I do not wish to make you uncomfortable, Wen,' he said, speaking to the ground. 'Sometimes my desire for you becomes too strong, that is all. I will not try that again.'

But I want you to try that again, Wen thought, though it was too late. She knew that she had vexed him. 'You must grow tired of my fears,' she offered. 'They come at odd times, I admit.'

'I only grow frustrated, for life is short and love is shorter, and we are running out of time.'

'Love?'

He shook his head and stepped before her. 'I know why you are fearful.'

'I fell off a roof.'

'I know.'

'You know?'

'I overheard you speaking to the Queen that night on the dock. You did not fall. You jumped.'

'You spied on our conversation?'

'I have been trained to make myself into a ghost.'

Wen stood silent for a long while, thinking. 'Titus, who are you really?'

His eyes darted around the shadowy space as if he could not find a place for them to rest. He touched his hands to his chest. 'I am a Roman man. That is all. Do you fear me?'

'Only a little.'

'Well, that is one small step.' He ran his hand through his crop of hair. 'I can teach you, Wen, if you will let me.'

'What can you teach me?'

'How to…not be afraid.'

'I would like that,' she said.

'Let us begin now. Give me your leg.'

'What?'

He motioned to the leg around which her sheath was tied, and she lifted it into his grasp. 'You still wear it,' he breathed.

'I never take it off.'

'The knots have held.'

'They were well tied.'

He removed the knife from the sheath and set her leg back upon the ground.

'It must feel strange to walk around in a simple toga without any of your weapons,' she remarked.

'But I am armed,' he said. 'Because I have you.'

With her knife, he cut a strap from one of his sandals. 'Now I am going to turn around and I want you to tie this strap around my wrists.' He turned around and put his wrists together behind his back. 'Go ahead,' he said. 'Wife.'

Obediently, she tied his wrists together, knotting the strap tightly. Titus turned to face her with his hands behind his back. He pulled against his restraint, his large arms flexing. 'Do you witness my total restraint?'

'I do.'

'Good. Now I would like you to kiss me.'

'Kiss you?'

'Kiss me, Wen, or I shall surely lose whatever *dignitas* I have left.'

She stood on her toes. 'I can barely reach you.'

Titus dropped to his knees. 'Is that better?'

She could not conceal her surprise. She stood a head taller than Titus now and for several moments she marvelled in the peculiar delight of the reversal. She bent to study his lips, then traced them with her finger. They were wondrously large, ponderously soft.

'Your lips are pleasing,' she observed.

'You may do what you like to them.'

Carefully, she set her lips down upon his. For a fleeting moment, she saw his arms strain against their tie, then go slack. *He cannot touch me*, she marvelled. She closed her eyes and focused on the taste of him—a delicious combination of beer and melon and some darker, muskier scent. She pushed her nose on to his neck and breathed him in deeply, taking her fill.

He let out a soft groan of pleasure. She wondered what she could do to inspire more such groans.

She stepped back and studied his face. Such a stern, heavy brow—no wonder she had feared him. How was it possible that such deep, soulful eyes lay nestled beneath it?

She ran her hands through his short, thick hair and was surprised by its silken texture. He watched her beneath heavy lids as she bent to kiss him once again, this time letting her tongue slide gently against his.

Her inexperience was vexing him, surely, because his breaths grew shorter with each sweep of her tongue and his body quaked with impatience. She was just running her tongue gently over his lower lip when he took a deep, heaving breath and plunged his own tongue deep into her mouth.

She pulled away in surprise.

'That is called passion,' he whispered. He sat back on his heels. 'You awaken it in me. Sometimes it is difficult to control and I apologise for it. You may continue.'

He closed his eyes and his lips stretched into a grin. She could not help but smile herself. He was trying so hard to make her feel safe.

She kissed down his neck—small, soft kisses that seemed to delight him. With each kiss she breathed in just a little more of his maleness.

She kissed behind his ear. 'What is that?'

'What?'

'That strange marking—it looks like hieroglyph, or a Latin letter.'

'It is a tattoo. I, ah, I got it as a child. It is a representation of my *familia*.'

'Of Tillius?'

'Yes, but an ancient spelling.'

She sensed there was more to the story, but she did not press. 'It is mysterious,' she said. 'Like you.'

She wondered what she might do next. She had always been curious about his chest. She dropped to her knees before him and reached out to touch it. His expression was sober—even strained—but he nodded with encouragement as she placed her hands on the twin flanks of his chest muscles.

'You have done much labour, or piloted many boats,' she said, for their size was remarkable.

'Yes, but none such as you,' he intoned.

She was not certain of his meaning, but the words had given her an odd feeling deep in her belly. He nodded with solemn approval as she traced her fingers down his stomach. Even through the thick linen of his toga, she could feel his rippling strength. He was a wall of contoured muscle, and she imagined kissing each sinew and seam of him.

She let her finger trace a leisurely course around his *umbilicus* and he drew a dangerous breath. 'Careful,' he growled, though he seemed to be speaking to himself. She recalled images of Egyptian gods, their large chests and slim waists, and of Greek gods with their bulging muscularity. Titus could have resembled any of them.

Wen was not naive. She was well aware that he was the kind of man sculptors wished to study and women wished to bed. His suitability as a mate had been vigorously avowed by both Iras and Charmion, and even the Queen seemed attracted by his divine proportions.

It was all the more reason to doubt that a man such as him could possibly desire a woman such as her. Yet that was what he claimed.

She placed both her hands on the tops of his legs and felt them flex. He said nothing, but looked more deeply in her eyes and flexed them again. It gave her a thrill, to contain such latent strength inside her hands. But it was the look in his eyes that made her bones turn to reeds.

She traced her finger along his lower lip, filling with the warmth that had so often disturbed her waking hours. It was not distress, she realised, but desire. She desired Titus. Beneath her panic and fear, beneath her uncertainty and confusion, it was there. Burning like a tiny fire deep in her belly.

He turned his head slightly and his lips closed around her finger. That fire flickered, filling her body with more heat than light, and a warm wetness between her legs.

She wanted to make him feel pleasure, but she did not know how. She had never spoken to another woman about such things. She had never had the chance. The men she served at the brew house often spoke of their pleasure with women, using the same words they used for violence. She had long ago ceased to listen.

She wondered if he wished to touch her breasts. Marni had suggested that they were appealing, and she had seen Titus glance at them many times. Her physical beauty was no match for his, but she wondered if the feel of the softest part of her might bring him pleasure.

She pulled her tunic up over her head and laid it carefully on his shoulder. She heard him gasp. She stepped backwards a few paces to gather her courage. She felt bolder already, however, knowing that he could not touch her. She was in control, and grateful for the power he had given her.

It seemed that Titus's lesson was working.

His lesson was clearly not working. In a single motion, she had removed her tunic and placed it over his shoulder and her breasts splayed before him like two ripe melons. This was no subtle introduction to love. This was a torturous tease meant to break his will.

She took a step closer, and his hands involuntarily strained against the bond that held them.

She was so very beautiful in the simmering shadows—so exposed, yet so mysterious—like a shade-blooming flower unfolding in secret.

Her small linen loincloth enveloped her most womanly places, but all else was abloom in the sultry air.

He wanted to touch her more than anything he had ever wanted before. He wanted to hold her in his arms and whisper to her that she was adored…and safe.

'Do you wish to touch me?' she asked, as if she were asking if he wanted honey with his grain. She looked down at her own nakedness. 'I mean, my breasts,' she clarified.

He could barely speak his reply. 'I do.'

She took another step closer, and he wondered how exactly she was going to allow him to touch anything. Did she plan to untie him?

If that was her plan, then he knew he must try to stop her, for he would not be able to control himself in his current state.

She was studying his face again—the siren. She was trying to read his thoughts.

He wondered if she could see that his desire was an invisible monster stretching out of the shadows, begging her to come closer.

Slowly, he lifted himself off his heels so that he stood on his knees. His desire stiffened. His lips hovered in the air just a hair's breadth from one of her nipples.

'You may touch my breast if you wish,' she offered. 'With your mouth.'

He could see that this was no longer a lesson for her, but her lesson for him. The objective was to teach him control—how to keep from crying, from dying, from spending himself right there, in the darkest, hottest, most torturous corner of the universe.

He took the soft brown fruit into his mouth.

'Oh,' she sighed, as he gently began to suck. His heart hammered and his arms tugged against the strap that confined them. He felt his desire lift the fabric of his toga in a rush of yearning. He wanted to pull her on to his lap and let her feel what she did to him.

He sucked a little harder. 'Mmm,' he said. He moved his tongue in soft circles until he heard her moan with delight.

'Now the other,' she commanded and placed her other nipple between his lips. She ran her fingers through his hair and brushed her body against his as he kissed and sucked.

'Wen?' he whispered between kisses. 'Wen, I want you so badly. Please.'

She rocked back. 'I do not know what that means.'

'Yes, you do.'

'I do not want it, then.'

'You are just afraid. Are you going to spend your whole life that way?'

'I do not wish to, but—'

'Touch me.'

Perhaps she meant to test herself. Perhaps she meant to test him. Perhaps she was only curious. Whatever the reason, she pulled her toga from his shoulder and placed it at her knees. Then she kneeled down upon it.

There they were, kneeling face to face in the shadows. They might have been two monks from some far-off land, kneeling to worship their invisible god. They might have been two statues, or two prisoners awaiting their deaths.

'You are trembling,' she said.

She wrapped her arms around him and pressed herself against him. She took a long, deep breath. He could feel the strong beat of her heart against his chest.

Then she reached down and touched him. There.

She wrapped her hand around his desire until he could feel himself pulsing against her grip through the layer of cloth.

'Stroke me,' he said. 'Please, *cara*, I beg you.' She paused, then moved her hand up the length of him. 'Yes, that is it.'

The scent of floral unguents perfumed her hair. He buried his nose between her braided locks and took it in. 'Squeeze harder. Please.' She tightened her grip. He could do nothing to aid her. 'Harder still, *cara*.' She squeezed a little more. 'Now move up and down. That is it.'

It was all he could do to keep his wits. Her naked breasts pressed against his chest and he imagined releasing himself from his bond and possessing them with his hands, his mouth. She continued to stroke him, but he could do nothing to close the space between them, for his hands remained bound.

'Kiss me, Wen.'

Obligingly, she lifted her lips to his, and he caught them. It was the most sensuous, delicious kiss he had ever experienced. Her mouth, so warm and wet, her tongue entwined with his. Her desire and his, so perfectly aligned.

'By the gods,' he breathed. He was already so close. He could feel the tremors, the undulating waves, threatening to crest. 'Do not cease your stroking. I beg you.'

His blood roared beneath his skin. He strained to contain his release, knowing that it was too late. He was beyond the point of control. As he thrust himself forward into the tightness of her grip, the bond around his wrist snapped and his arms burst free.

'Stop,' she cried.

He wrapped his arms around her body and rammed his desire into her stomach, pushing against her with too much force. His shaft throbbed with impossible need. He found her loincloth with his hands and fumbled to release the knot, desperate to find his home inside of her. Gods, how he wanted her. Needed her.

'Please stop,' she said, and he felt the warm wetness of tears upon her cheeks. 'Just stop.'

But he could not stop. His need was too great. He hovered at the top of a giant wave, beyond the point of control. He found her hand and placed it around him. 'Hold me tight,' he said. His shaft throbbed with an unresolved pain. 'Hold on,' he commanded. The wave crested, then crashed, and he spilled himself on to the ground.

He released her hand and she snatched it away.

He was panting like a dog. 'Forgive me,' he breathed.

'There is nothing to forgive.' She pulled herself to her feet and reached for her tunic.

'I embraced you with too much force.'

He had done much more than that. He had lost control. He had broken the promise that he had made to her. For a few dangerous moments she had felt his crushing strength and been unable to escape him.

'I failed you, Wen.'

'You did not fail me.'

'I harmed you.'

'No, you did not.'

Perhaps not her body, but he had harmed her trust. He buried his face in his hands and a howling sadness overcame him. 'I am not a dangerous man,' he muttered, as if trying to convince himself.

'I know that,' she said. She pulled her tunic over her

body and dusted it off. 'I do not know why I always become so afraid. I wish I could stop my fear, but I do not know how.'

He stood up, careful not to touch her, though his body longed for nothing more than to hold her close. 'You must face the very root of your fear in order to overcome it.'

'But how?'

Chapter Fifteen

She followed behind him into the street, her mind straining to comprehend what had happened. What had begun as a curious wading into the pool of pleasure had ended in an unnerving plunge.

A dull disappointment permeated her body, slowing her stride. She had not expected him to break his wrist bond. Nor had she expected him to press himself so violently against her. And when his hands had found the knot of her loincloth, a kind of terror had shot through her. For a moment, she was on the rooftop once again, surrounded by hard fists and stifling limbs and a man who meant her harm.

But Titus's actions had done her no harm and she knew no harm was meant. It was as if he had been overtaken in some great storm at sea and she had been his only anchor.

They came to a street corner. 'Which way to the palace?' she asked.

He shook his head. 'Not yet, my *cara*. This is our window. We must stop and look out. Do you not agree?'

She nodded, feeling an unexpected relief. Their parting would not come. Not yet.

'Follow me,' he said. He turned towards the harbour.

'Where are we going?' she asked.

'To help you overcome your fear.'

'We are going to find an evil Roman soldier and vanquish him?' she chided, though he did not seem to hear the forced jest. He was staring out across the causeway-divided harbour.

'We are going to the Lighthouse.'

'The Lighthouse?' A dozen different emotions stirred inside her. They were going to the Lighthouse! The great and noble beacon for the world and for her own life. She was thrilled.

She was also terrified.

They crossed the Heptastadion in a hired chariot. The long, low causeway seemed to stretch out for ever before them, dividing Alexandria's vast harbour in two and connecting the city to Pharos, its largest island. They seemed to be floating just above the water, like two birds frozen in their glide.

She leaned against Titus and wished for him to embrace her, but he kept his arms at his sides. He was clearly punishing himself for his behaviour in the alley.

'You did nothing wrong,' she offered as she touched his limp hand.

But he only gave her a sad smile.

'You must not be afraid to live,' she said, repeating what he had told her.

She repeated the words to herself, hoping they would make her brave. She was going to the Lighthouse at last. She would finally set foot upon the most sacred place in her world. She could already see the white plume of smoke twisting from its high perch and the sun glinting off its copper plates.

'We will climb as high as you are able,' said Titus, and they began their march up the long ramp that led to the entrance. 'I will not force you, but you must try to face your fear. That is the only way you will overcome it. Trust me.'

They rose gradually as they neared the entrance. There were crowds of pedestrians on either side of them. The chattering people bubbled with energy as they gazed around at the sights. The island faced the Great Harbour and, as they climbed farther up the ramp, the view of the city improved.

A smattering of boats appeared below—elegantly hewn galleys that lifted their oars from the water and raised their sails to the increasing breeze, until the harbour appeared as a pond playing host to fluttering white butterflies.

Just beyond the water, Wen noticed the tall white buildings of the Royal Quarter, including the elegant columns of what she believed to be the Queen's palace, all surrounded by the high, protective wall she knew so well.

She increased her pace, keeping to the middle of the ramp and refusing to look down as the land grew farther and farther away. They had not yet even made it to the entrance of the Lighthouse and already her knees were beginning to tremble.

There was a line at the entrance and, as they waited, Titus nodded encouragingly. 'You must not let your fear defeat you,' he said.

'Am I your wife or your legionnaire?' she chided.

'You are brave to do this, Wen.'

She did not feel brave. She felt as if she were made of glass, and that the slightest push would send her shattering upon the concrete. She wiped the sweat from her brow as Titus paid the fee and they were directed through the doorway.

What she beheld inside sent a shiver of awe through her body. She had expected to see stairs, but instead observed an endlessly spiralling ramp. 'Three hundred paces to the middle platform,' explained the attendant.

The ramp coiled upward in thick concrete spirals crowded with visitors. They were walking and talking excitedly, their voices echoing against the walls. Children shrieked, women cackled, and men boomed their exuberance. Wen thought she heard the bay of a beast.

'Is that what I think it is?' she asked Titus. But before he could answer, she spied the lumbering figures of two donkeys being pulled by reins. They carried coal and wood upon their backs.

'Fuel for the eternal fire,' said Titus. 'Shall we ascend?'

She gave a reluctant nod, and he took her hand in his as they started up the terrible ramp. They were only a few paces up when they passed a tall rectangular window and she heard the menacing groan of the sea breeze outside. 'Speak to me, Titus,' she said, feeling the needles of fear deep in her belly. 'Tell me something of the rest of the world.'

'The rest of the world,' he said, as if recalling an old friend. 'Well, I can tell you that it is wondrous and also terrible.'

'Why wondrous?' she asked, despising her obstinate feet.

'There are forests full of fearsome beasts and cities hewn into rock, and trees that would take twenty men to fell. There is an ocean so endless it makes the

Roman sea look like a pond. And there are mountains so high, Wen, that they are covered in perennial snows. They can scarcely be traversed.'

For a moment, her mind filled with wonder and she wished to ask him more. But visions of tall trees and high mountains filled her imagination and she began to feel dizzy. 'And why is the world terrible?' she urged.

'The world is terrible because of those who wish to control it. Kings and conquerors, I mean. They want it so badly that they will kill for it.'

She paused and gripped his arm, searching for some topic to distract her. 'The night in the labyrinth, why did you not kill the attacking guards?'

'Because I am tired of killing.'

She stared into his eyes and could see that he spoke truth. 'But is that not your purpose? As a commander, I mean. To kill?'

'It is Caesar's purpose, not mine.'

'I thought Caesar said that he was also tired of battle.'

'Caesar lied.'

'Oh?'

'Caesar relishes battle, for it brings him glory. He thinks nothing of killing. I have seen Caesar order the slaughter of whole tribes without any hesitation.'

The sun shone in the window on to Titus's face and it seemed as if she were seeing it for the first time. 'Then why do you follow him?'

'I do not follow him.'

'Then whom do you follow?'

'Come, let us go.'

They continued in silence. A hundred questions filled her mind, but they seemed to disappear with each faltering step. When they reached the next window, Titus peered placidly out to sea while she doubled over, trying to catch her breath.

'How are you able to do that?' she asked him. 'How can you gaze out the window so fearlessly?'

'It is a matter of trust. I trust that I am safe.'

'I do not know how to do that.'

'Then lie to yourself.'

'Lie so that I may trust?'

'So it is. Come, you must see this.'

She shuffled to his side, keeping her eyes upon the concrete floor. When she finally braved a glance out the window, she saw white clouds bubbling high in the northern sky. Closer to the horizon, they coalesced into a menacing grey. 'It is a storm. It appears to be nearing us,' he said.

'The first storm of *peret*,' she muttered. A cool breeze buffeted her face, and she closed her eyes and tried to breathe.

'The augurs of Rome would call it a sign.'

'And what does it portend?' she managed, keeping her eyes shut. The wind seemed to be getting stronger.

'There is a war coming. I fear that our time together has almost run out.'

There was the sudden shriek of a child. Just paces down from where they stood, a little girl had fallen and was sliding down the ramp, her legs greased with donkey dung. Time seemed to slow as Wen watched her small body flailing towards the edge, then pitch beneath the low fence and reach the bar.

'Hold on!' Wen screamed. Startled, the girl's mother noticed the girl dangling over the edge, her small hand gripping on the iron bar.

The girl's mother lunged, grasping her tiny hand just

as it was releasing from the bar. In a sweep of motherly strength, she pulled the young girl to safety.

Wen collapsed to her knees. She could not speak, or move, or even breathe. The world had begun to spin. There was a strong gust of wind and she felt the building begin to sway. There was nowhere to go. No escape. She stared down the ramp and imagined it covered in slippery dung. She felt a man's hands on her wrists, trying to pull her to her feet. 'No!' she screamed. Then she was falling, falling.

'You are all right, Wen,' Titus whispered. 'You are going to be all right.' He might as well have been speaking to himself, for she gave no sign of hearing. 'Please, be all right.'

She was lifeless in his arms. Her feet hung limp. Her long black braid swept along the ramp like a broom. The people eyed him with alarm as he made his way downwards. 'What did he do to her?' they whispered.

What *had* he done to her? He had broken her, that was what he had done. Her fear of heights was like a sickness. He had been a fool to think that climbing a steep ramp could provide a cure.

And she, in her pride, had been unable to refuse him. She had wanted to meet his challenge—to please him and show him her strength.

Had he not seen the colour leave her face? Had he not noticed how she clung so irrationally to the wall? Had he not witnessed the way she had choked for breath, as if she were drowning in the air?

It had been a terrible idea. He had goaded her into doing something she was not ready to do. Worse, he had wasted their last moments together.

He delivered her to Apollodorus just as the storm clouds extinguished the sun. 'Please tell the Queen that we visited the Lighthouse. Wen suffered an attack of nerves. I believe the Queen will understand and will know what to do.'

Apollodorus did not ask any questions. He only took Wen in his arms and began to walk away. 'Wait,' said Titus. A strange emptiness was invading him. 'Let me say goodbye.' He crossed to Apollodorus and took her whole body into his arms one last time. He placed his lips on hers and kissed her, and their window closed. 'Please forgive me, Wen,' he whispered. 'I will not bother you again.'

Caesar was yawning when Titus entered the General's chamber, having just awoken from the previous night's festivities. He was fondling an Egyptian wig and wore an odd grin on his face. 'Look at this, Titus!' he said. 'The Queen says it suits me.' Caesar placed the wig atop his head and laughed. 'What do you think?'

You look like a man in love, Titus thought.

'You look…like a man of the world,' Titus said.

'Ha! Good answer.' Caesar walked to his northern window and gazed out at the sea. 'A storm is coming,' he observed.

'General, I fear the storm is already here.'

'Speak plainly, Titus.

'Ptolemy's army marches for Alexandria.'

Caesar pulled the wig from his head and nodded. 'Cleopatra told me last night, though I did not believe her. I should have known when General Achillas took leave of the banquet.'

Caesar stared at the shiny wig in his hands. 'Still,

I am not yet convinced that he intends to attack, not while Ptolemy remains in my palace. I will send two messengers out to meet with Achillas and discover his intentions.'

'Let me be one,' Titus said. He had never feared war before, but he wished to do everything in his power to stop this one. There was simply too much to lose.

Caesar studied Titus closely, then shook his head. 'I cannot risk you. If Ptolemy's army means to attack, then we will need to send for help as soon as possible, and Mithridates of Pergamon will not deal with some lowly officer. But let us not get ahead of ourselves.'

That afternoon, Caesar chose two messengers to ride out to meet Ptolemy's army. Two others would remain with him in Alexandria to begin preparations for war, while the rest would prepare to depart: two would sail to Judea to seek aid, two others to Rome, and Titus would be dispatched to Pergamon along with a companion to be chosen from the ranks.

'But do not raise your sails yet, Commanders,' Caesar warned. 'Let us send our prayers to Mercury that our messengers will succeed. A happy Egypt is a happy Rome.'

As always, Caesar was a marvel of efficiency and composure, and for once it appeared to be in the service of peace. It did not take Titus long to realise the reason: it was Cleopatra. He was doing it for the Queen.

The messengers and other officers had departed Caesar's company in high spirits, hopeful for a truce. As Titus moved to follow them, Caesar spoke. 'Do not go just yet, Titus. Sit down.'

Caesar motioned to a leopardskin couch.

'You know that none of the Roman legions will come to our aid,' he said casually, pouring Titus a goblet of wine. 'Nor is it likely for anyone in Judea to send troops. If it comes to war, Mithridates of Pergamon is our only hope.'

Titus nearly spit up his wine. 'Apologies, General. I do not understand.'

'There is no incentive for Roman soldiers to fight in a war of Egyptian succession—you know it as well as I. And I am not offering any pay.'

'You are the leader of Rome's army. To come to your aid is the honourable path.'

'To a Roman soldier, the only honourable pursuit is pay or conquest of territory. I am offering neither.'

'What about the provincial governors? Will the soldiers not do what they say?'

'Yes, but only if they can see the benefit in it. In so many ways, a kingdom is better than a republic,' Caesar mused, sending a chill to Titus's core. 'The soldiers serve the King and the King rewards them for their service. It is so much simpler.'

But what if the King grows heartless and vain? What if he goes mad? thought Titus. He remembered his oath to Cicero and the other Senators.

'If we can get out of here alive, Titus, I have been thinking of taking Queen Cleopatra to wife.'

'General?'

'Does it not seem fated? Rome and Egypt united? We would rule so very well together. All the peoples of the earth would come beneath our wings.'

'And those who resisted?'

'We would have the largest, most powerful army in the world. Resisters would easily be eliminated!'

Titus's heart hammered as he tried to conceal his horror. It was his worst nightmare coming to pass: the Roman Republic overcome by a vainglorious tyrant. Caesar was waiting for a response. 'Your children would be beautiful,' Titus managed.

'Indeed they would,' said Caesar. 'And they would inherit the earth!'

Caesar gazed out towards the Lighthouse, as if imagining his own statue atop it. 'But let us not get ahead of ourselves. Gaining Mithridates's aid will be essential,' Caesar repeated. 'Without him, I fear we shall not make it out of Alexandria alive. It is up to you to secure that aid, Titus. There is no man shrewder and more convincing than you.'

Titus bowed to Caesar and took his leave. On his way to his chamber, he strained to comprehend what he had just heard. It was as if all his fears of Caesar's ambition had manifested in a notion that would change the history of the world. *I am thinking of taking Queen Cleopatra to wife.*

Titus scolded himself for not having seen it sooner. How impressed Caesar had been by the Queen's intelligence. How fondly they had looked at each other as they sat together atop the throne. The Egyptian wig— by the gods! Queen Cleopatra had successfully seduced the most powerful man in the world and now the two would join forces.

The consequences of such a union for Rome would be fatal. Caesar's popularity was such that he could simply seize the Senate and fill it with his supporters, turning the sacred Republic into something resembling a Greek comedy.

He returned to his chambers in a blur of dread. He

was staring at his sandals when he heard a knock upon his chamber door.

'What is it?' he growled.

'Commander Titus,' began the guard. 'Clodius Livinius Caepo begs an audience.'

'Clodius?' Titus swung the door wide open. Before him stood his young guard, his fine patrician toga covered in mud. 'Well met, Clodius!'

'Well met, Commander Titus.'

Clodius touched his fist to his heart in the formal salute.

Titus returned his salute, then seized his arm in a brotherly greeting. 'My heart is glad to see you, Clodius.' He motioned the young man into the chamber. 'Please sit down and tell me how you fared in the Queen's camp.'

Clodius took a seat at the edge of the nearest couch. 'Well enough, though I was quickly found out. Thankfully Mardion took me beneath his wing. He told me that I would not be punished as long as the Queen remained alive.'

'My identity was also discovered,' admitted Titus.

'Indeed? Was it Apollodorus who found you out?'

'Not quite. But you look famished. Let me get you some wine. When did you arrive?' He filled a goblet and placed it into the young soldier's hands.

'Gratitude, Commander,' Clodius said, draining his cup. 'Apologies for my thirst, but I have ridden without stopping all through the night. I was dispatched by Mardion himself yesterday, when Ptolemy's army abandoned Pelousion. I bring urgent news. General Achillas marches on Alexandria.'

'I already know,' he told the young soldier.

'But how?'

Titus smiled, thinking of Wen. 'I was visited by a lovely bird in a windowless room.'

'You speak in riddles, Commander.'

'Apologies, Clodius. Your haste is appreciated, as will be your aid in the siege to come. I shall have the steward prepare you a room and deliver you a meal.'

'Gratitude, Commander. But before I depart, there is one more thing.'

Clodius reached into the sheath of his *gladius* and produced a small, sealed scroll. 'I promised the messenger that I would give it to you myself.'

Titus noticed the Senatorial seal. 'Who gave you this?'

'A believer in our cause,' Clodius said, flashing Titus a sly grin. 'Or do you think that you are the *Boni*'s only spy?'

Titus reached for a chair to steady himself. 'What?'

Clodius bent his head to reveal the unmistakable B tattooed behind his ear. 'I believe I wear the mask of spy much better than the mask of patrician senator's son.'

'Much better,' said Titus, thoroughly impressed. 'I am bested, Clodius.'

Clodius smiled. 'You have no idea how long I have been hoping to hear that, Commander,' said Clodius. The young man bowed and took his leave.

Titus collapsed on to his sofa, still reeling from the news. Clodius had been working for the *Boni* all along, just as Titus had been. He gently opened the scroll, instantly recognising the sprawling script of Cicero, the leader of their cause.

* * *

Dear Watcher,
We are grieved to learn that the great bull has
decided to remain in the sparkling city. We as-
sume that he enjoys the smell of the roses there
and one rose in particular. It has become appar-
ent that he may try to defend that rose, despite
its lost cause, and then to unite with her to con-
quer the world.

We are certain you will be asked to aid in that
defence. In that case, we command you relinquish
your duty. Abandon the bull. Seem as if you are
going to seek aid for him, but do not do it. Let him
die with his flower so that the wolf may live on.
Yours in veritas,
Whisperer.

Chapter Sixteen

The storm still raged when Queen Cleopatra returned from her meeting with Caesar. She marched into her living chamber and threw off her soaking diadem.

'Ptolemy's army draws closer to Alexandria,' she announced. 'In two days, the Royal Quarter will likely be under siege.'

Apollodorus remained in the doorway, folding a dripping cloth. 'Tea of anise to warm her bones,' he called to Wen.

Wen hurried to the far end of the living chamber and set about stoking the brazier, grateful for something to do.

'Can you not force Ptolemy to call them off?' Charmion protested, wrapping the Queen's hair in a towel. 'He lives in this very palace!'

'It is Pothinus who truly rules, as you well know,' said the Queen. 'He conspires with General Achillas secretly. He will not rest until all of us are dead.'

Wen set the water to boil, her head swirling. *But I do not want to die, not when I have just begun to live.*

'Do you believe Caesar can defend us, Queen?'

asked Iras, wrapping a blanket around Cleopatra's shoulders.

'Yes, but he is terribly outnumbered. He has sent messengers to try to broker a peace.'

'They will be crucified,' said Iras. She led Cleopatra to the sofa and removed her sandals.

'I fear it,' said the Queen, shivering in her blanket.

'And what then?' asked Charmion, joining the Queen on the sofa.

'Caesar says that he has dispatched officers, including Titus, to appeal for military aid from nearby kingdoms.'

'Titus has gone?' Wen asked. She pressed the pestle down hard atop the anise seeds, turning them to dust.

'Not yet,' Cleopatra clarified. 'But he could leave as soon as tomorrow, depending on the success of the messengers.'

Wen dipped a stick into a honey pot, trying to conceal her panic.

'No honey for the tea, Wen,' said the Queen. Wen halted in confusion. The Queen loved honey with her tea. 'They will try to starve us out,' the Queen explained. 'We must start conserving now.'

Wen streamed the honey back into the jar. It moved so maddeningly slowly, immune to the race of time.

'Titus warned me that time was running out,' Wen said suddenly, staring at the honey. 'Now it appears that it finally has.'

'Why did Titus say such a thing to you, Wen, about time running out?' asked Charmion.

'I think you know why, Charmion,' said Iras.

'I suppose I do,' said Charmion, accepting her cup

from Wen with a resigned smile. 'You are a fortunate woman, Wen-Nefer of Alexandria, and I salute you.'

'Forgive me, Mistress Charmion, but in what way fortunate?' asked Wen.

'You need not call me Mistress, Wen, especially now that you have bedded the most handsome Roman in all of Alexandria.'

'Bedded? Do you refer to the carnal act?'

Charmion burst into laughter, making Iras chuckle. Even the Queen smiled into her steaming vessel.

Wen shook her head in mortification. 'But we have not… I have never…'

'You have never wandered the marshes with a man,' finished Iras, glaring at Charmion.

No, she had not. 'It is not for a slave to even think of such things, Mistress Iras,' she said.

'Please, just call me Iras.'

'You were with Titus the night of the banquet, were you not?' asked Charmion. 'I saw you leave the Hall of Delights together. And did you not spend all the next day together?'

'Yes, but he did not touch me,' Wen said. 'Or at least, he stopped touching me when I asked him to.'

Charmion nearly spit out her tea. 'You stopped him?'

'Clearly she is an innocent,' Iras clipped. She turned to Wen. 'Do you like Titus, Wen?' she asked gently.

'I do, Mistress—I mean, Iras. Very much.'

'You must learn to enjoy the pleasures of the flesh before it is too late,' said Charmion. 'Or are you not a woman of Egypt?'

'And why not let Titus be the one to teach you?' said Iras. 'He is certainly well made. Do you not agree?'

Wen buried her nose in her drink, pretending to take a sip. She did not want the women to see how her cheeks flushed with the very thought. Of course she agreed. She had so often considered the idea of Titus's strong, sheltering body that she could have sculpted it from clay. She finished her drink, then nodded meekly.

'Wen, I forbid you to let Titus leave this city without wandering the marshes with him at least once. You must not be afraid to live your life! What is that saying in Latin?'

'Carpe diem?' said Wen.

'You must do it for us,' cried Charmion. 'You must do it for your sisters—to cheer our hearts on this dark day.'

Tears came unbidden to Wen's eyes. She had never considered herself a sister to anyone. 'I am humbled,' she said. 'I wish for nothing else.'

'Then you must go to him before it is too late.'

'But surely he is busy preparing for his journey. I fear his guards will refuse me.'

'Do not fear, Wen,' said Cleopatra, speaking at last. 'I know a way.'

It was late when Titus heard the knock at his chamber door. Cicero's letter lay on the table before him like evidence to a crime. He tossed it into a smouldering brazier and jumped to his feet.

'Who calls so late?' he asked. He scanned the room for the location of his *gladius*. It was propped just next to the doorway.

'It is I, Apollodorus. I bring you a gift.'

Titus trusted the Sicilian with his life. Still, he hesitated. 'What is the nature of this gift you bring?' he asked. He now stood squarely before the door, his *gladius* in hand.

'The nature is…feminine,' said the Sicilian.

Feminine? Was the fool delivering flowers? Not likely. Titus assessed his preparedness for a fight. He wore no armour and the ponderous folds of his night toga would prevent him from making a fast escape. There was no helping it, however. As he opened the door, he held out his *gladius*, ready to strike.

Standing there before him was the tall, shadowy figure of Apollodorus and before him, a figure clad in white, her eyes the only visible part of her. But he knew those eyes. He craved them. 'Wen?'

'It is I,' she mumbled from beneath the cloth.

'It is as if you have been rolled into a carpet,' he said. The most desirable carpet he had ever seen.

'I am here to see if you might unroll me.'

He blinked, mistrusting his own ears. Unroll her? Did she have any idea of what she had just suggested? He searched her eyes. They danced in the torchlight, joyous and full of mischief.

Still, he was so thrilled to see her that he instantly forgot about having spent most of the day trying to forget her.

'Please come in. You are most welcome,' he said, and she flounced into the chamber with a bold purpose. *What purpose?* he wondered hopefully.

Just the thought of her presence in his bedchamber made his heart pound.

He watched her eyes scan the sprawling space, taking stock of everything. The balcony. The brazier. The wash basin.

The bed.

He was so taken by the activities of her eyes—the only visible part of her—that he forgot about her escort. It was Apollodorus's disgruntled sigh that shook Titus from his trance.

'Apologies, my friend,' said Titus, turning to the stocky Sicilian. 'You are also welcome, of course.' Against all his instincts, Titus gestured for Apollodorus to enter.

Thankfully, Apollodorus did not move. 'I cannot stay,' he said with blessed mercy, 'but I am grateful for your welcome all the same.'

Titus grinned with relief. 'I hope to see you again soon, so that we may reminisce about our journey and how the gods favoured us that night.'

But Apollodorus was not listening. He was gazing over Titus's shoulder, watching wistfully as Wen crossed to the foot of Titus's bed and took her seat. Apollodorus shook his head in wonder. 'The gods continue to favour you, it seems,' he whispered. 'Lucky jackal.'

Titus dropped his voice to barely a whisper. 'I will try to be worthy of her.'

'Do not merely try,' Apollodorus said in clipped tones.

Titus nodded gravely, then closed the door, pushing the bolt into its place. He stared at the thick metal for a long while afterwards, trying to arrange his thoughts. His hands had begun to sweat.

I was wondering if you might unroll me. That is what she had said, which meant that she wanted him to help her out of her *hetaira's* robe.

Which meant she wanted *him*.

Even if she had said nothing, the garment alone spoke volumes. Or perhaps more exactly, it asked a question, to which his answer was a resounding yes.

Yes, yes, yes.

His heart filled up to bursting, and he suppressed the urge to lift her into his arms. He wanted to tear off her robe and kiss every part of her, to make slow, torturous love to her until her whole body convulsed.

But, no. No, no, no. He could not do that, because he was leaving that very night.

The life seemed to drain from him as he crossed to where she sat. There were several sofas to choose from, yet she had chosen to sit on the low platform where he sat. Either she was too innocent to understand the meaning of such an action, or she had come to seduce him.

She bent to remove her sandals. Catching sight of her naked toes, he shivered with lust. He wanted to suck them, he realised. Each and every one of them, until she squealed with delight.

But what he wanted to do and what he needed to do were two very different things. He could not make love to her this night, not when his duty compelled him never to return. In truth, he was neither commander nor messenger.

He was a spy.

As such, his task was to follow orders—Cicero's orders, to be exact—so that Caesar would be defeated and the Roman Republic would live on. All of the needless killing Titus had done in Caesar's name, everything he had come to believe about generals and kings, had been leading up to this moment. The only thing preventing

Titus from fulfilling his purpose was the woman who sat before him, smoothing her gown.

'I did not think I would ever see you again,' he said carefully.

She stared at her hands, projecting an eerie calm. 'I did not know if you wished to see me.'

'Then you were mistaken.'

'You said that you did not wish to bother me again.'

'I did not think you would wish to be bothered.'

'I do wish it.'

'You do not know what you are saying.'

'You have helped me—'

'Shhh,' he said. He could not bear to hear her professions of gratitude.

'Will you not sit by my side?' she asked.

I must keep my distance...so that it will be easier to leave you for ever. She looked up suddenly, crucifying him with her eyes. Dutifully, he sat down beside her.

He placed his hand atop hers and a gentle peace spread out between them.

Finally, Wen spoke. 'I came here because I wish to wander the marshes...for the first time...with you.'

The statement hit him like a battering ram. If there had been any doubt in his mind, she had just wiped it away, along with a good deal of his composure.

'I see,' he said, trying to seem thoughtful. Inside him, the trumpets of a thousand armies were sounding. Wander the marshes indeed. They were words that he never thought he would hear, describing a thing that he had given up hope of attaining.

'Please,' she continued.

His heart pounded. He could not do it. He could not

accept such a gift from a woman whom he had just been ordered to betray. To abandon.

'You do not understand,' he said. 'I will be leaving soon. Perhaps even tonight.'

'That is why I am here now.'

'Wen, I may never see you again.' *I will never see you again—not if I do my cursed duty.*

'I wish to live, Titus—while there is still time. I wish for you to teach me how. Tonight.'

He swallowed hard. He could not do this.

He had to do this.

He was going to betray her. If he did not, then Caesar would become King, and all of the civilised world would regress into brutal monarchy.

'I cannot,' he said.

He watched a tear trace its path down her cheek. 'Do you not desire me?'

'I desire you,' he said, hardly able to speak. *More than I desire my own breath.*

'Then why?'

He searched his mind for some excuse. 'Because you are an innocent.'

'But I am not. At least…not in my thoughts.'

Another gut-twisting statement, clearly crafted to test his nerve. 'You have…thought of me?' he asked, not wanting to know the answer.

Because if the answer was yes—yes, she had thought of him in that special way, yes she had fantasised about him as he had her, kissing her, touching her, pleasing her—then he was surely lost.

But she did not answer his query. She did something far, far worse. She pulled his hand to her lips and kissed his fingers: first his small finger, then his larger one, then his largest finger, which she took into her mouth and began to suck.

A bolt of Jupiter's lightning travelled rapidly to his manhood, shocking it awake. Sorceress! She knew that drove him mad. He groaned and closed his eyes, begging the gods for mercy.

She had no idea that she had already vanquished him. From the moment he had seen her that night in the Queen's tent, he had fallen beneath her rule.

His only remaining defence against her was that she seemed to have no notion of the power she wielded.

Or perhaps she did, for in a single motion, she found the hem of her *hetaira's* robe and lifted it over her head.

He sat frozen in his seat, facing forward. He could not look at her. If he did, he was certain that his resolve would turn to ashes. He felt the curve of her hip pressing against the side of his leg. He was dangerously close to taking her in his arms.

Out of the corner of his eye, he perceived her naked flesh—her bronze skin and slender limbs and bulging round breasts. Her heaving stomach and some dark blur of flesh just beneath it. He did not dare look at her directly. He feared he might turn to stone.

'Why do you not wish to look at me? Do you not desire me?' she asked.

'I desire you too much,' he breathed. 'You must don your robe once more and depart.' But it was too late. He was already gazing into her eyes.

Her shining black hair hung around her face like a parted veil. He tucked one of the locks behind her ear and studied her delicate pink lips.

He followed her lips to her chin, then down the taut

pillar of her neck to its pulsing nape. Just below it, the twin peaks of her breasts protruded, challenging his will. His lust bubbled, along with an unusual reckless feeling. He let his eyes slip farther downward to the small black patch signalling the entrance to the realm of oblivion.

'Please,' she said, 'the marshes.'

He jumped to his feet and began to pace before her, keeping his eyes trained on the floor. 'You must depart.'

His tone was firm, and she felt panic creeping in. Could it be that he didn't want her? That she did not please him as much as she had hoped? 'Why? What is the matter?'

'Now.'

She reached for her gown to cover herself, then changed her mind. Slowly, she stood. This was no time to be meek. 'I will not leave until you tell me why. If you do not want me, you must say so.' She gazed down at her naked flesh, inviting him to consider her. But he seemed determined to consider nothing but the carpet upon which he trod.

'Wen, you are the only woman I want.'

'And you are the only man I want.'

He ran his hand through his hair. 'You do not know what you are saying.'

'Then teach me what I am saying. You told me to notice the windows that appear in my life. This is one, Titus. This night we can have together.'

Finally, he stopped pacing. He slid his gaze up her naked legs, then up a little more, and a windstorm of breath tumbled from him. 'By the gods,' he mumbled, and turned away. She heard the soft patter outside.

'The storm has arrived,' she offered softly.

'Indeed it has.'

He crossed to a table and filled a vessel with wine, drinking thirstily while he devoured her with his gaze. He slammed the goblet down suddenly, appearing to alight upon some idea.

'You must be in command,' he said.

'What?'

'You must tell me what you wish me to do and I will comply. Thus I can be assured that I will not take what you are not willing to give.'

Frustration bubbled inside her. 'But, I am willing to give all,' she said, having only a vague idea of what she meant.

'It is my condition,' he said gravely.

She paused, considering his proposal. She sensed there was some deeper reason for his hesitation—something unrelated to her innocence.

He was pacing again, avoiding the sight of her.

I have made him afraid to touch me, she thought. She had rejected him too many times, had unravelled before him too often for him to trust her now. She felt ashamed at her own cowardice and determined to show him that she could be different.

'Fine, I accept the condition.'

He stopped pacing and stared into her eyes.

She wondered how many women had to negotiate the terms of their own defloral. Then again, she wondered how many women had ever met a man like Titus.

'When do we begin?' she asked.

A small, sly grin played upon his lips. He was not

answering her question and the reason was clear: they would begin when she commanded it.

She spoke softly. 'I command you to remove your toga.'

His eyes flashed. He lifted his woollen toga up over his shoulders and tossed it on the floor. 'What now?' he challenged, but she was too overcome by the sight of his exposed flesh to respond.

He was a titan in truth—the very scale of him divine. It was no wonder the Queen's handmaids admired him. His sprawling chest heaved with his breaths and his massive arms seemed to tense and flex as she approached. His stomach was a maze of thick, knotted muscle, and below it—

She gasped, stopping cold. His manhood extended out before him like a sword—bald, engorged, enormous.

He took a step towards her and her fascination edged towards fear. 'Stop there,' she commanded. He was just paces away from her and she could see every large, bulging part of him.

She tried to take courage. He would not harm her—she was sure of it. He had never harmed her. He had only ever tried to keep her safe.

When she returned her gaze to his, his lids were low and he had assumed a menacing calm. The wind-buffeted rain was now pouring outside.

'What now?' he repeated in a low growl. 'What is your command?'

Surely she will relent, he thought slyly, and that was his intent. He had always loathed his largeness, for it startled the women he bedded. This night, however, it would be his greatest asset, for it would serve to deter Wen from her mistaken course.

Though she seemed alarmingly undeterred.

'Stay where you are,' she said. She approached him as she might have approached an unbroken horse. Slowly, carefully, she placed her fingers on his stomach.

His skin flushed with heat as she traced the hills and valleys of his muscles, growing bolder with each stroke of her finger. Soon she was standing at his side, staring down at the fullness of him, as if considering whether to indulge her curiosity further.

Touch it, he thought, trying to remember why that might be a bad idea.

His memory failed him. He could do nothing but pray—pray to gods he did not believe in for a thing he had never dreamed of attaining: her genuine desire for him.

And just as he thought them, his prayers came true.

She reached out and gently petted her hand down the length of his shaft.

He could not tell if it was the heat of the candles, the burn of his desire, or the simple unnerving fact of her naked body standing so close to his, but the dew of sweat surfaced on his skin.

'Come on to the bed and lie beside me,' she commanded, taking his hand. 'On your back.'

Obediently, he followed her to bed, letting her lovely round backside tease him to an even greater need.

He thought he had a plan—discouraging her with the sight of himself, then challenging her to take the lead. But she seemed alarmingly unfazed on both counts, and as he climbed on to the downy mattress and lay on his back he wondered why he had ever wanted her to be deterred.

She lay beside him and petted his chest, spreading around his slick perspiration until it was as if she were painting on the canvas of him. Gently, she placed her hands atop his desire. He groaned as she touched, then traced, then stroked him with a maddening curiosity.

'Turn towards me,' she ordered, and he rolled on to his side and gazed into her eyes. He had never felt so aroused.

'Touch my behind,' she said. To aid him in the endeavour, she wriggled closer.

He did as he was told. He slid his hand on to her bare backside and relished the feel of its firm roundness.

'Kiss me,' she said, and he dutifully placed his lips on hers.

And it was as if they had plunged back into the very same kiss they had shared outside the Library, which had merely been an extension of the kiss they had begun in the deckhouse, which was certainly a continuation of a kiss between gods, started at the beginning of time.

She kissed him languorously, listening to her instincts, which told her to get closer, then closer still. Moist with his sweat, she pressed herself against him and her body glided against his, writhing and twisting with her desire for more of him.

She had not expected to feel as she was feeling—so free and sensuous and wanting. She could have lain there all night were it not for the hot twisting feeling growing between her legs. She needed him closer still, though she knew not what command would achieve it.

'Touch me,' she said at last, uncertain of her own

meaning. She felt his finger travel down her stomach and stiffened with alarm as it gently entered her folds.

She shivered with surprise, followed by a thick tingling of pleasure. His movements were subtle and gentle, his finger like some instrument of pleasure playing the tune of her, a tune she had never before heard.

He continued to kiss her as he slid his finger gently all around her womanly opening, and she opened her legs wider, though she could not say why.

Somewhere deep inside her a drum began to beat out a slow, relentless rhythm. An invisible necessity blossomed within her. 'Yes, more of that,' she breathed between kisses, and he moved his finger more rapidly, tracing every part of her until she began to feel so restless with need she thought she might cry out.

'What now?' she said feverishly, but he would not answer her. Her hips heaved upwards, the drum inside her beating faster still. 'More,' she breathed.

Her bliss was imminent. She heaved and moaned, her body writhing beneath his touch. He only needed to maintain his rhythm, pulsing his finger in and out of her hot, wet depths until she reached that mindless precipice and plunged over it.

He should have been thrilled. He was giving her pleasure—the thing he wanted to do more than anything else. Still, something inside him faltered. She would be alone in it, then—her first taste of bliss. He would play only a small part. And when it was over, what then? It pained him to think that she might depart having no idea of the real pleasure he could give her.

Slowly, he withdrew his finger.

'No,' she gasped. 'Don't stop.'

He knew he had to act quickly. He had disobeyed her orders, had engaged in mutiny of the most treacherous kind, and had only moments before her ardour became confusion, her passion a barrage of questions and the moment turned to dust.

'Shhh,' he said. He eased on top of her and kissed her on the lips. 'Do not speak.' He took himself in hand. 'Do not think.' He found her soft fleshy petals. 'Just feel, my *cara*.' He watched her expression change as the tip of him pressed against her and with the guidance of his hand began to trace that hot, slippery path around her entrance once again.

'Oh,' she cooed.

'Yes,' he said. That was more like it.

He kissed her again, pulsing forward, letting her feel the warmth and pressure of him.

He had stepped into a dangerous realm. With himself in command now, he risked scaring her. Any moment, she could stiffen, or bolt, or cry out for him to stop, and the opportunity for their union would be lost. He needed to make that moment impossible. He needed to make her want him as badly as he wanted her.

He kissed down her neck, breathing hard. He took her nipple into his mouth. 'Ahh,' she cried, pushing her hips upwards. He pressed himself into her a little more, then withdrew, letting her feel his absence.

'No,' she said, and when he returned to her, 'yes.'

He glided his body over hers. He pushed himself into her just a little bit more.

The rain poured in a loud torrent—or was that the rush of blood in his ears? He throbbed with impossible need and nuzzled his face in her hair. 'I wish to be inside you,' he breathed.

'Please,' she said. 'I beg you.'

It was all the command he needed. He pushed as slowly as he was able, trying not to cause her pain. 'The pain will go away,' he said. 'I promise.'

She moaned, then sighed as he eased himself into her. 'Blessed heavenly Venus,' he said, feeling her warm wetness envelop him. He paused—melting into the paradise of her.

Was she still with him? He needed to know. He bent to kiss her again, questioningly, pleadingly, wondering if he had done wrong.

The kiss she returned him told him all that he needed to know. She plunged her tongue into his mouth without restraint, arching up her hips and coaxing him into slow, rhythmic, movement.

Now their pleasure was one thing—one hot, moving, pulsing thing that he never wanted to end. He pulled away from her lips to look into her eyes. They shone up at him like twin suns, filling him with their light, then became clouded by her heavy lids as she fell deeper into bliss.

Small, encouraging whimpers were escaping her lips, and she gripped his lower arms with a fierce concentration. He watched her, then she groaned, and he crushed his mouth down upon hers once again. She was going to come apart.

He was going to come apart.

She squeezed, he pushed, and suddenly they were tumbling over a beautiful cliff, shivering and convulsing together. He pulled her atop him as bliss flooded through him as she enveloped him in her arms.

And he knew that he never wanted to be anywhere else.

Chapter Seventeen

It was the middle of the night when the rain finally ceased. The slow drips from the palace eaves were like the final notes of a song that she did not want to end. He lay on his back beside her, and she watched the quiet rise and fall of his breaths. His face was soft and almost boyish at rest. She could have watched it until the dawn.

She was completely awake, utterly spent, and her *ka* floated on a river of light. She had lived her whole life never daring to dream of the joys he had shown her and now she could not rid her mind of him. Was this another facet of freedom? Or was this something sweeter still?

She stood and crossed to the table, and poured herself a cup of wine. There was so much she did not know about Titus—so much she longed to learn. Where did he live in Rome? What else had he seen of the world? What did he wish for and dream of in the night?

Who was he really?

She searched around the room, making a game of discovering his things. There was his *gladius* in its golden sheath, there his tunic, there his helmet so blue and bright.

Do not cling to him, Wen, she warned herself.

He had shown her another world—that was true. But that did not necessarily mean he wished for her to reside with him in it. A familiar sadness settled over her and at last she began to feel the heavy tide of sleep.

She glanced about the room one last time for something—anything—to remember him by, settling her eyes upon a brazier near her feet. Balanced near its copper edge lay a half-burned scroll. She pretended that the small, discarded document contained the answers to all her questions about him.

It did not matter that she could barely read whatever was written upon it. Some day far in the future, she would unroll the scroll and pretend that it told the story of their brief, beautiful love. She picked it up and tucked it into her sheath, then curled up at Titus's side.

When she awoke again, the sun was shining through the coloured windows, staining the bed cloth with its riot of colour. Wen heard the calls of the morning birds and the rumbling of carts in the courtyard below. But the sound of Titus's breaths was absent and the room was stiflingly still.

She sat up. He was nowhere to be seen. She scanned the large chamber, searching for signs of him—his red cape, his tangled toga, his strappy leather sandals. She found nothing. It was as if he had completely disappeared.

Then she spied the note lying on the table.

She put on her robe and returned to Cleopatra's palace, arriving in the Queen's living chamber just as Charmion was arranging the Queen's hair.

'Who might that be hiding beneath that lovely white carpet?' jested the Queen. She met Wen's eyes in the reflection of her mirror.

Wen removed her heavy veil and gave a shy smile. 'It is I, Queen. I have returned from my journey.'

'Was it a walk in a garden?' asked Iras.

'Or a skip down Canopus Way?' asked Charmion.

'Or a race at the Hippodrome, perhaps?' asked the Queen, searching Wen's expression.

'It was a flight through the air,' said Wen, 'over the endless blue sea.'

Iras swooned, falling on to a nearby couch. 'I believe you, Wen, for never have I seen a woman so flush with beauty and light.'

'It is true, Wen,' said the Queen. 'You are glowing.'

'Without your encouragement, I would not have gone to him at all. I owe you all a debt.'

'It is I who owes you a debt, Wen,' said the Queen. 'Your advice has proven quite effective so far, both in politics and…other things.' Wen searched the Queen's eyes and thought she detected their own kind of glow.

'But where is Titus now?' asked Charmion.

'I do not know,' said Wen in despair. 'I fear he is gone.'

Wen removed Titus's letter from beneath her belt and handed it to the Queen. 'My reading skills are poor, my Queen. I do not know for certain.'

The Queen unfolded the parchment and began to read. 'Dear Wen, as I write this I am watching a goddess at rest. She is sleeping so very peacefully on my bed. I worry that if I blink I might discover that I have only imagined her. The name of this goddess is Wen and I worship her most ardently. She is the most beautiful, intelligent, magnificent woman I have ever known.'

'Oh!' cried Iras.

The Queen grinned, then continued. 'I hope she will understand why I cannot say goodbye. I fear that if I wake her, her kiss will have the power to keep me here, when my duty calls me away. Ptolemy's army marches on Alexandria and I must recruit an allied force so that I may keep my goddess safe. I promise that I will do so and that I will return. Truly, Titus.'

The Queen returned the letter to Wen with a mischievous smile. 'You have entranced him, my dear. I would have expected nothing less.'

'Oh, Wen, are those not the most beautiful sentiments a man has ever written?' gasped Charmion.

Wen glanced down at the looping Latin script, puzzled.

'What is it, Wen? Why are you not delighted?' Cleopatra asked.

Wen stared in wonder at the Queen. 'You are able to read Latin?'

The Queen's eyes grew big in the copper mirror. She turned to look Wen in the eye. 'You have found me out, Wen. I should have known that you would.'

'But, my Queen, why did you ask me to be your translator?'

'Because I needed you to be part of my ruse.'

Wen struggled to understand, but emotion clouded her thoughts. She had been tricked. By the Queen herself. Duped. 'I needed to appear not to understand Latin,' Cleopatra explained. 'It is how I was able to spy on Caesar and know his true mind. You have been a necessary part of that ruse, Wen, and I am grateful.'

Wen tried to understand. Still, something about the Queen's explanation did not ring true. 'But why…me?'

The Queen started to answer, but there was a sudden shriek from the courtyard below, followed by a chaotic rustling. Wen followed the Queen and her handmaids to the edge of the balcony and peered out. Three large, fiery balls had landed in the bushes, their flames already travelling up one of the trees.

'It has come,' said the Queen. 'My brother's army has arrived.'

The fireballs were followed by a rain of arrows and the people of the Royal Quarter rushed indoors while Caesar's legion hastened to douse the flames.

'Do not fear, Sisters,' said Cleopatra. 'And listen while I tell you a secret.'

The Queen retreated to her couch, where she calmly explained that Caesar's preparations for war had begun many days ago in secret. 'There was a reason he was in a hurry to give the feast,' she said. 'That very night, while the citizens of Alexandria clustered at all the temples and feasted on free bread and beer, and while all Alexandria's nobles and landholders made merry in the banquet hall, Caesar's soldiers had quietly moved much of the city's grain within the walls of the Royal Quarter.'

Wen listened in wonder. As the city's residents feasted and revelled, their Roman occupier was stealing their grain.

'That is not all, My Sisters,' continued the Queen. 'The day Caesar sent his messengers of peace out to meet with General Achillas, he finished constructing dozens of catapults and ballistas for our defence. They are being positioned as we speak. They were constructed and stored in secret in Caesar's villa.'

What was more, Caesar had spent the past few days constructing an elaborate military buffer zone outside the Royal Quarter wall. He had destroyed all buildings lying within fifty cubits of the wall and the materials were used to construct several maze-like fence structures riddled with hidden traps.

'There is a reason he is called the greatest General in the world,' Cleopatra said in triumph.

Wen felt reassured by the Queen's words, though she sensed the fear behind them. She also noticed what the Queen did not say. She did not say that General Achillas was relentless and clever, though he was well known to be. Nor did she say that Caesar could hold out for ever.

The days passed. The women watched and waited. Some nights, Cleopatra would go to Caesar's rooms and not return until morning. 'We are safe and protected, Sisters,' she assured her women. 'As long as Caesar lives we shall be safe.'

More days passed and no aid arrived. Caesar's barber found a scroll addressed to General Achillas written in Pothinus's own hand. His treachery finally proven, Caesar had Pothinus beheaded.

Not that it helped matters. Ptolemy's soldiers were entering the harbour late at night, stealing the royal warships one by one.

When Caesar discovered the scheme, he remained calm. 'Whoever controls the harbour, controls Alexandria,' he explained to the Queen.

The next morning, the residents of the Royal Quarter awoke to the thick smell of smoke coming from the harbour. That night Caesar had deliberately set Alexandria's entire military fleet ablaze.

In the fire, part of the Library ignited and Cleopatra wept as she watched great tongues of flame destroy what she had always held so dear.

'What matters most is that we are alive,' she told her sisters, as if trying to convince herself. 'Is that not true?'

Wen nodded, though she recalled what the Queen herself had taught her: that there was a difference between being alive and living.

Wen thought of Titus every day. She studied each of the words he had written to her, imagining the large, gentle hand that had fashioned them.

She envisioned him crossing the sea in some small, fragile boat, his hands gripping the oars as he and his small entourage journeyed to find help.

She went to the Royal Temple of Isis and made the requisite prayers and offerings, begging the Goddess to keep him safe. She watched the Lighthouse, trying to take heart. *The flame is not yet extinguished,* she observed. *He will follow it back to me.*

The weeks became months. Their morale declined along with the royal food stores. Ptolemy's troops were endlessly creative and every day they found some new way to threaten the men defending the wall of the Royal Quarter. A battle was fought in the harbour and Caesar emerged victorious. But while Caesar controlled the harbour, Achillas had the city and his army would not relent.

The next day, a rain of fireballs plunged into the

Royal Quarter in numbers greater than Caesar's men had yet seen. Apollodorus looked ashen as he stormed into Cleopatra's living quarters.

'Come with me now—by order of Caesar.'

The Queen and her women gathered their belongings and followed Apollodorus below the palace, where Cleopatra's royal bath house stretched. It was a labyrinth of massage rooms, steam rooms, hot pools and lounging areas that had not functioned since the siege.

'You will be safe from any fires here,' explained Apollodorus.

They made their camp around the large cold-water pool and waited. They spoke softly, straining to hear what was happening above.

Iras lit several candles and they passed the time with games of chance. First they played senet, then rods and cones, then on to dice. 'Will I be killed by my husband-brother?' the Queen asked the dice morbidly. 'Two for yes, three for no.'

It was no use. They could not cheer themselves up, or escape the growing fact that Caesar was losing. Nobody said what everyone was thinking: that these might be the last moments of their lives.

Wen had never allowed herself to wish for freedom, but now the desire invaded her body like a fever. She began to loathe the walls that surrounded them and the guards who kept them inside. She knew that their captivity was for their own safety, but safety did not seem so very important any more. She thought about what Titus had said about freedom—that it could never be given, only taken.

Iras and Charmion joined Apollodorus on a mission

to retrieve food from the palace kitchen. After they had gone, Wen approached the Queen. She was sitting at the side of the pool, letting her legs dangle in the cool water. 'May we speak, my Queen?' Wen asked, feeling the tickle of boldness in her stomach.

'Of course, Wen, sit down.' She patted the concrete edge of the pool, and Wen took her seat.

'I come to you with a request,' Wen began. 'A rather large request.'

The Queen was watching Wen curiously. 'Yes?'

Wen's throat felt dry. She had practised this moment a hundred times in her mind, but now none of her carefully selected words would come to her. 'Queen Cleopatra, I wish to tell you that I am indebted to you and will always be so. My life began the day you brought me from the brew house and I wish to serve you for all my days.'

The Queen nodded solemnly.

'I may be uneducated,' Wen continued, 'but I know what I observe. I see the care you have for the people of this great kingdom and your reverence for its ancient culture. You have treated me with the same care. Indeed, most days you seem more like a sister to me than a master.'

Wen hesitated, fearing that she had given offence. But Cleopatra only smiled, encouraging Wen to continue. The words began to pour forth. 'That is why I ask that you release me from bondage. I will remain in service to you for all of my days, but I wish for it to be of my own free will. And if I am to die, I wish to die a free woman. My Queen, I wish for you to set me free.'

Wen closed her eyes, unable to meet the Queen's

gaze. When she dared open them again, the Queen was lunging to embrace her. 'Oh, Wen, you make me so proud!'

Wen almost choked with her surprise. 'Proud?'

'You have passed the test I have put you to and more quickly and gracefully than I ever could have believed possible.'

It was not the reaction Wen was expecting and she wondered if she had been misunderstood. 'Do you refer to the test of serving you faithfully? The test of a servants' worth?'

The Queen smiled. 'I refer to the test of freedom.'

Wen wondered if the Queen had gone mad. 'I was not aware of such a test, my Queen.'

'You were free from the moment Sol purchased you from your master.'

Now Wen could hardly speak.

'Do you remember Sol's words?' Wen stared down at the mosaic adorning the depths of the large pool. It was an image of Aphrodite emerging from the sea foam. 'He showed me a scroll. He said that it attested to my conscription by Cleopatra Philopator the Seventh.'

'Conscription. What does that mean?'

'Recruitment?'

'Yes.'

'You *recruited* me into your service?'

'I did. It has always been your choice. You just did not believe you had it.'

'But why did you not tell me?'

'I am telling you now. I have been waiting for you to ask.'

'I do not understand.'

'True freedom is not something that can be bought

or traded or granted by another. It must be desired and then taken by the person who would be free.'

Wen had been in the Queen's service for a full season now—over four months. In that time, Wen had acted overly boldly, spoken out of turn, violated the rules, laughed loudly, drunk thirstily and let herself feel desire, never realising that they were part of a larger change taking place within her.

'Then I am free?'

'You do not sound so certain.'

Wen was certain—suddenly irretrievably so. 'I am free,' she said, and the words were like a song rising up from her heart. She felt her eyes filling with tears.

'You have been free since the moment you stood before me, Wen. You just did not believe it.'

Wen swished her legs in the water, wondering if Cleopatra considered the implications of her words. 'I know what you are wondering, Wen,' the Queen said. 'If I believe that you should take your freedom, then why should not everyone? My answer is that everyone should. If I did not believe that, then I would not be Greek! But such a thing cannot be achieved without the peoples' will.'

'The people must take their freedom just as I have taken mine?'

'Yes.'

'Do you really believe that one day the people of Egypt will take their freedom?'

'I do,' said Cleopatra. 'They will take it from a monarch—someone like me. They will do as the Romans did five hundred years ago.'

'Do you not fear it?'

'I do fear it. But I do not believe it will happen for many, many years. The Egyptians love their kings.'

'And queens.'

Cleopatra smiled graciously. 'What will you do with your freedom, Wen?'

Everything I have ever dreamed, Wen thought, hardly knowing where to begin. She thought of Titus's letter. 'I would like to learn to read Latin.'

'A worthy goal!' the Queen exclaimed, clapping her hands together. 'We will begin as soon as we are allowed to return to my chambers.'

'You will teach me?'

'Of course! Now tell me, what else will you do?' asked the Queen.

But Wen was already doing it. She had plunged into the frigid pool.

The Queen shrieked, 'Can you swim?'

Wen splashed to the surface, flailing her limbs wildly. 'No, my Queen—but I do not care! I am free!'

The next day, the fireballs ceased. Cleopatra ushered Wen into the palace library, where she retrieved a large scroll from one of her shelves. 'These are the songs of Catullus, the Roman poet. They were procured by my father when he was last in Rome. They are wonderfully lurid. I shall point to each word as I read it and thus you shall learn.'

'I would like that very much,' said Wen, watching Cleopatra unfurl the scroll. 'Is it not the duty of a scribe or teacher to perform such a task?'

'The roles and riches of this life are illusions,' Cleopatra said with a brush of her hand in the air. 'They matter not.'

'I admire that saying,' Wen mused. 'The High Priestess quoted it often.' The Queen blinked, betraying an emotion, then recovered her expression.

The Queen knew the High Priestess, Wen realised suddenly.

The Queen motioned Wen to a table and the two women sat next to each other on polished wooden stools. Cleopatra unrolled the dusty scroll before them.

'Now that I am free, Queen Cleopatra, may I ask you why you sent for me?' Wen blurted. 'At the brew house, I mean. Why…me?'

Cleopatra smiled slightly, smoothing the parchment. 'I think you know the reason. I think you have known it all along. Let us see if you can guess it.'

Wen knew how the Queen delighted in games, but she suddenly felt foolish. She did not know the reason. She had no idea at all. She began to speak, hoping to find some hint of the answer in the Queen's reaction to her words. 'The man you sent to retrieve me,' Wen began, 'the man who called himself Sol—he said that you were interested in my holy birth.'

'Yes,' the Queen said invitingly. 'Go on.'

'I am a child of the Temple of Hathor, born of the Festival of Drunkenness. The High Priestess was my mentor and teacher.'

'Yes, she was.'

But how would the Queen possibly know that?

'The man who sold me to the slavers said that the High Priestess had been killed by the late Pharaoh Ptolemy, because she had loved the usurper to his throne.'

'That usurper was my older sister, Berenice,' said Cleopatra. 'The High Priestess loved her like a daughter.'

Wen nodded thoughtfully. It seemed quite possible.

The High Priestess spent most of her time in Alexandria and seemed to delight in the presence of young people. Wen had always wondered why the Priestess spent so much of her time in Alexandria. Now she finally knew the reason—she was instructing the royal children.

'But Berenice was not the only one of Pharaoh's children that the High Priestess loved.'

'You knew her?' Wen asked, searching the Queen's eyes with growing excitement.

'Of course I knew her, she was our holy teacher,' said the Queen. She smoothed the scroll's edges lovingly. 'The High Priestess taught me to read—and not just words on a page. She taught me to listen and to observe. And also to seek. Everything I know that is of use, everything I believe that is of value, all that success that I have had in my life is all thanks to the High Priestess.'

'Then we are connected,' Wen cried, 'for she was my teacher, too!'

'She was more than that, Wen,' said Cleopatra. 'She was your mother.'

Everything had changed and nothing at all. Somewhere deep inside herself, Wen had always known that the High Priestess was her mother. Still, to hear the words had been a revelation that had lifted her *ka* into the sky.

She was not nobody, as she had believed all of her life. She was somebody. She was Wen-Nefer of Alexandria, daughter of the High Priestess of Hathor. Though such a high birth did not change who she was in her heart. As her mother would have said, it mattered not.

Still, Wen was grateful, and her gratitude came in great, crashing waves that often resulted in tears. Each morning, the Queen read to Wen from her scrolls, the Latin words dancing off her tongue like music. And every afternoon they would sit down and sip tea and remember the woman who had shaped both their lives.

'But how did you find me?' Wen asked one morning.

'I knew that your mother had a daughter—a girl of my same age—for she spoke of you often. She said that you were very clever and that one day she would present you at the palace. She said you were brilliant at reading people and that you would make a fine advisor one day.'

Wen shivered with pride. 'She said that? About me?'

'She did indeed, though that day never came. You see, my father had to keep raising taxes to service his debt to Rome. Then the River failed to rise and the people of Alexandria began to riot. My father departed for Rome, hoping to borrow more money, and while he was gone, my older sister Berenice usurped the throne. Your mother had nothing to do with my sister's treachery. She was not even in Alexandria at the time. But when my father returned from Rome, he was so angry at Berenice's treachery that he killed her and everyone who had ever known her, including your mother.'

'Ptolemy's purges.'

'I wept for her, Wen, for I had loved her and, after I became Queen, I resolved to find her only daughter. I knew that you had been sold into slavery in Alexandria, along with the other temple children. Before I was exiled I heard a story of a brave beer maid who jumped off a rooftop of a brew house somewhere in the Egyptian Quarter. She was my age, had a scar on her leg and she was known to be perceptive and clever.'

'But how did Sol know I was the right woman?'

'The roles and riches of this life are illusions. I told him that the right woman would know how to finish that saying.'

'I thought everybody knew that saying.'

'No, it was your mother's alone. She taught it to us.'

Wen's spirit filled to bursting. She was her mother's daughter—a free woman, an advisor to a queen. Her life had become so much more than she ever could have dreamed and she prayed for the siege to end so that she could continue to live it.

She yearned for Titus. She stared at the words he had written, comparing them against the words she knew. Slowly, the markings began to acquire meaning. The strong *T* of Titus, the low-sloping *p* of *promise*, the lovely round *r* that began the word *return*.

But when?

One day, Ptolemy's troops flooded the palace pipes with sea water and the residents of the Royal Quarter found themselves with nothing to drink. Caesar and his men went to work digging wells, but fear settled on the legion like a fog. They had successfully defended against the siege so far, but without a consistent source of fresh water, the soldiers were lost.

Wen descended to the baths with her empty pots. She lifted her skirt and was bending at the edge of the pool when she noticed the sheath tied to her leg. Just behind the knife, a small piece of paper protruded.

It was the scroll that she had stolen from Titus's bedchamber. She had forgotten about the small memento and now it peeked up at her like a gift from the gods.

She tucked it safely beneath her loincloth, then filled her vessels with water. Soon she had settled herself beside her Latin alphabet to see if she could decipher the small message.

The paper had been damaged by both fire and water, and it was a wonder that its words were still legible at all. She compared them against words that she had memorised from Catullus, along with the sounds of the Latin alphabet.

Slowly, the Latin markings began to make sense. A terrible, devastating sense. It was a letter, quilled by someone who called himself the Whisperer. His long, elegant script confirmed a fine education and the Senatorial seal at the bottom of the page marked him an important man. In the letter, he urged someone called the Watcher to abandon his post. He said that the bull, whom Wen guessed to be Caesar, should be allowed to perish along with his rose, whom Wen could only assume was Cleopatra.

Which left only the identity of the Watcher for Wen to determine. But she did not have to guess it. She knew that the Watcher was Titus. He had been ordered by someone in the Roman Senate to abandon Caesar and all efforts to help defend against the siege.

To abandon her.

Her heart seemed to plunge from some high place. It fell and fell as the realisation took hold: *Titus is never coming back.*

Chapter Eighteen

Wen spent the next few days too stunned to speak. She read the letter over and over again, hoping that she had made some grave error in its interpretation. Perhaps the bull was not Caesar, but an actual bull. Or perhaps the bull was Ptolemy, and the rose was Cleopatra's younger sister Arsinoe, who had recently defected to Ptolemy's army.

But none of these possibilities completely fit. The only interpretation that made sense was her first: Titus had been ordered to betray Caesar by abandoning him to defeat.

Wen knew that she should show the Queen the letter, but she could not find the courage. She wandered around the Royal Quarter, heedless of the danger, trying to arrange her thoughts. The Queen had grown thin and listless in recent weeks and had visited Caesar's chambers less and less often. Wen feared for the Queen's spirit. She did not wish to be the cause of her lost hope.

Coward, she told herself. The Queen deserved to know. At the very least, it would enable her to prepare a secret escape. But a part of Wen still could not believe it was true. *I will keep you safe*, Titus had promised her. *I will return*.

Just days before, Caesar had released Pharaoh Ptolemy and allowed him to return to his army.

The hope was that the young Pharaoh had spent enough time between the walls of the Royal Quarter to see the futility of destroying them. It had been a desperate measure—a last-ditch effort in an unwinnable war.

And it had all been for naught. Ptolemy had instead rallied his troops outside the walls of the city, preparing to make a final strike.

It was only a matter of time now. The once-mighty fortress of the Royal Quarter was crumbling and would soon be overcome. There was no more water, no more food. Their only hope was aid from abroad.

Their only hope was Titus.

Wen found herself at the docks, staring up at the Lighthouse. It beckoned as always, its thread of smoke spiralling to the heavens.

Come, it seemed to say.

Wen stepped into a small rowboat and began to row. She had nowhere to go and nothing left to lose.

'Beware the heirs of Romulus and Remus,' her mother had cautioned before she died, but the words had been a riddle in Wen's young ears. Now, finally, she understood, though it was too late. She was already in love and doomed to die.

Her boat found its inevitable course and she was soon making her way on heavy legs up the ramp to the Lighthouse. She had no money to pay the entrance fee, but even the Lighthouse had been touched by the war and there was no attendant in sight.

Ra was already making his descent to the Underworld as Wen began the slow climb up the spiralling ramp. A familiar fear began to bubble within her, but she brushed it away. 'Lie to yourself,' she whispered, remembering Titus's advice.

Her fear seemed insignificant now, with her death looming so close. She stopped to gaze out of each window, swallowing her nerves and studying the sky as it grew pink with the memory of Ra's light. She had been lying to herself all along, she realised. About him.

She plodded slowly, for she lacked energy, having eaten very little for many days.

I serve the Roman Republic. That is what he had told her when she had confronted him about his mission and it occurred to her that he had not lied. There had been many other clues to his true purpose—she had just not been willing to see them.

Now she could only see her sandals, how they shuffled slowly up the cracking concrete.

She strode out on to the first deck as if floating on a cloud. There was not a single soul in sight and she stared down at the limestone-white city painted in the rouge of dusk. It was beautiful, even in its cloak of war. The theatres and gymnasiums, the synagogues and temples—they stood out amidst the smoke and destruction, decorating the streets with their stony purpose.

Titus had been right. Kings should not rule the world. They were rarely good, always corrupt, and they played with people's lives like children playing with toys. Queen Cleopatra was an exception to the rule and even she had agreed that people should rule themselves, should seek their own freedom.

Wen departed, continued up the ramp. *Freedom is an endeavour,* Titus had told her. *A thing that is earned.* Wen had earned her freedom, or so she believed, though she wondered if she would ever be free of him.

She climbed and climbed, the lie of her own courage slowly becoming truth.

She heard the roar of the flames before she saw them and felt their searing heat upon her face. She stepped out on to the top of the Lighthouse to a grand show of light.

The fire was larger than she expected and wilder— a great white bonfire, barely contained by the high dome that topped it.

Wen stepped around the inferno on careful feet, keeping to the platform's perimeter and hugging the low iron fence that separated her from certain death.

Sweat dripped from her brow, blurring her vision. She willed herself not to look down and stopped to observe the tongues of flame dancing so near.

Visions of Titus plagued her. Titus taking her hand in the Reception Hall. Titus sitting beside her on the Library bench. Titus in his bright blue helmet, parading like a peacock. She could not purge him from her mind, no matter how hard she tried. Nor could she condemn him, for he was doing what he believed to be right. She could only hope that wherever he was, he lived and thrived.

Is this how it feels to love? she wondered.

Behind the large flames, she spied two large metal panels.

Looking closer, she saw that they were mirrors—large polished reflectors mounted on wheels. *The copper mirrors*, Wen thought. They travelled on metallic tracks and hung on high bars, so that they might be adjusted to any position or angle to signal passing boats.

Now one of the mirrors gave a mighty groan and seemed to move of its own volition. Soon an ancient figure stepped out from behind it, shuffling towards Wen.

At first, Wen could not tell if the person was a man or a woman. But as she neared, Wen observed her pear-like shape and long, white hair, which was scattered across her shoulders like ash. She pointed at Wen with a coal-blackened arm. 'Tourists are forbidden here.'

'I am not a tourist.'

'Then who are you?'

'I am nobody.' Wen paused. *No. Not nobody.* 'I mean to say—I am Wen-Nefer of Alexandria. Who are you?'

'I am Mut, the Keeper of the Flame. Why have you come here, Wen-Nefer?'

'I have come to seek freedom,' said Wen. *From love.*

Mut shook her head gravely. 'No, no, no,' she said. She linked her bony arm with Wen's and led her to a sheltered area behind the mirrors.

'Here we are protected from the flames,' explained Mut. She gestured to a mat, and Wen sat down, letting the ocean breeze cool her skin.

'Welcome to my home,' Mut said. She scooped a cup of water from a large pot and offered it to Wen.

'Yes please,' Wen said, accepting the water grate-fully. She took small sips and gazed out at the white-washed city, which was rapidly disappearing into the darkness of night.

The old woman settled herself on what appeared to be a sleeping mat and wove her loose white locks into a tidy braid. The light of the flames danced on the side of her ancient, wrinkled face.

'I did not know that a woman kept the flame,' said Wen.

'Woman, man—at my age it matters little.'

'How old are you, may I ask?'

'Ooowww,' said Mut, flashing a toothless grin. 'Older than the River is long, my dear. And how old are you?'

'I have seen one and twenty floods.'

'Then you are too young to seek your freedom,' Mut said, glancing downwards.

Wen realised that the ancient woman thought Wen planned to jump. 'Apologies, Keeper,' Wen said. 'I do not mean to jump. I came here to find freedom from my fear. I am afraid of...of high places.'

'Oh, is that all?' said Mut doubtfully. 'Well then, congratulations, my dear, for you are as high up as a person can get—in Alexandria, at least.'

'Gratitude,' said Wen, though she felt little joy.

'There is another reason you are here.'

'I suppose that I came to gather my courage.'

'A tester,' said Mut.

'A what?'

'A person who has ascended in order to test herself. A tester.'

'Are such people common?'

'No, they are very rare.'

'Why?'

'We tell ourselves stories about our lives. We gather them up like Isis did the pieces of Osiris after Seth destroyed him. We put these pieces together to make meaning.'

The Pieces of Osiris, Wen thought.

'These stories shape who we believe ourselves to be. Most people tell themselves stories to make them feel comfortable. Stories with limits. A tester tells herself a challenging story—a story with a lesson at its end.'

Wen studied the old woman, wondering what lesson she would teach.

'The last person to climb to this high perch was over twenty years ago—a pretty young Egyptian woman much like you, though her linens were fine and a golden cobra snaked up her arm.'

The High Priestess of Hathor, thought Wen. *My own mother.*

'Now tell me why you are trying to gather your courage.'

'I must tell someone that she has been betrayed.'

'Do you know this for certain?'

'Yes,' said Wen. She gazed into Mut's eyes. 'No.'

'Then you are wasting your fear. If you are going to be afraid, be afraid of something real. Like crocodiles or plagues of locusts.'

'What if I am right?'

'Then you must not allow the betrayal to break your spirit. If you are strong, then betrayal matters little. Just remember, within everything is its opposite. What you perceive as a betrayal may not truly be one.'

In the last bit of light, Wen noticed the old woman's eyes—they were the colour of the sea, deep and blue, and she thought she could discern the shape of a spiral within them.

'Have you always been the Keeper of the Flame?' Wen asked.

'Of course not,' said Mut. 'I have lived a hundred different lives. The roles and riches of this life are illusions, my dear. They matter not.' With that, Mut stretched out on to her mat, closed her eyes and began to sleep.

Wen's heart filled with wonder. She suspected that she had just met the source of her own wisdom. She yearned to speak more with Mut, but the old woman was already deep in slumber. Soon Wen was yawning herself. She lay back on her mat and fell asleep to the sound of the flames.

She awoke to the caress of Ra's fingers, and the shock of her high perch. She glanced at Mut's sleeping mat. It was empty. The ancient woman was already at work.

Wen gazed out across the land in amazement. The view from the second deck was much grander than from the first and she forgot her fear as she took in the glory of Alexandria.

There was the grand Canopic Way, the city's largest street. And there was the blackened Library just near it, still standing despite the flames that had destroyed one of its sides. There was the battered Royal Quarter, its gardens destroyed, but its buildings still blindingly white. Wen could see the sprawling gymnasium, the steps of Serapeum Hill and the columns of Alexander's tomb. She could even see the street where the brew house stood and thought she could discern its small roof.

It was all so very miniscule, so very trivial from such heights. Even the terrible roof from which she fell seemed almost comical in its size, like a small pebble on a large, rocky beach. That was when she knew that she was no longer afraid—not of heights or betrayal or even death. Nor would she ever be again, for she had become truly free.

She gazed out beyond the city walls and towards the east, where the natural border of Lake Mareotis ended and the land spread out in large, grassy fields.

There among the greens and browns she beheld an army at march. There must have been ten thousand men—all walking in perfect rows towards the gates of the city. Her heart began to pound. She squinted her eyes, dreading the sight of Ptolemy's ceremonial head-dress. Instead she perceived a tiny blue point against the fallow fields. It was unmistakable, even from so far away, as was its wearer. *Titus*.

'Titus!' Wen shouted.

Mut hobbled to Wen's side. 'What is it, my child?'

Wen could hardly think. She could barely speak. 'Please, Mut, may we move the mirrors?'

Chapter Nineteen

He should have known better than to fall in love with an Egyptian. He should have known better, yet there had never really been a choice. She had surely cast a spell on him—one of those ancient Egyptian curses they whispered of in Rome. By the time he realised her hold on him, the magic was at work and the only way to lift it was to do his duty and abandon her.

And he would certainly never do that. Never, ever, in a thousand years. Curses on his duty and his philosophy and his wretched *dignitas*—he would not abandon the woman he loved.

The battle had been short and mercifully decisive. Ptolemy's exhausted forces were no match for Mithridates's fresh, well-provisioned ones. The prince's men fought bravely and well, and quickly sent Ptolemy's troops running for the River. For the first time in his life, Titus thanked the gods, for he knew that Wen would live.

Caesar's own exhausted legion met Titus's at the battle's end. 'It took you long enough,' Caesar said.

'I should say the same,' Titus jested.

The Senate would have to think of another way to be rid of Caesar. Titus would not be the one to betray him.

Together they commenced their march towards Alexandria that morning and soon spied its high walls.

Titus was searching the base of them, hoping to catch sight of a welcome party, when a beam of light hit him in the eye. High in the northern sky, he beheld the Lighthouse's flickering flame, enhanced by the reflection of its copper mirrors. He could hardly believe it. He had never seen the flame directed towards land. He did not even know it was possible.

'It appears that at least some of the citizens of Alexandria are happy to see us,' he mused.

'Happy to see you and the troops you bring,' corrected Caesar. 'Though I will certainly take credit for the victory.'

Titus smiled. 'I would expect nothing less.'

'You may at least have your spoils.'

'What spoils are there to be had from a besieged city?'

'I think you know,' said Caesar.

When Titus arrived outside the Queen's palace, he burst into the Reception Hall. 'Well met, Titus!' said the Queen. She stepped down from her throne. 'You have come to our rescue once again. We are indebted to you for our lives.'

'It is my honour to serve you, Queen.' His eyes darted about, searching for Wen.

'I assume you are not searching for my sphinxes,' said the Queen.

'Apologies, Queen Cleopatra, I was searching—'

'For Wen,' finished the Queen. 'I know.'

'Is she here?'

'She is not in the palace at present, though I can say that she has been awaiting your arrival for some time. She told me to tell you that you must find her. She said you should follow the flame. Take the most direct route.'

Puzzled, Titus walked down to the royal docks and stared up at the Lighthouse. The flame was no longer being directed towards land, but its familiar plume of white smoke twisted up from beneath its wide dome.

Are you there, Wen? he wondered.

He wandered down the dock, finding himself stopped where they had disembarked on that fateful night. Incredibly, their small sailboat was still there, still roped to the dock. He untethered the vessel and stepped aboard, resolving to take it to Pharos Island where he would dash up the spiralling ramp and seek the woman he loved.

But when he pulled back the deckhouse curtains, he realised that he had already found her.

'Titus!' she cried, leaping into his embrace.

He could not contain his joy. It burst from his pores and threatened to obliterate his armour. He squeezed her as tightly as he dared, burying his face in her hair and breathing in her scent. Tears came unbidden to his eyes. 'It is as if I have been imagining this moment for a hundred years,' he said.

'And I for a thousand,' sobbed Wen. 'Did you see me signalling to you from atop the Lighthouse?'

Titus set her upon the deck. 'That was you?'

'Yes! The copper mirrors can be moved. There was an old woman. The Keeper of the Flame. She told me not to fear. Oh, Titus I could see your blue-crested helmet!' She was breathless, the words tumbling out of her. 'And the Queen knew my mother. And we ran out of water. And I learned to read and—'

'Shhh,' he said. He parted her lips with the force of his own, letting her feel the wind of his breath inside her. It carried the message of his longing for her, a message she received with a joyful sob.

'Can I tell you a secret?' he asked.

She exhaled hard, then took a step back. 'I already know. You are a spy for the Senate. You are trying to preserve the Roman Republic from the threat of Caesar's kingly ambitions.'

She might as well have delivered him a body blow. 'How on earth do you know that?' He looked around nervously, though they were snugly within the deckhouse, with only the seagulls outside to hear them.

'I am an advisor to the Queen of Egypt. It is my job to know such things.'

He stepped forward. 'You are an advisor and a sorceress.'

She stepped backwards. 'And you are a very good liar. Now tell me why.'

'Why?'

'You were ordered to abandon Alexandria. Why did you return?'

'I—'

'You betrayed your own philosophy.'

'I—'

'You let Caesar's ambition win.'

He was utterly confused. 'How do you know that I spied for the Republic?'

'I read you like a book, Titus. But that does not matter. What matters is that I agree with you.'

'You agree with me?'

'My mother was killed by a ruthless king, though her only wrong was educating his daughters. Kings are dangerous. They are like masters. They cannot exist if people want to be free. That is why I must know, Titus. Why did you return? Why?'

She would not let him come any closer until she had an answer, for she believed that was what she deserved. 'Because I love you, Wen.'

'You…love me?' She looked around the room, blinking in confusion.

'I have loved you from the moment I saw you.'

Stepping backwards, he watched her legs crashing against the lounging platform. She lost her balance and collapsed on to the mattress.

'Are you all right?' he asked, crouching at her feet.

'But you gave up your dream.'

'You are my dream.'

'You shunned your true duty. You failed to do what was right.'

'It is going to take more than a single spy to save the Roman Republic. It must come from the will of the people.'

'Is that what you truly believe?'

'It is.'

She seemed satisfied at last, though her expression was vexed. 'You love me?'

'And I will prove it to you,' he said. 'Touch my heart.'

Slowly, she lifted her hand and laid it across his beating heart. 'Do you feel that?' he asked.

'Poon-poon, poon-poon,' she said.

'That is the sound of my love for you. It never goes

away, no matter how far apart we are. It is like the flame of the Lighthouse—it will always be.'

He lay down beside her on the mat and grazed his fingers gently up and down her arm. The tiny, soft hairs swayed beneath his touch like a field of wheat. Encouraged, he bent forward and planted a series of kisses down her neck. He was rewarded by a soft moan.

'How I have missed you, my *cara*,' he whispered.

'And I have missed you.'

He dared to move his arm about her waist, drawing her atop him and pushing her tunic to her waist. His hands wandered across her soft thighs, then visited her shapely hips, then explored the small of her back until they found themselves caressing her soft bottom. His heart thrummed. He wondered if she felt it, too—this strange Pandora's jar of desire, twisting open.

He pulled her lips on to his, waiting at the ready for her tongue, which settled just inside his mouth with a delicious uncertainty. Gently, he coaxed it into his own mouth, and soon their tongues were moving together in an easy, sensuous rhythm.

There was no helping it: they were matched. There was something about their kissing that resembled a dance, or music, or the crashing of waves on the shore. They were like no other kisses Titus had ever experienced and he felt that he could stay here for a thousand years, his lips locked with hers.

With a little encouragement, she scooted up his legs and came to rest straddling his waist. He could feel her feeling him and the jar twisting open just a little more. A wave of alarm traced her expression, followed by that small twinge of delight that sometimes played at the edges of her lips. He arched his hips slightly, letting her feel what she did to him. Her whimper of surprise was so resonant with desire that he thought he might be undone right then.

'You want me,' he whispered, letting his hands graze across her breasts.

'Not at all,' she said. And there it was—the twinge. Only this time it was playing at the edges of her voice and it made his insides coil with lust.

He resolved to make love to her slowly, torturously, and watch her thoughts turn to silt. It was as if all of the women he had ever known had only been preparing him for the goddess who now sat atop him in her victory pose.

'We are matched, Wen,' he said, marvelling at the rare and precious truth of it.

He only wondered if she could comprehend what that meant. There were millions of people in this world—in Alexandria alone, in fact—and she could spend her whole life searching without finding one who suited her half as well as he did. She leaned a little closer, closing her eyes and breathing him in. Then she collapsed on to his chest and laid there, her ear atop his heart.

'You love me,' he said.

The control was all hers now. She could do whatever she wished. More than anything, he wanted her to kiss him. On her own. Without any coaxing.

'The boat is moving,' she said.

'Yes, I untied us from the dock.'

'You what?'

'Before I stepped aboard, I untethered the deck line. We are floating free now, Wen. There is no telling where we may land.'

Her eyes blazed with excitement, and her lips stretched into a heavenly grin. 'I love you, Titus,' she said. Then she leaned over and placed her lips upon his. Softly. Gently. Deliciously.

And they floated off together into the wine-dark sea.

* * * * *

*If you enjoyed this story
you won't want to miss these other great reads
by Greta Gilbert*

*ENSLAVED BY THE DESERT TRADER
THE SPANIARD'S INNOCENT MAIDEN*

COMING NEXT MONTH FROM

✶HARLEQUIN®

✦ISTORICAL

Available April 17, 2018

All available in print and ebook via Reader Service and online

THE OUTLAW AND THE RUNAWAY (Western)
by Tatiana March
Celia finds necessary refuge in brooding Roy Hagan. Life with an outlaw is
no place for a sheltered young woman, but as Celia gets closer to Roy she
learns what's beneath his steely exterior...

A NIGHT OF SECRET SURRENDER (Regency)
Gentlemen of Honor • by Sophia James
Celeste Fournier once gave her innocence to the man she loved. Years
later, that same man, Major Summerley Shayborne, is in danger! Their
reunion revives locked-away feelings, and now she'll risk all to save him!

LADY CECILY AND THE MYSTERIOUS MR. GRAY (Regency)
The Beauchamp Betrothals • by Janice Preston
Lady Cecily Beauchamp is irresistibly drawn to the mysterious
Zachary Gray. Knowing her family will forbid their match, Cecily should
resist. But the spark between them ignites a passion neither can deny!

AN EARL TO SAVE HER REPUTATION (Regency)
by Laura Martin
After being caught in a compromising position, Lord Harry Edgerton and
Lady Anna Fortescue get engaged to prevent a scandal! Unable to resist
Harry's charms, Anna realizes the betrothal may have its benefits...

A WARRINER TO SEDUCE HER (Regency)
The Wild Warriners • by Virginia Heath
Meeting confirmed rake Jacob Warriner brings schoolmistress Felicity Blunt
gloriously to life. Yet is Jacob merely a mischievous scoundrel, or is there
much more to this Warriner than meets the eye?

THE KNIGHT'S FORBIDDEN PRINCESS (Medieval)
Princesses of the Alhambra • by Carol Townend
Princess Leonor can't escape her tyrannical sultan father. Count Rodrigo is
entranced by Leonor and will do anything to protect her, but the risks are
great: she is the daughter of his sworn enemy!

**YOU CAN FIND MORE INFORMATION ON UPCOMING HARLEQUIN® TITLES,
FREE EXCERPTS AND MORE AT WWW.HARLEQUIN.COM.**

HHCNM0418

HOME on the RANCH

YES! Please send me the **Home on the Ranch Collection** in Larger Print. This collection begins with 3 FREE books and 2 FREE gifts in the first shipment. Along with my 3 free books, I'll also get the next 4 books from the Home on the Ranch Collection, in LARGER PRINT, which I may either return and owe nothing, or keep for the low price of $5.24 U.S./ $5.89 CDN each plus $2.99 for shipping and handling per shipment*. If I decide to continue, about once a month for 8 months I will get 6 or 7 more books, but will only need to pay for 4. That means 2 or 3 books in every shipment will be FREE! If I decide to keep the entire collection, I'll have paid for only 32 books because 19 books are FREE! I understand that accepting the 3 free books and gifts places me under no obligation to buy anything. I can always return a shipment and cancel at any time. My free books and gifts are mine to keep no matter what I decide.

268 HCN 3760 468 HCN 3760

Name	(PLEASE PRINT)	
Address		Apt. #
City	State/Prov.	Zip/Postal Code

Signature (if under 18, a parent or guardian must sign)

Mail to the **Reader Service:**

IN U.S.A.: P.O. Box 1867, Buffalo, NY. 14240-1867
IN CANADA: P.O. Box 609, Fort Erie, Ontario L2A 5X3

HRCBPA18

Get 2 Free Books,

HARLEQUIN

SPECIAL EDITION

Plus 2 Free Gifts—

just for trying the Reader Service!

Get 2 Free Books,
Plus 2 Free Gifts—
just for trying the
Reader Service!